RED MOON:

Secrets of a Sixties Schoolgirl

Pamela Mariko

FORDHAM PUBLISHING
Australia

i

Published by:
FORDHAM PUBLISHING
Australia
First published August 2015.
Reissued August 2019.

ISBN: 978-0-6485634-0-2

This is a book based on the author's life from 1964-1967. It is not entirely factual. Names of individuals have been changed to protect their anonymity, along with names of schools and areas. In some cases, events have been compressed or the timing changed; in others, two people have been woven into one. 'Sandra' being sent away for 'bad' behavior is fabricated for the purpose of storytelling. Dialogue is as real as can be remembered, with embellishment, or is fictional.

DEDICATION

For Mum

TABLE OF CONTENTS

CHAPTER ONE:

LONG DARK NIGHT

1966 UK

I suppose I could've slashed my wrists right then. A tarot card stared face up from the bathroom floor. The Hanged Man.

I sank further down into the bath water. Jackie would find me, limp, in red water. Then Aunty Mary would have to tell Mum. I imagined Mum's white face. She'd have to sit down before she fell. She'd feel that kick in the stomach we've both felt before, the kick that constricted your lungs, grabbed you by the throat, and made your face crumple.

I wiped my face with the flannel. Suddenly, I missed Mum. It was the first time I'd been away. I put the razor down by the Hanged Man. I couldn't do it.

"You're not going to drink *all* the remaining miniatures, are you?" my cousin Jackie called through the door of the shower block. She was talking about the gin she'd managed to buy from the off-licence. She said it should help bring on my period.

"Two tonight, instead of one. Last try." My voice wobbled. I bet she knew I was crying.

"It'll be all right," she said in that soothing older person way. "I'm going back to the caravan. If it *still* doesn't work, don't worry, you'll only be about twenty-nine when she or he is fourteen. You'll be able to go down *The Tiles* together."

Very bloody funny. Her footsteps echoed out of the stone building. Lots of pop stars went to *The Tiles* club in Carnaby Street. I'd be able to go when I was older now that we lived near London. If I wasn't pregnant.

I sat up and took one of the little gin bottles out of my pink sponge bag, unscrewed it and swigged. I made a noise like a balloon going down and spat some out. How do people drink that stuff? It tasted like perfume. I swigged again and screwed up my nose. Saliva came in my mouth like I was going to vomit, but I didn't. I stared up at the ceiling.

Please God let me come on.

If you do, I promise I won't do it again until at least this time next year – when I'm nearly sixteen. Honestly.

And with protection next time.

I don't even mind if you make it happen when I'm wearing my white trousers, and I'm on stage in the Young Teens Talent Quest competition in front of everyone. Just *please* let me come on.

"Please." My whisper echoed through the steam to the white walls. I drank the rest of the miniature bottle and put the empty in my sponge bag.

Water lapped around my throat and shoulders as I sank back into the heat. As if *God* would listen. Besides, I said I wasn't talking to him anymore after what *he'd* done to Mum and me. Especially me. He even took my best friend away, right when I needed her, but that was only the second worst thing.

I rested my neck against the enamel and folded my arms across my chest. The glassy surface of the water gently rocked back and forth with my breath. The shadows of light and dark in the moving bath water made me remember the afternoon sunlight through the trees – the day I got the *really* bad news. It was almost two years ago, before I was a teenager.

But you never forget.

1964 Sheffield

That autumn day, weak sunlight feathered through branches and falling leaves as I got off the school bus. I had an apple crumble in my bag – in a dish that is. Proudly made in domestic science class. Couldn't wait to deliver it to my mum and dad. Especially Dad; he liked apple crumble. It was his favourite dessert.

I walked up our road and ran my hand along the edge of our cold stone wall; you know, sauntering along looking at our pretty front garden. As I did that, a voice in my head said, "Daddy's dead." It wasn't a female or male voice. Just a voice. I thought, why did I think that? It was weird. Really weird.

Something else was weird too – the lounge curtains were drawn.

I walked slowly up our driveway and in the back door. Grandma's back disappeared into her room. I didn't even get a chance to say hello. Mum said, "Take your things straight into the lounge, darling."

I opened my mouth ready to argue but something made me shut it again. I don't know what. Mum and I sat together on the long brown settee and she held my hands.

"I have some very bad news. Something awful has happened to Daddy." Her eyes became glassy pools. "He dashed across the road to buy cigarettes during the coffee break," she said. "A car was coming too fast round the roundabout; it hit him. He – died."

The air was thick and still. The dark wooden clock ticked on the mantelpiece and distant chirping of late-to-bed thrushes faded away. There was a shove at our front door and then the newspaper met the hall carpet with a thud.

Dad's evening newspaper.

The letterbox clanked back into place and stilled.

There had to be some mistake. He'd been *there* in the morning; how could he just *not* be there at teatime? "He can't be dead," I whispered.

Mum's pretty face crumpled and her soft brown curls bobbed as she gasped out some strange breaths.

My mouth dropped. "But, I made him an apple crumble."

Tears ran over Mum's cheeks. She drew me into her arms.

"He wouldn't have felt anything," she sobbed.

A terrible longing knotted in my chest. *My dad.* "I want to see him."

"It's not a good idea, darling. People don't look the same after…their soul isn't in the body any more…"

A slither of tears wet my face. "I wonder where it goes."

After we'd cuddled up on the settee and talked for a long time and it was dark and cold outside, there was a knock at the door. It was Uncle John, Dad's best friend. They'd been friends for years.

"Jean. I'm so sorry," he said in the hall and Mum started sobbing again.

I went and got my apple crumble and took a dish to him when he sat down in Dad's easy chair. "I made this in domestic science for Dad. It's his favourite. I'd like you to have a slice in his place, Uncle John. I made it ever so well."

Uncle John took the spoon and dish and started eating but then big tears ran down his face under his tortoiseshell glasses. Eventually he put the bowl down and had a real cry making sounds like an animal in pain. I didn't know what to do because I'd never seen a grown-up man cry before so I asked Mum if she'd like me to put the kettle on.

After he'd gone, Mum tucked me in for the night but I woke up and stared at the ceiling. It was so hard to believe.

And *that* was just the beginning of my long, dark night.

CHAPTER TWO:

GOD AND BILLY

I didn't want to go to school after the weekend. I shouldn't have had to go. But *they* thought I should go – so I didn't get behind.

Mum and I kissed goodbye. "It *would* be easier if the headmaster told everyone in assembly, you know," she said.

Panic punched me in the stomach. I imagined hundreds of students in the big hall. *Andrea Hampton's father has been killed.* "No! Only *my* teacher and the headmaster. You agreed. I don't want people to know." Especially Brendan James. I frowned. "I don't want to be different." Not everyone was going to read Friday's stop press, *City Man Killed,* or Saturday's longer version showing Dad's photo. I curled my fingers in my pockets. I hoped.

Mum gave me a bright smile. It'd fade from her lips the minute I was out of sight.

I kissed my Grandma. She lived with us all the time, back then.

"Go nicely," she said, whatever that meant.

We were three little women: the maiden, the mother and the crone all doing usual daily things, but it was different now.

"God bless," Grandma added.

God bless. Like he had already? I turned towards the street. Autumn's carpet of gold and russet had blown away and crisp, brown leaves were hurled through the foggy sky. I looked back at our driveway as I reached the bus stop. It was hard to believe what had happened. I turned back and tucked my chin into the collar of my coat, head lowered against the onslaught of the north-midland winds.

Against life.

How would it be when I walked through the school gates? It was just a normal school day for everybody else. Not for me. Nothing would ever be the same again for me. Everybody *else* had a dad. A sensation began in my chest and crept outwards, pushing against my skin as it rose to my neck.

Two glowing orbs shone through the morning fog. The bus headlights. I rolled my tongue behind my lower lip, dipped my head down further into my neck then stomped onto the bus platform.

Mr Fillmore taught science. He was tall and nice so I was doing my best to pay attention but it wandered out of the window towards the horizon.

The classroom was on the first floor and the school was high on a ridge above the city like our house. Beyond the houses and towards the far hills you could see some blast furnaces and other industrial chimneys. Two of the largest were slightly curved, big at the top, bigger at the bottom and narrower around the middle to upper part. One was lighter brick so appeared white and newer, whereas the other one was blackened with age and smoke.

There were thin, red brick straight up-and-down chimney columns behind the blackened one.

These towering furnaces, which the poet Blake called satanic mills, bellowed smoke into the distance, yet even that veil of charcoal was lighter than how *I* felt inside. It spiralled round and round and beckoned me out, into the sky and beyond the grey to mingle with the higher clouds.

I saw my dad, smiling, looking down. We were in a garden – he on one side of a hedge and I the other.

Suddenly there was a big noise and the classroom door flew open. My stomach jumped as if I'd been asked to read. We all turned and looked. Miss Hubbard burst into the classroom with a really mad face.

"Could I have a minute, Mr Fillmore?"

He nodded and put his chalk down, but frowned.

Miss Hubbard faced the class and her thin, letterbox red lips moved. "Who was sitting one row from the back, second desk from the window, in art class this morning?"

She spoke as if she were in an auditorium without a microphone.

Everyone froze.

Oh, hell. My arm sort of half went up as I slid further under the desk. I could see Mr Fillmore thought, 'Oh, hell' as well. He wouldn't have wanted it to be me. Anyone but me, at the moment.

Miss Hubbard leant forward and rested her knuckles on the front desks. Her skin didn't fit her body but was stretched over her cheekbones and hung from her jowls.

8

Her albino eyelashes stood out like a demonic curse on her hawk-like face.

"How dare you walk away from such a disaster, Andrea Hampton?"

Disaster?

"You spilled paint on the desk this morning and didn't clean it up properly," she bellowed, her face getting pinker. "That paint seeped through the lid into a girl's desk." She said each word really slowly as if she was talking to a two-year old.

"You *thoughtless* girl. Another student's exercise book got wet. You should have reported the incident and cleaned it up properly."

I bet they could hear her three classrooms away.

I rolled my tongue behind my lower lip. My hair shielded much of my face when I lowered my head. Only my nose poked through the curtain. Okay. I knew I'd done it. The paint had oozed through the crack by the hinges. I didn't ask to come to school. I had other things on my mind, didn't I?

"Look at me when I speak to you. I'll see that you're punished for the terrible act you've committed. You'll be writing 100 lines every lunch time on how to treat other people's desks. DO. YOU. UNDER*STAND*?"

I wanted to pick a bogey out of my nose and flick the pale green, hardened mass between her lips.

My eyes burned behind the lids and I could feel the skin under them crease ever so slightly as I lifted my chin sideways. It wasn't the end of the blooming world, was it? My top lip moved upwards at one corner.

I couldn't help it.

I looked at her as if she were an unusual breed of insect that I might study in the science lab. It was only sodding *water* paint. Anyone would think I'd oil painted obscenities over the whole school, or on her new car.

She turned from pink to crimson so that her ginger-white lashes and hair were luminous.

"Don't give me that look! Consider yourself in detention for dumb insolence, as well."

I didn't give a toss.

"This *is my* teaching time," Mr Fillmore said to her.

She opened her red mouth and Mr Fillmore stepped towards her. "You don't need to labour the point more than you already have, Miss Hubbard."

Miss Hubbard's high heels click-clicked as she flounced out. After she'd gone Mr Fillmore looked over at me.

"Are you all right, Andrea?"

I nodded and tried to smile.

"Do you need to go outside? Just go, if you feel like it. Have a walk around."

"I'm okay, Sir."

"Don't worry about her – I'll see her later," he said, then shook his head as if he couldn't believe how awful she was.

He would see her, too. He'd tell her about me and then she would simply die of embarrassment. She would have to come back and apologise. She would have to grovel.

Grandma went over to the window. Her grey perm blended with the sky outside.

"Let's shut it out, shall we?"

Mum took the poker from the fireside stand. "Definitely." She poked and stabbed the coals in the fire.

Grandma drew the heavy maroon velvet curtains.

"We'll be cosy in here."

Her chin wobbled. She was trying not to cry.

Mum sat on the settee with me. Sunset reds leapt and spiralled into the air above the grate. Grandma sat down and clasped her hands on her knee. They said in social science class that red was the colour of life. We stared across the hearthrug's crimson symbols and into the fire: a portal of volcanic colour to another world.

I called it the Fire Escape.

The clock on the mantelpiece marked the silent minutes until the kettle whistled from the kitchen. "I'll make it." I dashed off, made a pot of tea, put the knitted tea cosy on and brought the tray in. "It's brewing."

Billy the budgie chirped: "Do you want a cup of tea?"

The cage was in the corner. His little turquoise body and yellow head bobbed up and down. "He's not saying all his other lines today. He must know something's different."

No-body answered.

Grandma picked up the teapot. "I'll pour."

"I'd better let Billy out for his afternoon exercise," I said.

After checking the windows were all closed I opened Billy's cage door and put my finger in. He hopped on then sprung to my head and did a dropping. He always went on my head. It was because I was smaller than everyone else. "Thanks for your calling card." I took a Kleenex and removed it.

11

He zoomed around the room chirping then hung upside down on the mirror and looked at himself.

"B-i-l-ly," Mum called, but in a sad voice.

He flew to her shoulder, played kiss and turn then jumped onto her hand and made love to her thumb.

"He has to have some fun; he doesn't have a budgie wife," she said, and then her mouth pulled downwards.

Poor Mum.

Grandma looked at her apron then took a white lace handkerchief from her cardigan sleeve and dabbed at her eyes. "The Lord works in mysterious ways."

Mum looked away then reached for her amber glass ashtray and took a Park Drive tipped out of its packet, lit it, and inhaled.

I stood with my back to the hearth, facing them. "God was there for *Billy* last winter."

They didn't answer but they both sort of nodded at the fire and I knew they remembered that sad time.

Grandma had let Billy out for his daily fly round the lounge; then she went out the back door to put some washing on the line. She had one of those thick stoles around her shoulders. So thick, she couldn't feel Billy's claws gently resting in the mohair on her back.

They both went up the garden path.

Freedom!

Billy spread his wings and soared into the pale, refrigerated sky, leaving Grandma calling, "Billy!" her finger raised in perch form to the heavens awaiting his return.

We all cried. Grandma said, "He'll come back. God will see to it," and off she went to her bed-sitting room to have a talk to God. Mum stifled an eye roll and said, "Don't get your hopes up, darling." Then Grandma emerged with her Divine inspiration: to fund a display advert in the *Telegraph and Star,* describing Billy. She looked over her brown-rimmed glasses at us and said, "We must all pray."

I had, but I wasn't going to tell anyone about it.

The phone call came three days later. A lady who lived three miles away had seen the advertisement in the newspaper. She'd found a turquoise budgie with a yellow head on her washing line. As it happened (and this is where God came in) the lady had lost her own budgie some months previously and just happened to have an empty cage.

She coaxed our exhausted Billy onto her finger, talking to him constantly as she backed him in through the door. He gladly went in the cage. The lady phoned us but wanted to make sure he was ours, so Mum had to talk over the telephone, going through Billy's repertoire: "Billy, Billy's a good boy; do you want a cup of tea? You're beauuuutiful," and more.

Apparently, Billy's head bent on one side and he started chirping, then head-butted the phone.

Mum and Dad took our cage and drove out to the house. Billy had a little brown bruise on his forehead but was otherwise unharmed. They brought him home and when we had made sure all windows and doors were closed, we let him out for a fly – and he did a dropping on my head. Yep, he was our Billy all right.

Grandma said we had to give thanks, and a nice way to do that would be to sing a hymn.

My dad and I shuffled about. I knew the dimple in his cheek meant he was bursting to giggle, like me. Still, we all agreed it would be kind of 'right', so I chose *All Things Bright and Beautiful* and we stood in the lounge and sang the hymn with Billy in our midst, to give thanks to God for his return. What a happy day. Not like now.

Mum and Grandma were still staring into the fire.

"You always said God worked miracles. If he could do something complicated like rescue a lost budgie from the icy-white sky before he got attacked by big crows and magpies, why couldn't he stop someone getting run over?" I snapped.

Grandma opened her mouth but no sound came.

We all jumped then because the doorbell rang. Every time we answered it there was another neighbour in a suit or best coat. They would say, "Oh Mrs Hampton, I am *so* sorry for your loss; if there is *anything* we can do," and then they would talk in hushed tones and sometimes the ladies cried with Mum.

Mum answered the door. Uh-oh. The vicar.

As if there was anything *he* could do. Checking up on Mum, he was, making sure she hadn't lost her faith. Well, she had. She told him on Saturday when he came to pray for Dad's soul. Not that she was a regular churchgoer, you know, but she went with Grandma sometimes. She couldn't go anymore.

"God's love is everywhere," the vicar said as he sat down in Dad's easy chair.

I remained standing.

Was it in Miss Hubbard? Was it under the bed and in the wardrobe when dark night shadows seeped from under and within the furniture? Was it there in the scary dreams I'd had since Dad died – where lions and tigers chased me from room to room and house to house? "Where were this God and his love when Dad raced to get a packet of fags? Why didn't he stop the speeding car?" I muttered.

"Andrea!" Mum hissed.

Well, he wasn't there then, was he?

Damn right he wasn't.

"Shall we all pray together?" The vicar said, kneeling on our carpet.

I stayed on my feet, folded my arms and narrowed my eyes at him. *Don't give in Mum*. Don't kneel and bow to this God who took Daddy away. Don't.

Mum dropped to her knees, head in hands. She was sobbing.

They needn't think *I* was going to get down there.

"Dear Lord…" The vicar looked skyward.

While he was praying, I rolled my eyes, first to the left, then up, then down again to the right as if I was watching a bird in flight or following the arc of a rainbow. At the same time, I expanded my chest and gathered as much air as I could to sigh. My breath expelled between a 'ha' and a hiss.

The vicar went on about God looking after Dad in heaven. He'd need to do a better job of it than he had on earth.

I knew what brand of cigarettes Dad wanted to buy: either Park Drive tipped in the white and red packet or Woodbine in the pale green packet. He may have gone to buy five in a paper bag but if he felt really flush, he'd have bought a whole packet of ten. They smelled rich and comforting, like woodwork and newspapers on Saturday. He didn't even smoke cigarettes often. In the evenings he liked to smoke his pipe. That was the best smell of all; it wafted through the house like a blanket of security.

If Dad came back to see me, he'd have the pipe between his teeth when he talked to me and he'd give it a little tug with his lips every so often. When he smiled the dimples would appear on each side of his face, deepening like little black holes. I looked at the vicar's black bib. *That* reminded me of other black holes, like graves and holes in the sky that might lead to heaven.

Was that where he went? Was it?

"Amen," the vicar said.

His knee joint cracked as he got up. Thank goodness he didn't sit back down. I didn't want him spoiling the chair's scent with his musty old book smell. The headrest still had a whiff of Dad's Brylcreem when you huddled up to it.

Smells were funny things; they made you remember people and places. I couldn't smell shoe polish any more. Mum and I just gave the shoes a quick rub now.

I would have given anything to smell Dad's Imperial Leather aftershave in the bathroom and the honey on his breath at breakfast. I never used to like the smell of honey. I giggled and wrinkled up my nose when Dad ate honey on toast – it smelled funny.

I missed it the most.

The vicar walked towards the door. He nodded at me. "Andrea," he said. I remained standing with my arms folded across my chest.

I knew what that white collar and black bib meant.

The white was a small band of good and nice things like the white sky when the sun broke through but didn't last very long. The black shirt part was the huge void of death – and life, for the people left behind. It was the void of this God who shook our foundation and threw us into the severe, dark night.

I puffed my chest out under my tightly folded arms and narrowed my eyes even more.

"Hope to see you in Church," he said to Mum. He didn't say it to me. I pulled my mouth into a one-sided smile. Didn't think he would.

I had other plans – and they were nothing to do with Church.

CHAPTER THREE:

RISE AND FALL

Boring school again. I could hardly wait until break. Mandy was waiting outside the classroom, leaning against the wall. Her long hair was the colour of the cream at the top of the milk bottles delivered to our doorstep. She looked a bit like Marianne Faithful.

"Thank goodness it's break-time," I said. I could talk to her about how to get off with Brendan James; that'd cheer me up a bit. I took hold of her arm as we walked along but she kept it close to her side so I couldn't link mine through. "What's up?"

"I don't know how to say this, Andrea." She stopped walking along the tiled corridor and looked down at her shoes so that her hair fell forward and hid her face.

"The thing is I went out with June the other day. I'm *fed up* because you don't want to do stuff on the weekends."

Was she daft, or what? "I can't at the moment." She meant that I'd stopped going for walks with her on the 'Crags' – the edge of the moors. It was where the boys went. And I'd stopped going to the youth club too, right when we'd just got friendly with a couple of lads. Now I didn't want to go. Well, I didn't. Not for the time being. I wanted to stay home with my mum, make paper cut outs, draw, and even, dared I admit it, talk to my dolls. I wouldn't tell Mandy *that*. We were pretty mature for twelve-and-a-half-year-olds.

She lifted her rosy face. "So I can't be your best friend anymore."

Surely she wasn't going to desert me? "I don't understand. We've been best friends since we were five when you lived in Baker Street and me in Roma Road."

"June's persuaded me to be best friends with her."

My stomach curdled. June was always trying to get Mandy to herself. She was supposed to be best friends with Sandra. "What about Sandra?"

Mandy's blue eyes went from me to her shoes again. "June decided you and Sandra can be best friends."

June was a little cow. She thought she knew it all just because she had an older sister who went to work and 'did it' with her boyfriend. "But…" It was like drowning, water stuffing up my sinuses as I tried to hang on and keep my head above the surface. "What about tea tonight?"

"Apologise to your mum for me." She looked up again. "I'm sorry; got to go."

Her back disappeared down the grey corridor and people started pouring out of classrooms. I swallowed hard, turned to the wall and pretended to study the notices. How would *she* have flaming well felt if it'd been *her* dad that got run over and killed a few weeks ago?

Wind stung my face and blew through my hair.

I pressed my heels into my pony's sides and we soared through the crisp, bright skies into the meadow. "You and I against the world, Flash."

The moment was as nice as it could be, all things considered.

The grey-white behind the thick clouds brightened. There was a faint shine like a distant yellow torch finding its way through a blanket of mist. Like magic, the mists faded to a really pale blue-grey, like you might see on a paint sample card: blue-grey white, as opposed to creamy-white or oyster white.

Then the yellow-white ball brightened, and the fields, which were a grey-green shadow, sharpened to verdant green.

"Isn't it *lovely*?!" Grandma would say and all the people in the shops and streets would go, "Ooh, I say, in't it nice?" Others would say, "Aye, that it is." The weather was a bit like life. It rose and fell in a big wavy line, or like cantering, rising up and down in the saddle. The 'up' bits were when things got a bit better for a while, then the sun went in again and you hit the saddle, so to speak.

I reined Flash in from a canter to a trot and my backside bumped down against the leather as we turned onto the Roman road. It was made of pinky-rust gravel. Romans made it ages ago and it had a ditch either side to drain away water. It went from near Upper Greenwood, past the stables and all the way to the howling windy moors.

As we got nearer I could smell the stable. If I were blindfolded I could easily believe it to be the smell of the school toilets on a warm day, or of the sanitary rags that some girls flashed around the changing room to show they'd started their periods. *I'd* rather be private when I hooked the loop of the pad onto the sanitary belt.

Because I knew it was the stable and not the bogs or the rags, it was kind of a comforting, damp-earthy animal smell.

It was the sort of earth smell that took you from the silken green moss in the cracks on the old stone walls deep down into the earth, sinking into the smell of roots and soil and rain, so far down that you'd reach the root house of Mr and Mrs Mole and Mr and Mrs Beaver.

I breathed in the earth as we turned into the muddy drive towards the stables. It became a leathery smell as we passed the tack room. "We're home." I reached forward and patted Flash. "Glad Heather lets me rent you." She had five horses. Couldn't ride them all at once, could she? I jumped down and his nose nudged me in the chest. He was velvety-soft around the mouth. "Love you too. Okay, saddle and bridle off."

When I turned on the tap to fill the metal bucket, the whole pipe rattled like a drum beat. Blackbirds and thrushes sang nearby and there was a distant rumble of the number 51 bus, then silence hummed over the fields.

In the country, time sort of stood still.

Flash moved his head and dropped his nose over my shoulder – near my neck. I liked that. "Oh, Flash." I squeezed my eyes as the sad things came into my mind then rested my head against his warm, tan neck. "At least I have you."

"Hiya. I took Woden up the moors."

Heather burst into Flash's stable in her Wellingtons.

I jerked up, turned my back to her and reached for Flash's brush while I waited for the burning in my eyes to go. "Did you ride through the heather?" It was purple and mauve and blew and bent with the wild grass for miles.

21

"Near. You have to be careful. Those bogs can suck you into the ground and swallow you up. Hey, there's a kids' gymkhana down the road. Remember being in them?"

It seemed like a lifetime ago. I'd cringe if I were even seen in *jodhpurs* now. *Imagine* if Brendan James saw me getting off the bus like *this*. Die.

I put on a happy face and turned around. Heather was pretty in an unusual way. She looked foreign or even a bit black but she wasn't. She had olive skin and round, golden-brown eyes, a turned up nose and very white teeth. Her hair was short and brown and she had pierced ears with little gold rings in them.

"Last one I was in, my mum spent weeks sewing my herald's costume and matching banner. They had different coloured squares top right and bottom left with black crossed swords emblems on the gold parts; shield and daggers on the maroon. Around the tunic's edge, Mum sewed black arrows into cotton wool – like ermine. My banner hung from the trumpet Dad made out of a tube and baking funnel sprayed gold," I said.

"Did you win?"

"Blooming winner was a little girl in her Sunday best, white nylon dress, riding her white pony. The only thing that could be considered fancy dress was her wand. Obviously she waved it in the right direction."

"I bet Hayley, the riding school owner was knocking off the fairy's dad," Heather grinned. "I've groomed Woden. Back to Upper Greenwood. Or 'Apper' as Miss Hubbard says."

"Upper is supposed to mean we live in a posh area, especially the way she says it. Most people say 'uppa', like the 'uh' sound that old people make when they get up, don't they?" I finished brushing Flash. "You are lucky to have horses but it's a lot of work."

"Wait 'til winter. Now you're renting him, no matter how black and bitter the mornings, you'll still have to come before and after school, same as me."

Even with frozen fingers I'd have to pick out the grot from his hooves every day. It was a much bigger job than when I used to go riding at the stables. "I hope it doesn't interfere with the youth club time. Mandy and I used to go on Thursdays." I straightened up. "We got chatted up by older boys. Sandra's not allowed."

"Bugger lads. I'd rather have horses!"

I nudged my face up to Flash's tan neck to hide my expression. "See you tomorrow," then I whispered to Flash, "I like Brendan, but you're my *best* friend in the world."

Mum marched through town like she was still in the Women's Royal Air Force. Rule Britannia! She was cross that I was arguing about buying size eight trousers.

"You'll grow out of them. It's a waste of money. The ten will last longer."

I didn't want a baggy-looking bum. I *had* to have nice tight-fitting jeans like everyone else. Besides, I wanted Brendan James to notice me. He was older – about fourteen, but he looked seventeen. A poster advertised *Goldfinger* at the Gaumont. It'd be fab to go and see a James Bond picture with *him*, then sit snogging in the back row.

My gaze wandered to mannequins in the shop windows.

23

"Are you listening?" Mum asked.

I was next to her. How could I not hear?

Mum stopped in her tracks, right there in the street. "Don't ignore *me*. Do you realise I've given up my Saturday for you?"

I froze. What else would she do?

"You ungrateful child. I'm doing my best to make sure you have the things you need and that's the response I get." Her voice escalated to her former WRAF Corporal Hampton pitch. Any minute she'd say, "ABOUT TURN!"

I bet my mouth and eyes looked like three colourless dots with a nose in the middle. We were in *town*. Everyone would hear. "I'm not ungrateful and I know you're doing your best..." I mumbled with my head down.

"Why have you started this 'not answering' behaviour? Do you hear me?"

Who wouldn't? People were turning their heads to look at us: young families, elderly people, bus conductors hanging off their platforms, people in wheelchairs, kids, teenagers. All of them turned as if they had severe neck problems. I'd die if I saw someone from school. *Oh God*, don't let *Brendan James* come by.

I pouted and turned away.

"That's it, I've had enough. Here!" She thrust some money into my hand then strode off. Walked off! My mum! She left me in the middle of town. Right. I was going into the shop to buy the size eights.

I couldn't get it off my mind.

I went into the changing room. I'd have them and I didn't care what she thought. They were hipsters and really fashionable. I'd wear them with a skinny-rib

24

jumper. I glanced in the mirror. They looked great – really tight, but my face was all pinched and furious. Deep, sad yet angry eyes stared back at me. I didn't *mean* to hurt Mum's feelings.

"I'll have these, please." I handed the size eights to the shop assistant. I couldn't stop thinking about Mum. How upset was she? What if she ran away?

She was all I had.

I didn't even want to do the rest of my shopping. A sea of unknown faces swarmed in the streets. Families; mums and dads.

From lowered lashes, I looked at girls my age. Girls with their arms linked, laughing, looking in windows and having fun. Friends. Pairs. I still had my friend Sandra, who was June's best friend before June dumped her for Mandy, and I had other friends, but not a special best friend like Mandy. I didn't know what I'd do if I walked into my ex-best friend Mandy with her new best friend. I'd hate it if I saw her and June out shopping together. I'd look the other way. That's what I'd do.

I looked at my shoes and the uneven cobbles of the city pavement as I walked to the bus stop. What if Mum wasn't there when I got home? My stomach felt funny. What if her bus crashed and she died like Dad? I shouldn't have given her the silent treatment. What if I never saw her again? If our last words were cross words...

Head down like an upside down mop I clomped down the bus stairs clutching my shopping. Flaming white trousers.

I ignored people I passed in the street. Instead, I watched the little blades of grass that sprung up in

25

between the pavers. One step on each paver. I walked quickly, stapling my pain into my lips until I saw the maroon door of our house, then I slowed down a bit as I walked up the drive.

I put my key in the lock and waited for the metallic click. It was only closed, not locked. I pushed the door a little and walked in. All was quiet. "M-u-m," I called. She wasn't in the kitchen. No welcoming hello. No, 'Do you want a hot drink?' I prodded the lounge door. She'd had a cigarette in there, but she wasn't there.

My record player lid was open and one of Dad's favourite records, The Bachelors' *No Arms Can Ever Hold You* was sitting on the turntable. On the side table Roy Orbison's *It's Over* was out of its record sleeve. Last time I played that Mum cried. She asked me to take it off.

Why had she got it out?

Grandma's door was closed and I couldn't hear any talking. She was either having her afternoon nap, or talking to God, or... What if everyone had died?

"M-u-u-m." My voice wavered. She wasn't downstairs. I walked upstairs, slowly. Her bedroom door was slightly ajar. She was on the bed. Her shiny brown curls tumbled on the pillow.

My stomach got that plummeting sensation as if I wanted to wee. Was she moving?

"Hello," I said. It was almost a whisper.

She turned and half smiled. A smile that said, "You've been very difficult but I still love you." Her face was pink and her eyes were puffed. She'd been crying.

I wanted to hug her so much I could have just about jumped on her. I pulled my mouth in a kind of smile. "Are you all right?"

"I was just having a lie down. I must've nodded off."

I sat on the bed and made big eyes. "Sorry I didn't answer before." I folded my arms. Mum propped herself up and saw my package. "I've decided you can pay for your own clothes; I'll give you a bigger allowance."

"That's fab, Mum."

She put her arm around me. "You'll get to understand the value of money that way."

We had a bit of a hug – well, quite a big hug really.

I swallowed hard and got up. "I'm going to put my things away and change my dolls' dresses."

After I'd closed my bedroom door I hung up the white trousers and got out my dolls: Jenny, Diana, Lorna, Susan and Sharon. "Let's change your dresses and comb your hair, then." I wasn't *playing,* I was just caring for them. Once the last press-stud was fastened I sat them in a row. "I think I'm horrible to Mum because I *feel* horrible," I whispered to them.

Outside, twilight was descending. Through my bedroom window Dad's tool shed in the garden became a silhouette like Dr Who's Tardis about to dematerialise. I imagined him making some cabinets in there and Mum walking up the garden path and taking him a cup of tea. It wasn't *fair*.

I opened my bedside cabinet and took out my box of treasures: Dad's army medals, his cards to me and some ceramic horses and soldiers from his boyhood. There were many more at Granny Hampton's. I stroked everything and put my face near but nothing had Dad's smell. If only Mum hadn't given Dad's clothes to the poor people I could have had a jumper to sniff. I closed the cupboard on the box, picked up my dolls and held them all on my knee. My eyes squeezed tightly shut over the wetness and I pressed my lips into each one in turn. "Everything will be all right." I put them in their beds on the wardrobe shelf then drew my curtains on the shadowy garden.

I bounced down on the settee beside Mum and she put her arm around me. It was cosy by the glow of the fire, especially now we were friends again.

"Mum." My eyes smarted. "I had a *fab* ride this morning. Thank you for paying for Flash." Better not to talk about the afternoon.

She cradled me to her.

I let the heat in my throat lessen. "Remember Dad wouldn't let me go to see the Beatles a few months ago because he said there would be too many people there and I might get squashed?"

"We were right, despite what you thought. It was chaos. Mandy and Sandra's parents didn't let them go either, did they?"

"June went."

"Only because her older sister let her tag along."

I snuggled up to her. "Herman's Hermits are coming to City Hall with Wayne Fontana soon. Sandra said she could go if I could. You wouldn't have to worry, Mum. They're nowhere *near* as popular as the Beatles so it wouldn't be wild. Besides, I'd be with *Sandra*." Mum knew Sandra wouldn't do anything rash.

"I'll talk to her mum and let you know." She stared into the fire. "Aunty Jenny has invited me to dinner with them and another friend – a friend of Tom's, in a few weeks. Would it be all right if I left you with Grandma that night?"

I looked up from where I was nestled under her arm. Go out? On her own? What other friend? Mum was thirty-seven. I know she had Dad, but she wouldn't really want to go *out* with anyone at *her* age, would she? "Who?"

"I don't know. A man from Tom's work. They think I need some company. I don't really want to go, but perhaps I should. What do you think?"

She was asking *me,* woman to woman. "It's not a *date*, is it, Mum?" I shook my head.

Her eyes had that distant, staring look.

"No, darling, nothing could be further from my mind. Just dinner at Jenny's and conversation."

I stared at the gold, orange and red flickering flames. It was the perfect opportunity. "Okay, Mum. You go and have a nice time." I'd invite Brendan James round. I would. *Yeah.*

The red hearth smouldered, its warmth lovely. I knew *exactly* what it was I wanted to do now. I snuggled back under Mum's arm, my face against the warmth of her jumper to hide the heat in my cheeks. Good job her dinner wasn't this week. "What day in a few weeks will it be?" *My* night needed to be planned weeks in advance.

Oh yeah.

CHAPTER FOUR:

SILENCE, STICKS AND SONGS

Mum always made me go early for the bus so I wouldn't be late for school. It was starting to rain: soft drizzle spilling from charcoal clouds onto grey rooftops and November trees, which spiked into the mists.

A gust of wind made me drop my chin. I stared at the wet pavers. Sandra arrived and grunted hello. I looked up and mumbled back. She was pale and skinny, a bit like the model Twiggy with short hair the colour of corn. Pretty, really, but she was so quiet you wouldn't know she was there. She had long, dark eyelashes and sometimes you felt she was looking at you from beneath them.

"Let's be best friends," she said without smiling.

I bet her mum told her to say that. "Let's. We were always friends anyway."

"June found me boring as a best friend 'cos I'm not allowed out as much as you three."

"Mandy got fed-up waiting for me to feel better about Dad." Blooming June picked her moment to steal *my* best friend.

"My mum said they were cruel."

"Yeah."

We stood with our hoods up until the double-decker bus came, then went upstairs.

"Said on the wireless rain'll get worse later on," I said to the side of her hood.

"Better not lose the brollies."

"What did you do at the weekend?"

"Nothing."

"I went riding on Flash. Don't tell anyone."

"Why?"

"I'm nearly a *teenager*. It's not fashionable at *our* age to ride. It's for ten year-olds, or real Princess Anne or Heather types." Mandy used to say she'd rather ride a boy, but she hadn't done it yet. "I love Flash though." I sighed. "He makes me feel better."

"I won't say. I like horses."

She turned and stared out of the window.

The engine's rumble and the conductor jingling coins were the only sounds. Sandra had nothing to be fed up about but she was so moody *and* quiet. It was like being with a little girl. I felt so old.

"Next Saturday I'm going to my cousin's. She might give me advice on how I can get off with Brendan." Mandy and I used to talk about boy things. "How's your tortoise?"

"Cold. We made him a house in a shoebox with air holes inside the coalbunker. We only use the smokeless fuel one."

"When d'you wake him up from hibernation?"

"Spring."

"Lucky him, being able to sleep away winter." I started to get up. "Next bloomin' stop."

31

We walked through the school gates. Mandy and June were leaning against the railings. They both had on the same jackets. Obviously went shopping on the weekend. June had styled her short dark hair as if she was growing it to be like Mandy's. She was small and dainty for her age, like Sandra.

I glanced at Sandra's chest. My bust was bigger than hers and June's but not as big as Mandy's, unless I stuffed something in the ends of my bra. June, Sandra and I did that sometimes. Suzy Brown had bigger ones than any of us, and Lucy Bell who went out with Brendan's friend had a pair like a grown woman – I'd seen them in the school shower.

Mandy and I looked more right together because, apart from having tits, we were taller than Sandra and June and looked older. My hair was long like hers, except golden brown that glowed a reddish colour in the sunlight. When we had sun.

Sandra and I huddled further into the hoods of our duffle coats.

Mandy moved away from the railings and took a step towards Sandra and me. June's arm slipped through hers and pulled her off in a different direction. Mandy widened her eyes and wrinkled up her forehead at me, her mouth opening in a sigh, as if to say, I tried.

Sure.

Wind whipped around our faces as Sandra and I turned the corner towards the school entrance. I lowered my head further. I hated that wind. I hated school and I hated the way June had Mandy all to herself. The bell went and Sandra parted with a nod; she went to the 'A' class and I to the 'B'. I filed in, blended in, with all the other grey skirts, grey cardigans, grey stockings – not the boys, of course, who wore grey trousers and jumpers. The whole world had gone grey. I was like a pebble from the beach, tumbling through a hole with all the other grey pebbles, into the pit of learning.

First period – RI. Who wanted to listen to religious instruction? Not me. Definitely not me.

There was a clatter of scraping wood as we all sat at our desks. I got out my exercise book and pens then slid a little further down in my chair. Made myself comfortable. Folded my arms.

Miss Lane clapped her large pink hands then held onto the back of her chair as if she was about to deliver a sermon in Church.

"Qu-i-et!"

Her voice was like a man's; not shrill, auditorium loud and stressed like Miss Hubbard's, but tennis court loud, and very male. She hadn't plucked that hair out of the mole on her chin, either. She started on about the Bible. There was a faint waft of fresh air from the smallest opening at the top of one of the windows.

All the other windows were closed and condensation began to run down the inside of the glass panes. By the end of the class everyone would have breathed in everyone else's fart, including Miss Lane's.

"Make sure you're paying attention. The Bible is the most important book there is."

I glanced at her then gazed out of the window at the thunderous clouds. The drone of Miss Lane's words became a far-away sound.

It was those two industrial chimney columns that held my attention. The two huge ones were nearest. Smoke bellowed into the air and hurtled down between them, banging between the dark and the light, making circles like rings around a planet.

I'd been allowed to stay up and watch 'The Outer Limits' on the Thursday night before Dad died. It was scary, about men on a strange planet who'd mutated and had eyes like fried eggs. When it was over, I sat on Dad's knee and gave him a hundred kisses. I might have given him ten, or two, normally, but I counted out one hundred.

Then I said to Mum, "I'd better give you your hundred now!" But it wasn't so imperative. I gave her a few then she said I could give her the rest of hers tomorrow otherwise I'd never get up for school. Lucky I gave Dad his, because he wasn't there the next day. I hoped those hundred kisses kept him going.

That was the only goodbye I gave him. Uncle Lance told Mum that *I* shouldn't go to the funeral because funerals weren't suitable for children. Instead, I went to Aunty Jenny's house. She wasn't my real aunty. She was a friend of Mum's. That was the only day I had off school.

Rain fell against the windowpanes and filled the sky. It mingled with the smoke bellowing from the old chimney columns. Everything became colder, paler – emptier.

There was a deathly hush. I sensed people were looking at me. I blinked. It was like when you heard an alarm clock. You knew something was ringing, but you weren't quite sure what it was or if it was something you had to take care of. Eventually, you realised. I began to realise now that my name had been called twice. A voice whipped through the silence.

"Andrea *Hampton*."

That was the third.

I prised myself away from my daydream. All eyes *were* on me. I looked down at my grey jumper rising and falling when I breathed and let my hair fall over my face.

"Look up when I speak to you."

She must have been seven feet tall in her flat, round-toed black brogues. Her long, grey skirt flopped to her mid-calves and almost covered her thick, pinky-beige stockings. She had on a long, greenish-grey cardigan – the thick, hand knitted sort, over a sensible off-white blouse.

Her grey hair was parted on the side, almost straight, and gripped back on the longer side. No make-up. There were actually *two* of those moles on her chin, one with two hairs springing out of it; the other had just one hair but an extremely long, dark grey one like a spring coil. Someone once said there was a mile of hair behind every mole.

She made Miss Hubbard look like a fashion queen.

"Read the page we are discussing," she said.

My heart and stomach parachuted. Page? Book? Me? My finger travelled over an open page until someone whispered the page number and the line.

Her face was livid pink.

"What have I been talking about?"

I looked at the desk. *I* didn't blooming well know, did I? I raised my head. "I don't know, Miss."

"Come here this instant," she said.

35

My eyes travelled up to the ceiling then down to the wall on my right as I pulled my mouth to the side, making a dimple. I slowly pushed the desk, giving it a good scrape along the floor, then stood and sauntered over to her.

I saw what was coming: the stick. I raised my chin as I reached her desk.

She was round-shouldered most of the time. Her thick cardigan pockets stuffed with man-sized handkerchiefs pulled her shoulders forward and down. Perhaps the snot in the hankies had hardened to lead weights.

She took her cane, held it in her right hand and actually straightened her shoulders and stood to attention, rigid like a Nazi soldier.

"Hold out your hand."

As if I cared. I did as she said without batting an eyelash. I had fallen from trees, cut my legs on jagged pipes playing on the new building sites, felt a horse's hoof on my shin and been plunged into the darkest well of misery while a life floated away like a balloon. Did she think a bit of wood across my palm was going to stop my attention wandering?

One strike. It was over in a second. My iron mask was tilted to the ceiling. *One strike and you're out, you old bag.*

"Sit down," she said.

Fuck off. I narrowed my eyes and glided away as if I had a book on my head. I'd tell my mum. She'd come to the school.

Mum didn't agree with caning girls, unless they were really bad, as in throwing things at teachers or stealing.

Cathy Compton threw things at teachers all the time. She even put up her fists up to them and swore to their faces. I never did stuff like that. Cathy Compton's mum said to Mr Fillmore on open day, "I don't know where our Cath gets this fookin' swearin' from."

I settled down in my seat, folded my arms and looked out of the window.

Hairy gob would have to grovel after this. *Miss Hubbard* had already given me a public apology. Privately, she said she'd cried in the staffroom when Mr Fillmore told her about me. Lane is worse; she manhandled me. I'd *get* her.

I was smouldering like the chimney columns, partly from anger, but there was something else too: an energy. I wanted to hit, scream or burst.

The bell rang like a fire alarm and everyone sprang off their chairs clattering bags, books and wooden desk lids. Especially me – I gave mine a *really* good bang before I lifted my chin and swept out.

"She'll get into trouble," Sandra said.

I managed a smile and we started walking down Greenwood Hill. "I hope. I think we've missed the first bus, don't you?"

"Yep." She lowered her voice and leaned into me. "Don't turn round, but guess who's not far behind you?"

I hardly moved my lips. "BJ?"

"Yep."

I kept my voice low. "It seems only yesterday we used to get off at Carrington Crescent with Mandy and June then walk through the lane to Carrington Road." Brendan

James lived on Carrington Crescent, opposite the lane. But he always got off a stop later, on Carrington Road, then walked through the lane to his house. He used to pull his leather Beatles cap down and collar up – he knew what was coming. *We* had it all planned.

"I'm not going to push you into him, Andrea."

"I didn't ask you to. It needed the four of us to make it fun. I'm just *saying*."

Footsteps neared. Brendan and his friends were chatting, right behind us.

"Hello, girls."

He never spoke to me when he was on his own. I half turned. "Hello."

"You've missed the bus," he said.

"You have too, then."

"Come 'ere a minute," he said as we passed the big old Church.

Sandra kept walking but gave me a sideways smile. Before I could turn around Brendan grabbed my free arm with one hand then cradled me and my bag with his other and pulled me backwards towards the Church's driveway.

His friends and some girls from my class walked by and called, "Mmmm!" and "Whoo!"

My back was against his chest. "What's going on?"

He steered me towards the leafy bushes, away from the others. "You'll find out in a minute."

Then we were alone.

Brendan James turned me around. He looked so much like John Lennon. His nose was straight and his mouth thin, like John's. You couldn't exactly call him good looking, but there was something about him.

38

He bent and kissed me on the mouth, like they did on television. His hard chest pressed into me. I breathed in, not quite a smell, as such, but – I don't know – just something very male. The scent of soap was still the scent of soap, a wool jumper was still a wool jumper, but there was a different aroma about them when used by a boy. When used by him.

I was so stunned that I didn't even move when he put his hand inside my blouse and down my bra. I brought my elbows up but it was too late. I could have *died* with embarrassment.

I had cotton wool in the ends.

Aunty Mary and my cousin Jackie cleared our Sunday dinner plates away.

"You sit down, Jean," Aunty Mary said to Mum. Uncle Lance passed Mum an ashtray. It was the first time we'd been visiting since the funeral. Poor Mum; it used to be the four of them.

"I expect you girls would like to abscond," Uncle Lance said. He always used posh words. Head teachers did that.

"Come on," Jackie said and I sprung off my chair and followed her into the front room. Being two years older than me, she was more mature than June, Sandra, and even Mandy. She had a boyfriend, Bob, but they didn't do it.

The heavy royal blue curtains hid some of the watery gloom, although the sound of the rain on the windowpanes made it all the more cosy inside, especially with the glow of the small TV lamp to warm our background.

Jackie held the switch down on the gas fire then pressed the ignite button. There was a slam like wind exploding and then flames leapt into action. Jackie picked up a few single records. "Which shall we play?"

I lolled down by the gas fire looking at her records in the green Columbia and Parlaphone record sleeves and a couple in the orange and white Decca covers. "Any of the Beatles."

Jackie clicked the arm back on her red and white record player and the Beatles 45, *She Loves You* dropped down and started to play. My record player was the same but turquoise and white on black legs. We each got them as Christmas presents from our parents. The black legs were really mod and had little gold bits on the end where the legs sat on the floor.

Jackie nudged me as she sat down on a scatter cushion. "I heard you got the cane. My mum would've gone to the school too."

"Mum wore her new suit – the one that's nipped in at the waist and makes her look tall and slim."

"The deep pinky-red one?"

"She had on her best black high heels too."

"Fab."

"A stark contrast to Miss Lane. *She* had to say sorry to me in front of the deputy, Miss Smart."

"Dad says they're not supposed to cane girls."

"She's not allowed to any more – or else. Smart said so. I love this record."

"I like *Please Please Me* best," Jackie said.

"I think John Lennon's fab, don't you?"

"I prefer Paul." She closed her eyes and pretended to faint. "Oh, Paul!"

"Turn that thing down," Jackie's dad shouted from the dining room.

Jackie's lip went up as mine would but she didn't answer back like I'd started doing.

"Remember when our dads used to comb their hair forward and take the mickey out of the Beatles?" she said.

I smiled at the reds and yellows in the gas fire. "Your dad always corrected their grammar, saying, 'What sort of English is that – I wanna?' And my dad said his 78 records were *real* music. Or The Bachelors."

"He liked *I Believe, Diane* and *No Arms Can Ever Hold You*, didn't…" she trailed off.

I looked at the carpet.

Jackie put her arm round me. "Your dad was such fun when he went, *Yeah, Yeah, Yeah* and *Ooooh* like the Beatles, with his quiff forward."

My heart lifted. "Then our dads straightened up, folded their arms across their suit waistcoats and talked about something else, as if they'd never acted silly! Let's play *I Wanna Hold Your Hand.*"

She put the record on and we sang along until we got the giggles. I leant towards her. "There's this boy at school called Brendan and he looks like John Lennon."

I sprawled out on the rug nearer the gas-fire. "Mandy, June and Sandra used to push me into him in Carrington Lane. He used to wobble on impact, look ahead and pretend nothing had happened. Now we've stopped harassing him, he looks at me. In fact, he's got his own back. He *got* me, down Greenwood Lane. Before I could stop him his hand went down my bra. It was the new pink and white cotton one from Marks and Spencer's that Mum bought for me. Oh, I could die."

"They always try and do that."

"But I don't fill it out. I had *cotton wool* in the ends. He felt it."

Jackie's head rolled back and her laugh began as an almost silent screech. It made her eyes screw up closed. She rolled around the floor, laughing and hugging her stomach until tears ran down her face. I laughed too, and neither of us could speak. Finally, we sobered up.

"The next day when I walked past him at school, one of his mob said, ''Ere comes cotton wool job!'"

"I would *die*."

"I wanted to vanish like the Tardis but I turned back with my head in the air and swept my eyes over the four of them. I looked down my nose as if they were specs of dirt on the pavement."

"Good."

"Brendan sagged at the knees and hunched his shoulders and arms in a withering act. 'If looks could kill,' he said. I let my snooty look linger over them before I walked off."

"The sooner you get a proper date the better."

"I'd love it if Brendan took me to the pictures and we snogged in the back seat. Brendan's friendly with this other girl in his year. She's got hair that looks as though she's got her finger stuck in an electric socket. And she's fresh from the farm ruddy, with fat legs too!"

Jackie narrowed her eyes. "How *could* he? You'd better do something before he gets serious with the Frizz. Let's get my tarot cards out."

"What are they?"

"They tell your fortune. They're French. Dad let me have them as language practice."

"Fab."

Jackie went into the hall and came back with a nylon headscarf over her head.

"Shuffle them up then place them face down. Right, now, facing you, turn up the first six cards, first here. Right, the second crosses it, third above, fourth on the right, fifth here on your left, that's it, and that one below. Now turn them over from left to right.

"Hmm. *L'Amoureux*. You are thinking of having a love affair and it'll probably happen," she said.

My cheeks were on fire. "It's upside down to me."

"I haven't studied the reverse meaning but I think it's not as good as if it were the right way up."

"Oh."

"Deaths of circumstances, new ones starting and something to do with the moon; I can't work that one out," Jackie said.

I placed four more cards down the right side like she showed me. "I'll have to get some."

She stuck her chin out and spoke in a deep, witchy voice.

"Looks like your goal will be fulfilled."

"I was thinking of asking Brendan over the night Mum goes out."

"When's that?"

"Three Saturdays away."

"I have a better idea. *My* mum and dad are going out the Saturday after next; that's sooner. I'll have a small party. Invite Brendan. I'll make sandwiches, you bring some crisps and we'll get Bob and Brendan to bring some light beer and cider. You can't carry much. You'll have to go on two buses."

Invite Brendan. I could hardly breathe.

Jackie played with a strand of her long red hair.

"It won't *really* be a party – it'll just be the four of us, but you needn't tell Brendan that."

The Beatles' *It Won't be Long* started playing.

"I'll die if he says no," I said, but I didn't think he would. Why should he? I felt nearly fifteen like Jackie. I'd wear my new paisley mod dress, lacy stockings – and a bra.

No cotton wool.

CHAPTER FIVE:

THE DIARY

Late 1964

I checked my face in the hall mirror. "Bye, Mum. The 51 is coming up."

"Have a nice time with Jackie and your school friend, Brendan, darling. Make sure you're on the last bus." She held the door as I rushed out.

I waved from the bus platform. School friend. She made it sound like he wore short pants and played ball in the playground.

Excitement pounded in my heart with every step to the top deck. There were plenty of free seats so I sat next to the window and put my bag on the spare seat. Did Brendan think I was silly on the phone when I invited him? I tried to be grown up. His mum was really nice and bright and said, "Yes, dear, of *course* you can speak to him." Then she called out as if she were calling a puppy, "Bren-dan, ph-o-n-e!"

My insides had felt like I wanted to wee, but worse, and my hands were sticking to the receiver of the black telephone.

I made myself sound friendly, like Jackie said I should, and asked about his day and how the homework was going. We never talked like that. He must have thought, 'What?' Then I said, "I've just had a couple of fab weekends at my cousin's place. She's fifteen. We do a lot of stuff together." Then I blurted it out.

"That's what I'm ringing about really. Jackie is having a party in two weeks and I wondered if you'd like to come?"

Don't let him say no.

"Fab. I'd love to," he'd said.

Love to.

I brought my thoughts back to the present, looked at my shoes and checked out the lacy stockings. Got the new suspender belt on. We pulled up at his stop and I spied a Beatles cap through the bus window. A dark navy form with leather shoulders sprung onto the bus platform; all six feet of him. Something jumped in my stomach and my cheeks warmed. Brendan *James, eeeeek!* It would be like being with John himself.

He strode down the bus aisle and raised his eyebrows as he lowered himself into the seat beside me and his body touched mine. Saliva in my mouth came quickly and I had to swallow several times. It was that wool – the navy woollen Beatles jacket. It was slightly damp from the drizzle and very male.

"Hello. I've been looking forward to this."

His voice was deep like a man's. Close up, his blue eyes were dark and sparkling. The mouth that was usually straight had a slight tug at each end and there were creases at the corners of his eyes. "Glad you caught the bus all right." A dull veil lifted from me like a light bulb had come on.

Jackie said ask lots of questions because boys liked to talk about themselves. He asked questions too and we laughed together. It was nice to laugh with a boy.

"Does your mum know you go to parties?" he asked.

The traffic rumbled outside and money jangled as the conductor passed by. Parties? "I don't usually mention it when I go." I'd never been to any unless you counted Christmas parties at auntie's and uncle's houses, playing Ludo or the local youth club. "Do you?"

"Some. I go to the Esquire Club quite often."

You had to be sixteen to go there. He could pass, easily. His shoulders were well above mine as we sat side by side. "I don't think I've been to that one…" I trailed off.

"I'll take you sometime."

His hand grasped mine, but casually, as if he did it all the time.

"Do your mum and dad go out much?"

I almost couldn't breathe. He was going to ask if he could come around sometime so we could snog. I wouldn't tell him about that night Mum was going out – yet. She didn't usually go out. Mum and Dad never did, really. What could I say? Mum was trying to go out occasionally? Then he'd ask about Dad. I didn't want him to ask where Dad worked. I couldn't tell him what had happened. I couldn't. Not Brendan *James*. He wouldn't know what to say. He'd cough politely and feel terrible. It'd be awful. "Occasionally." *Don't ask about Dad.*

"Does your mum work?"

I almost laughed, relieved. "She's a secretary. Does yours?"

47

"Same. In an office."

The air was still and the bus growled. My eyes creased in concentration. *Don't ask.* No please, please not.

"What's your dad do?"

I smiled but only to hide my thoughts. His eyes were intense, his mouth serious, straight, his nose front on, waiting. Waiting.

I couldn't say, could I? It would spoil the evening. I half turned to the window. Oh, help. My mouth opened as I turned back to him and I had to say something. "Ellisons. Yeah. He works at Ellisons. He does the pays and stuff." Well, he used to.

"Accountant?"

I made a fist with my free hand inside my pocket. "Not quite, but something like that." I turned to the window, craned my neck over my shoulder and pretended to look back at something across the street. I removed my fist from my pocket and waved. "A boy I used to know..." I didn't even like to ask about his dad in case he started on mine again. "Are you staying on for O levels?"

"Doubt it. I'm in the top third but I want to earn money."

"I'll stay on for O levels because I'm really good at English and art. Pity about the rest." I laughed. So did he.

"So, how many people are going to this party?"

I sort of gulped. "I'm not *absolutely* sure – but – not many, I think."

"What, you mean, maybe like four to ten people or something?"

I hoped he wasn't disappointed. "Probably six or eight," I lied. Jackie was going to have a pretend phone call come in saying four of them couldn't make it.

He nodded. And smiled. We both smiled. I think he knew I liked him.

Freddie and the Dreamers' *You Were Made for Me* was playing as we arrived and Jackie opened the door. Bob was behind her in the hall. "Jackie, Bob, this is Brendan, and Brendan, this is my cousin Jackie and her boyfriend Bob." I went bright red because I'd never had to introduce a boy before.

"How d' y' do?" Bob said, extending his hand. The boys shook hands and had a laugh about something. "Come in. I'll take those. Would you pass a glass for Brendan, Jackie? I've got plenty of light beer as well. We've just been listening to the Stones. Like 'em?"

They knew he did because I'd said so.

"They're my favourite now," he said.

Bob showed him into the lounge while I helped Jackie set out the food. She'd made cheese and pineapple pieces on cocktail sticks and stuck them in half a grapefruit upside down. "It looks *fab*. I'll make us a shandy."

Jackie followed me into the lounge with the food. The Rolling Stones' *Not Fade Away* played. Brendan and Bob loved it, as did the boys at my school. It was because Mick Jagger purposely stuttered, f-f-f, before the word fade. It sounded like he was going to say the bad word.

I sat on the velvety sofa next to Brendan and Jackie settled on Bob's knee. It was fun to talk and laugh all together, in between eating and drinking.

49

Brendan put his arm around me and it was strong, protective and nice. Bob leant over Jackie and they started snogging.

Brendan pulled me to him and his lips came close to mine. I nearly got the giggles. I'd liked him for so long and now he was with me I could almost burst. He closed his eyes as our lips touched so I closed mine then our heads moved round and round like they did in films. I got the hang of it, except he was a bit sloppy and I wanted to wipe my mouth but I couldn't really do that in the middle of it.

"We should get a juke box so we don't have to get up every few records," Bob said.

"Fab idea!" Brendan said then whispered to me, "Is there somewhere more comfortable we could go?"

Jackie and I had already thought of that: downstairs for her and Bob, her bedroom for me. "Oh, not sure, I'll have to ask," I whispered against his ear then called across to Jackie. "Do you mind if we go somewhere a bit more private?"

I inhaled that same aroma – that soap and cotton maleness, as we walked up the stairs and turned on the landing to her bedroom.

Once inside I drew the curtains so that we were in total darkness, protected even from the dull glow of the street lamps.

"Come 'ere," he said, and pulled me onto the bed. His tall body covered me.

The more we kissed, the more I got to like it. We even talked a bit in between. No wonder all our mums and dads liked to be in bed together. At last, I was *really* with Brendan James. I might marry him one day. His hands

50

heated the paisley silk, kneading and grabbing, but not too hard. It made my breathing heavier and I closed my eyes. I wouldn't go all the way yet, but I couldn't help pushing myself into his hands as he snogged me. When he unzipped my dress and slipped it off one shoulder, cool air fanned my body. I filled out the bra I had on, and I knew he could tell. I smiled.

I slung my riding hat down on the bench top.

Mum was sitting at our new peacock blue, Formica kitchen table, her hand on her forehead. She looked up. "Hello, Andrea."

She sounded tired. I banged the back door shut behind me. "Brendan James has invited me to a Christmas party! What's up, Mum?"

"I'm afraid I've had a bit of a shock."

"What?"

"I want to know why Brendan was in your room when I was out."

How did she know? I told Grandma I was going to have an early night. I was. I just wasn't alone. Grandma watched *Dixon of Dock Green* in her bed-sitting room on Saturdays and had the TV quite loud. I made *sure* Brendan didn't walk on the creaky floorboard because she was underneath.

He actually didn't need to walk much at all. We fell onto the bed and started snogging straight away, desperate for touch because nothing more than a paisley grope had happened at my cousin's. We'd had to catch the last bus back.

I gave a blank stare.

"I know it's true. Your diary happened to fall off the kitchen table ..."

"You looked in my diary?"

"Not purposely, Andrea, it slipped off the table and fell open at that page. When I picked it up, I couldn't help but see it."

Oh yeah, right. She told *me* not to lie.

"Now what did Brendan do in the bedroom?"

I wanted to laugh. We hadn't 'done it' – yet. I folded my arms and leant against the kitchen cabinets. "Well, if you've read the diary I expect you know."

"Don't be cheeky."

I looked at the patterned linoleum on the kitchen floor.

"This is not appropriate behaviour at your age."

"I'm nearly thirteen."

Mum rolled her eyes to the ceiling and muttered, "Bloody hell."

"YOU'RE A CHILD. Good heavens! Do you remember we talked about love, intimacy and intercourse when you asked me some years ago?"

How embarrassing. "Yes." She said the man puts his willie in the woman's hole, and I went, *uuuurh,* but I was only ten. I kept my eyes on the linoleum. "You said it was nice when two people love each other."

"And were married. Now, what happened?"

My cheeks were on fire. "I'm not telling you – it's private." My voice reached a really high pitch. "You shouldn't have looked in my diary." I know what it said. It said, Brendan put his hand down. Not the top either. He put it down *there*. And I think I wrote, he had it out. I

52

curtained my face with my hair so that it became one with my folded arms.

"Did anything happen?"

"N-o-o." But I'd let him *next* time. Now that my face was cooling I looked up and sauntered over to check if the immersion heater was on so I could have a bath later. I clicked the switch on. "I'm going to have a bath, Mum."

She stood and waved the diary. "Come back here."

I stopped in my tracks.

"If I find any more rubbish like this, I'm going to have it read out in assembly next term."

She *wouldn't*.

No, she wouldn't. She was just trying to scare me.

Would she?

I looked at her as I might have looked at a tightrope when about to cross between two skyscrapers.

I'd absolutely *die*, she knew that. Imagine that being read out in front of him, his friends, the Frizz, even Mandy and June, who were not exactly speaking at the moment. Everyone would laugh.

She raised her eyebrows and gave a single nod.

Bloomin' 'ell. I wouldn't put her to the test. I'd never leave incriminating evidence around *ever again*. I'd hide what I wrote.

I slunk out of the kitchen. "I told you he's invited me to a Christmas party. That means he's my boyfriend..." I muttered from the bottom of the stairs.

"Do you want to end up like Suzy Brown?" she shouted after me.

Suzy was in my class and got pregnant. She had green eyes, a long fringe and a permanent fed-up look, which made her look older than most of us. She did it with Brendan ages ago. She'd done it with everybody. I didn't know whose baby it was but she'd been sleeping with older boys who went to work.

"She'll be sent away to St. Agatha's to have that baby; afterwards it'll be adopted. It'll ruin her, the silly girl," Mum called.

Suzy wasn't looking forward to it. She said she'd have to work in the laundry. She didn't even work at school. There weren't any other girls quite like Suzy. Some girls let the lads have a bit of a grope in the back seat of the pictures and four or five of them had gone all the way but most girls just talked about it – about what it would be like.

I put my transistor radio outside the bathroom door on the landing because I wasn't allowed to take it inside. The disc jockey on Radio Luxemburg was playing some of my favourites. I didn't want to miss any Beatles songs so I turned it up. Now it was loud enough to hear from the bath. I closed the door, sank into the warm depths and splashed around. Herman's Hermits' *I'm Into Something Good* came on followed by Wayne Fontana and The Mindbenders' *Um Um Um Um Um Um.*

Finally, I let the water out and dried myself off, slipped my padded dressing gown and slippers on and headed towards the bedroom.

Voices. Mum's, and a male voice. A strong, deep male voice. I fastened up my dressing gown and hung over the landing banister. It sounded like Brendan's voice.

I crept down a few stairs and sat on a stair by the handrail so I could make out the conversation coming from behind the closed lounge door.

It *was* Brendan's voice.

"No, Mrs Hampton. Yes, Mrs Hampton. No, Mrs Hampton. Yes, Mrs Hampton. We were both very foolish, Mrs Hampton. No, I'm sorry, I won't. Thank you, Mrs. Hampton."

What had Mum *done*?

The door opened. I backed up the stairs in my soundless slippers and hung over the top balustrade. Brendan must have sensed me there; he had a quick glance up. He didn't quite roll his eyes but the look said, *Bloody 'ell*, or worse. I widened mine in the same way. The door clicked shut behind him.

I waited a minute, the sludgy underworld bubbling inside me, before I stomped downstairs like a soldier in the SS and burst into the lounge. I narrowed my eyes. "What's going on?"

"I've spoken with Brendan about how wrong it was to be in bed with you, Andrea."

"How did you get hold of him?" I screamed.

"I looked him up in the phone book and rang. I said, 'You get round here in fifteen minutes or I'm coming to see your father,' and he was."

"How *could* you? How dare you?"

"Do you realise he could go to prison for interfering with a minor?"

"I'm not a child and I'm going to a party with him."

"Oh no, you're not."

"You've ruined my life," I spewed out at her and slammed the lounge door. I hoped it broke.

She followed me upstairs. "Andrea, be reasonable…"

To hell with that. I turned back. "I hate you."

55

"I thought you might," she said, her mouth pulled in a sad yet determined line. "Don't slam the bedroom door."

I did, but not quite as powerfully as the downstairs door. Then I turned my face to the wall and looked at the picture of John Lennon out of the *TV Times* pinned up there. The Beatles' *Misery* played in my mind.

Christmas Eve tomorrow. No party. No Brendan. Christmas Day on Friday. No Dad. I might as well just starve myself in my room. There was nothing worth venturing out for. And I definitely wasn't speaking to Mum. How could I?

I wasn't going to have Christmas.

I was going to stay in my bedroom.

CHAPTER SIX:

CHRISTMAS

I wasn't going down.

I wasn't.

Why should I? Some bloody Christmas. I felt sorry for Mum. I knew how awful it was for her: her first Christmas without Dad. How did she think I felt? We could have been friends if she hadn't told Brendan off.

I didn't know why she made such a fuss; I was almost thirteen. Some girls in Africa got *married* at my age so it was normal to want to be felt up by the lads. Girls at school liked it. I wasn't the only one who felt randy. Besides, I hadn't actually *done it*. I wouldn't let him go all the way *yet*, even if he had a rubber Johnny.

Brendan didn't even look at me when I walked up to the cricket field the other morning. He put his collar up and Beatles cap down and looked straight ahead. That was the day I would have gone to the Christmas Eve party with him. Now he camouflaged himself with collar and cap when we passed.

He had probably told the Frizz about my mum. I bet they laughed about me. Maybe he even took *her* to the Christmas Eve party while I was confined to the barracks. I bet *her* mother didn't read *her* diary.

There was no chance I was going downstairs to open my presents. I didn't even want them, and as for *hers*, I'd left them in a pile with Grandma's. She could please herself.

I turned the transistor on and *I'll be Home for Christmas* played.

Be home. I should run away.

"Andrea," Mum called from the bottom of the stairs. She could call all she liked. I propped myself up in bed with my scatter cushions and looked out across the gardens. Brendan was just a few streets away. I wondered what sort of day he was having.

There was a tap on the door like a little mouse scratching. Not quite the threatening ogre she was to Brendan – and me. Mouse-taps.

I kept my eyes fixed on the window. "Go away."

"Andrea, please." She opened the door.

I wasn't going to turn my head. Instead, I stared at the bare, black December branches, demonic forks in the sky. I didn't even blink when she walked around and sat on the bed.

The Christmas song finished and Peter and Gordon's *A World Without Love* came on.

"Darling, I know you're upset and angry with me, but I did what I did for your own good. Someday, when you're a parent, you'll understand," she said quietly and it almost made me feel calm.

I swallowed and concentrated on not looking, rigid like the black forks that held my attention; then I turned and glared at her. "You've ruined my life. He's not even speaking to me. I'm not interested in Christmas." My eyes returned to the devil's pitchforks in the grey-white void beyond Dad's tool shed.

"Could we call a truce just for today and Boxing Day?" Her voice was faint and shaky. "It's such a sad day for us all, quite apart from the Brendan business, isn't it?"

Because she had that catch in her voice, *I* wanted to cry even more. I kept my face in 'freeze' mode.

"Grandma's very sad, too. Come on, come down and open your presents. Let's call a truce for two days then you can go back to not speaking to me. Even wars have breaks on Christmas Day, you know."

It'd be cosy down there with Mum and Grandma.

"Come on. Perhaps we can discuss the Brendan issue in a few days if you want to, but please, for now, let's make up as best we can. Daddy wouldn't want our Christmas to be like this, now, would he?"

Every trick in the book. There was a tug somewhere in my chest. I thought of Dad in his pale green weekend shirt, then in his best pale blue one. He'd have worn that today. A pins and needles sort of feeling spread through my shoulders then crept up to my throat. My dad would never have let me go out with Brendan. God knows what he would have said if *he'd* found my diary. I'd have been housebound 'til I was thirty.

I folded my arms extra tightly across my chest and turned further away so that I looked over my shoulder at the wall behind my bed head.

"Please, Andrea, come on."

I suppose I *could*, but I wasn't going to be *nice*. I pretended to scratch my face and quickly brushed away an escaping tear. I gave a big sigh. "Just for two days."

She leant forward and hugged me. I half-smiled, pulled away and got up. After I buttoned up my padded dressing gown, I put my slippers on and stamped downstairs.

I kissed Grandma and we said Merry Christmas to each other, but very softly.

She looked all pinched around the mouth and a bit red-eyed, as if she'd been crying.

Mum followed me to just inside the lounge door. "I'll go and make us a nice milky coffee to have while we open our presents," she said.

Grandma put her hand over mine. Her eyes welled up. "I don't know what's happened, precious, but your mother needs your love. She misses your father so much. Try and make up nicely. Everything will work out eventually."

I suppose she meant God will see to it. Well, he hadn't brought Brendan to my door with claims of undying love – ravings that he couldn't live without me no matter what my mother said. "She's *ruined* my life," I snapped.

Grandma drew her chin into her neck and widened her eyes; they were big blue pools. Then Mum walked back in with the tray and Grandma sort of blinked and smiled.

"Oh, coffee and biscuits; lovely idea, darling."

She helped Mum organise the plates.

"Shall I be Father Christmas?"

Mum laughed. Even I laughed; then I remembered, and pulled my face back into a mod pout. Father Christmas was always Grandma's role since Grandpa died and she came to live with us. Only this year she wasn't dressing up in a red dressing gown with a red crepe paper hat and cotton wool around the hat and her mouth.

This year was a plain-clothes year.

1965

Georgie Fame's *Yeh Yeh* sounded through the gold grid of the transistor on the windowsill while Mandy, June, Sandra and I stood looking out the window.

"My mum's sad about Sir Winston Churchill dying," June said.

"Mine too. All people their age really liked him."

"And the sounds of winter '65 are coming to you live from the North Sea," disc jockey Mike Ahern said on the radio.

"I love Radio Caroline," I said. It was a pirate radio station.

"It's great to have mod songs from our own British radio station. They're so fab. No wonder the BBC radio stations hate them," Mandy said.

June turned the volume up. "Too bad. No one can do anything. They're three miles out at sea, not in British waters. Mandy likes Mike Ahern. He's got glasses. I prefer Rick Johns."

She turned it up more when the Beatles *I Feel Fine* came on.

"Not too loud, my grandma's in the other room remember." Only the week before June wasn't even my friend, now she was acting as if she owned the place. She wanted a chance to meet lads, that's what she wanted. When June heard I was having a party, she said, "Let's all be friends again – even though *Mandy and I* are best friends. It's silly not to be on speaking terms at our age."

Well, she started it.

She turned the knob back down. "Sorry. The boys should be here soon. It would be nice to meet a boy. I'd like to do it soon." She flicked her hair behind her ear. "My sister does it with Paul, of course."

Mandy smoothed down her Cilla Black dress. It was similar to mine. "Does her Paul use a rubber Johnny?"

"I think so. You have to be careful."

"My mum and dad use them," Sandra said.

"I think mine did." I looked at June. "When we were seven, *Mandy and I* found one in a jar in her mum's bedside cupboard. Remember, Mandy?"

Mandy put her hand over her mouth and giggled. "It was re-usable and Mum used to wash it out. I saw. I asked what it was and she said, 'Never you mind.'"

"That little squirt in my class with the runny nose, Joe, said he went to buy some at the chemist and the young lady assistant said, 'What do *you* want *them* for?' And he said, 'Cum round back and I'll show y.' He probably wiped his nose on his sleeve while he said it."

"He's gross," June said.

Mandy nudged me. "Lucky you got the green light."

"I've been quiet the rest of the holiday; looked after Flash, helped at home and been round to Sandra's."

Mandy and I exchanged a look.

"Your mum would be happy with that."

"I asked if I could have a few friends around when she went out, including Brendan. I said, 'Promise, cross my heart and hope to die, I won't let him touch me.' (Below the waist, I thought, crossing my fingers behind my back).”

I wouldn't, either, this time. A promise was a promise. It'd be a little more than a few friends, but there was no need to get into specifics with Mum. “She said, 'As long as you're sensible. You can get to know Brendan in a more proper way.'”

Mandy looked back over the table at the dining room door. That was my grandma's bed-sitting room. “Sounds like something your grandma would say. The food looks nice.”

“Her mum always does a good spread, doesn't she? Look. The girls are here, I'll get the door,” Sandra said.

“Thanks. I'll load up the record player. Turn the radio off.”

Brendan's friends arrived. I got flutters in the stomach as I went into the hall. There came the Beatles cap. A surge of warmth rushed to my cheeks.

Brendan pulled a scared face as he stepped over the threshold. His eyes darted around. “Am I still in the bad books?”

“Mum's out,” I assured him. “She's cooled off a bit, anyway. Come and have a drink.” I guided him through to the lounge.

“I've brought these.” He put some light beers on the sideboard. “Looks like most of the lads managed to get served in the off-licences.”

“I bet some asked their big brothers to buy it. We've got plenty for people I invited.”

“More than four?”

The skin under his eyes creased when he smiled. I giggled a bit.

"Who brought all the soft drink?"

"My mum provided it."

"She let you have the party?"

"She said I could have a few friends over…"

"Andrea *Hampton*…"

I gave him a cheeky smile. "I have to go and talk to some of the others, but I'll come back." I had to play it a bit cool like my cousin Jackie said. She knew.

Please Please Me blared out from the record player and Brendan mouthed the words to me, the lines deepening either side of his nose.

My navy blue skinny rib hugged my ribs and made my bust look big – well, bigger than it was. The jumper looked groovy tucked into my grey hipster bell-bottoms with the really wide belt. Brendan's eyes followed me. I bet he was mentally rolling off the skinny-rib, but we'd have to start from square one: being friends. If he'd wait.

I had to concentrate on what was going on. I'd made extra sandwiches and canapés, which was good because those Mum made had already been eaten. There were a few more people than she'd catered for.

"Where have all these boys come from?" I whispered to Sandra.

She shrugged.

June leant towards me. "Some of these are gate-crashers."

The mainly lemonade shandy Mum had provided was disappearing fast. Some boys hadn't even brought their own drinks. Tight bums. New boys were coming. I didn't know them. People were letting them in.

"Where's the beer?"

I was sure several of them said it because it was like an echo. Cheeky so-and-sos. They hadn't brought any.

"We don't know them," Mandy said quietly.

"I think you weren't invited," I said, re-opening the front door.

"Word gets around," one said, walking around looking at things in the hall. Our things. Mine and my mum's.

The gritty pop-pop of a few motor scooters vibrated up our driveway and came to a halt. While I was trying to get rid of the last lot of unwanteds, big boys with parkas on pushed their way inside. Mods. They were about seventeen and good looking. At least they had some cider and beer in their parka pockets. I let them go through to the lounge and I followed, as if I was a visitor. They looked around, talked to my girlfriends and were okay, except they filled the place up a bit. June was in her element.

The drink had nearly run out. People were putting their drinks down where there weren't any mats. Mum would go mad if they left rims. The mods were okay, but how would I get rid of the other ones I didn't invite? I thought we'd dance the twist and the shake to Beatles records and have fun – about twelve of us. There must have been forty people. It was *really* noisy. The fog of cigarette smoke was overriding the soft, warm glow of the lamp. It wasn't awful, but it wasn't exciting like I thought it would be. I hoped I'd put out enough ashtrays.

Suddenly, there was a roar like something between a machine gun and an electric saw. It made me jump. Motor bikes. I dashed back into the hall. We couldn't have mods and rockers under the same roof. Their headlights shone through the small window in the middle of the front door as the jack-hammer sound came to a halt.

"I'm sorry," I said to the big bikie with the black leather jacket and silver studs, "But I can't let in any more people. You weren't invited." He must have been the leader of the gang. The Shangri-Las' song, *Leader of the Pack* was about a boy with a motorbike, but he died.

"Any booze here?"

"It's all gone," I lied.

He eased one big boot inside. "Let us in out the cold for a few minutes, love."

Other bikies followed. I was getting fed up. I looked for Brendan and Kev. "Can you do something?"

"They'd kill us," Kev said.

"We'd have the rest of the gang after us. We'd be mincemeat," Brendan added then he leaned closer and whispered, "They won't be able to nick all the beers; I hid some in your pantry."

People were everywhere. Then the unthinkable happened. I put my hand up to say, 'No, don't…' but it was too late. Some boy from our school opened the dining room door.

"Bloody 'ell, there's an old lady in there," he said.

Oh dear. I'd forgotten about Grandma – until now.

Mum had told her I was having a few friends around and that I'd be sensible and responsible. Would she mind staying in her bed-sitting room? There'd be a *bit* of noise, she'd said. But this wasn't a bit. Grandma wouldn't be able to concentrate on *Dixon of Dock Green*.

The boy wobbled and burped then closed the dining room door.

It opened again.

Oh die.

Oh carpet, swallow me up.

Grandma walked through into the hall in her pink furry slippers. Her maroon, tweed wool dress was partially covered by her stole; she'd become bent since Dad died. There was a lull in the conversation, which dwindled to a deathly hush.

Thank God she hadn't got a hair net on.

They all moved back, making a pathway for her. Many spilled out into the hall behind her, adding to the number of boys lolling against the walls and staircase. Some sniggered and make rude comments. Grandma made a beeline for the front door.

Yea as I walk through valley of the shadow of death, I shall fear no evil.

"I'm sorry it's a bit noisy. Where are you going?" I whispered.

"Going to Mrs South. I'm going to phone your mother," she said without looking at me.

As the front door clicked shut after her, I turned and faced a sea of gaping faces. "You'll have to go now."

"Soon," someone said. They filed back into the lounge laughing and talking. Some of my girlfriends whispered that they were going; they were a bit scared because the rockers had been looking menacingly at the mods. I wasn't in the lounge much, so I didn't know. I was on door duty.

The only girls left were Mandy, June, Sandra and two others but those two were picking up their coats and gloves. I didn't have time to talk to them or Brendan. I was too busy watching what people did, where they put their drinks, flicked their ash and if they were nicking anything.

Screeching sirens almost burst my eardrums as headlights flooded the area outside the front room window again.

"Uh-oh," someone said.

"Uh-oh," I agreed.

There was a one-two-three knock at the door.

A big uniformed police officer stood there. He peered inside. "Is your name Andrea Hampton?"

"Yes."

"It's your party?"

"Yes."

He plodded inside. I hadn't invited him, either. The other policeman plodded behind him. That one had narrowed eyes and a flat face like a gangster.

"How many of these people did you invite?" The first one asked as we walked through to the lounge. The gangster followed and his beady eyes darted around. I pointed through the lounge door to my three remaining girlfriends, Brendan, and five of his friends.

"And the rest?"

I shook my head.

"Now, Andrea, has anyone been taking any little purple pills?"

"No."

"Has anyone been passing a cigarette around?"

68

"They've had their own packets and filled up a couple of ash-trays." I pointed to the modern, square amber glass ashtrays that Mum liked.

He looked over at the other policeman then back to me. His eyes were like bulging marbles beneath his helmet. He gave me a big smile that stretched his lips almost flat then nodded ever so slowly. "But, was there any *particular* cigarette, just going round by itself?"

Did he mean like the *Invisible Man*? When his bandages came off all you saw on the TV screen was the cigarette walking about by itself. I knew very well what he meant, really. Mum often reminded me not to accept a cigarette that people might pass around to share because it was a drug and dangerous. I might die and she didn't want to lose me as well, so I promised. No one here had brought one of those, I was sure. "No."

That officer clicked the light switch on. Bright light flooded the room and shone on our rust, maroon and gold patterned carpet. "Check pockets anyway," he said to the gangster-face, then walked over to the record player and clicked the 'eject' switch. The arm lifted from the record and the Stones' *Not Fade Away* f-f-f'd to a halt.

There were lots of moans like cows and 'Aw bloody 'ell's' and 'boos' from all the boys.

The gangster looked in the nooks and crannies around the lounge and kitchen then sniffed the air. He shook his head at the nicer, talking officer then turned to the boys and held up his hand like a traffic warden.

"You lot line up. Turn out your pockets – all of 'em."

He checked the contents then shook his head. I bet the helmet straps under the chin were really uncomfortable. The nicer one turned to me.

"Is there any damage anywhere?"

I did a quick scan. "I don't think so."

He looked at the uninvited boys. "Right. You lot go; go on."

More, 'Aw *bloody* 'ells'.

"NOW."

They booed the officers as they started to file out. *I* was pleased.

The nice officer faced the six invited boys and my girlfriends.

"Start clearing away some of this junk, then you can go too."

He nodded around the room at the paper plates, bits of leftover food, ashtrays and bottles then he tipped his helmet towards me and lowered his voice in a kinder way.

"I want you to check again for damage when it's a bit clearer."

The others scurried about filling rubbish bags with the throwaway stuff and bottles. Mandy took the serving plates to the kitchen and rinsed and stacked them. The boys collected beer bottles and cardboard cartons then took them to the bin.

"*And* the ashtrays," the policeman said.

The room looked better now. Things were in their place. Instead of being cluttered with bottles, the mantelpiece had its usual clock, two small vases and Mum's amber ashtrays.

"You can all leave now."

My face fell. "Can't the friends I invited stay?"

It nearly cracked his face, but he smiled. "I think not; your mother will be home within half an hour. Your grandmother will stay with neighbours until your mother comes home."

The gangster pulled his mouth in a tight line and nodded.

I bit my lip and looked down. Mum would be disappointed in me. I turned to the nice one. "Can *Brendan* stay 'til my mum comes home? It's okay; he knows my mum." Did he ever.

Brendan was a few feet away, trying not to choke. Out of the corner of my eye I watched him bring his knuckles to his mouth and cough politely.

"Mrs Hampton has met you before?"

"Oh yes, Sir. If you don't mind, I'll help clean up a bit more and be here when Mrs Hampton gets home so Andrea doesn't have to face the music alone."

Brendan knew when to mind his Ps and Qs.

The nicer policeman looked him up and down. He wagged his finger at Brendan. "Don't you be getting up to anything."

"No, Sir."

CHAPTER SEVEN:

WINTER WORLD

That was Mum's key in the door.

Brendan had high colour in his cheeks. He wasn't guilty. We'd only been talking. He kissed me a couple of times with his arms around me but he didn't get fresh. Now he edged away to the other end of our long, brown modern settee. I bet we looked like a couple of wide-eyed bookends propping up the vacuum in between.

There were voices; Mum's and a man's.

The door swung open and Mum entered the lounge. A tall man followed her in. Brendan and I edged further into our settee arms so that we became one with the material.

I made big eyes. "Hel-lo Mum." *Don't shout at me in front of him.*

She sort of smiled back with tight lips.

Brendan shot up as if he had a chilli pepper up his backside. Mum would like that. Not the possibility of Brendan having a chilli pepper up his bum (although she might) but his manners in standing up when she entered the room. Yeah, she'd like that.

With this look on her face that wasn't quite a smile, she raised one eyebrow. I didn't know how she did that. I couldn't do it. Both mine went up if I tried.

"Hello, Brendan."

The unknown friend of Aunty Jenny and Uncle Tom towered behind her.

Brendan stepped forward, probably thinking he was my dad. "Good evening, Mrs Hampton. Good evening, Sir."

He offered his hand to the stranger, who shook it.

"I'm terribly sorry about the trouble," he said to them both. "It wasn't Andrea's fault. There were just a few of us here having a quiet shandy and listening to records, when all these gate-crashers arrived." He looked at Mum's friend and wrinkled up his forehead. "Honestly Sir, there were too many of them for us to do anything about it. We were out of our depth, my mates and I."

Mum's date nodded and went, "Hmmm," like he was playing a part. Well, he was. He had dark hair and glasses – kind of serious-looking but quite handsome for an older person, I supposed. He looked around. "Do you think there's any damage, Jean?"

Mum shook her head. "We'll have coffee in a minute." She turned back to me. "You've done a very foolish thing, Andrea. It could have been so much worse. We'll be having a talk later."

"I'm sorry, Mum, honestly. How could I have known all those older boys would find out about my small get-together? I didn't even know them. I've cleared most of it up. *Brendan* helped me." That, together with his gentlemanly manners, would help.

She gave a quick nod. "Thank you, Brendan."

Everyone was silent. Seconds ticked by and Brendan cleared his throat. He looked at me and then at Mum standing there with her arms folded.

73

"Er, well, I'd better be off."

I walked him to the door.

"*Goldfinger* is *still* on at the Gaumont," he muttered.

I'd seen it with Sandra and her mum and dad now, but that didn't matter. I nodded and tried not to beam too much. He was going to ask me out – to snog.

"It's been one of the longest running films…" He bent as if he was going to kiss me goodnight, then changed his mind and straightened up.

"See you, Andrea."

"Race you!" Heather said, urging Woden into a canter.

She was such a tomboy.

I clicked my tongue a couple of times as we entered the green field. "G'n boy."

We charged through grass and pale sky, past the mossy stonewalled walls and stiles. The wind blew my navy and yellow anorak up like a balloon around me.

"At least your mum didn't stop you going riding as punishment for the party," Heather puffed out.

"True. No big party for my thirteenth though; just Mandy, June and Sandra to tea on the day." We'd play Beatles music and pretend to be each other's favourite Beatle. "I should be nicer, I suppose. I'm lucky to have Flash. My mum probably wishes she had a goody-goody two shoes daughter like Jocelyn, Aunty Enid's daughter. They live down south now, but s*he* says," I put on a squeaky voice, "Yes, Mummy, No Mummy, three bags full Mummy."

"Bloody Pollyanna."

"Brendan James only sat next to me once on the bus, since the party." Mostly he sat with older girls in his own class – like the Frizz. I couldn't stand it. I'd have to tell him how I felt one of these days.

We cantered through the field and back onto the Roman road's gravel path. Heather galloped ahead. I leaned into the canter, sped into the wind, sun and space. Country walls and trees blended to one fast moving colour and then I was forward, flying, upside down.

My head thudded. I looked up at blue sky and heard the screech of tyres.

"Y'all right love? Don't move your head or neck for a minute."

A man was running towards me from his parked car.

I moved my eyes to one side. Lucky I had my riding hat on. "Think so." Flash walked a step nearer and hung his head and soft nostrils near my face. He made a little breathing rumble.

I reached out and stroked his face. "All right, Flash."

Heather rode back. "You okay?"

"Nothing hurts." I moved my head left and right. "Flash tripped. He was unsteady today."

"She did a somersault right over his neck and landed on the top of her head," the man said. "Do you want me to take you to hospital to check your head?"

He might be a bad man. "No, thank you." I pushed my arms into the gravel, sat up and took my riding hat off.

Heather moved my hair around with her hands.

"No blood or bumps," she said to him.

"It's a good hat. I'll go home as soon as we settle the horses."

"You're sure you're all right?"

I got up and held Flash's reins "Honestly. Thanks for your help."

He went back to his car.

"I'll walk with Flash, Heather. There might be something wrong. He stepped this way and that when I tried to put his saddle on, and his ears went back."

"He does look thinner."

"His spine cut into my thingy when I rode bareback last week."

"Lucky you."

The stable smell welcomed me as we turned into the dried-mud driveway.

"Fancy falling down, Flash!" I hung up the saddle and bridle then turned on the noisy old tap over the bucket. The dampness in the air tickled my chest as I breathed. When I wiped Flash down he felt bony under my hand. There was less of him padding his ribcage than there used to be. I took the brush. "Stand still, Flash. I'm in charge. What's wrong?" I had to boss *someone* around. "You like to be brushed." I stopped. "Heather! Come and look at this." There were tiny fingernail-sized bare patches dotted about his body. I'd noted a few when I saddled him, but now I could see there were more. On top of his weight loss, it made him look sick. "Easy, boy."

A tear formed in the corner of his big blue-brown eye and slid onto his cheek. He looked at me for a long moment then hung his head.

"I didn't mean to be bossy. I won't brush." I put it down and turned to Heather in a panic. "Look! Is he sick?

Does he need medicine?" I fumbled for a hankie in my anorak pocket and blew my nose.

"Hadn't seen *that*. I'll tell my mum. She'll know."

Heather walked back to her own horse. I pressed my face into the side of Flash's once glossier tan fur and we kept our heads together for a few minutes. "Perhaps we're both suffering from the gloom of the winter world." I heaved a sigh. "Got to go and finish homework. If I miss a day with you, it's because I'm off school with the sniffles." I patted him and looked into his soft eyes. "I'll make up for it next time."

Mum looked up from the kitchen table where she was reading the *Telegraph and Star*.

"Nice ride?"

I sat down. "Great. What's for dinner?"

"I want to talk about your homework."

"Almost done." I looked away.

"You're doing too many things now: up at dawn every morning to groom Flash, and an hour after school. You want to go to a friend's house *and* the youth club during the week, as well as weekend visits. You're finishing homework late at night. Something has to go – and it's not the homework."

I jerked out of my slouch. "Mum! Don't make me *choose*! You've only just started letting me go to the youth club again." That meant more chance of bumping into Brendan.

I love Brendan. I love Flash. "I *love* my horse. I just want someone to…I don't know."

Mum lit a cigarette then closed her eyes and drew on it.

"Put the kettle on and the tea in the teapot. You know, I think you didn't realise how much work having a horse was going to be."

How did she know? My cheeks warmed as I put tea in the teapot. I went back to the table and Mum gave me one of those, I-wasn't-born-yesterday nods.

"Dad brought back a kitten from a litter when I was three. You didn't let me keep *him* either."

"It did its business on the kitchen floor. I worked part-time." She sighed.

"I adore Flash, Mum. He's sick. He's thin and his fur is coming off. His big eyes looked right into me today as if he knew *everything* about me and as if he even knew something I didn't. It was *really* strange. Do you know what I mean?"

Mum looked at the sky through the kitchen window.

"I think so."

"Remember when I was seven, about the dog? You had to go to the phone box during the night to ring the hospital because you had a 'feeling' Grandpa had worsened, and a big dog waited outside the box."

"There were no buses. I had to walk through a bad part of town to get there. I tried to shoo it away, but it wouldn't go."

"It walked all the way to town with you, and every time you stopped, it stopped. When you got to the main road in front of the hospital, it looked both ways, crossed the road before you and walked up the hospital steps to the door." Even as I said it, I got shivers down my spine.

78

Mum's eyes were watery.

"The doorman asked if he was mine. It just turned around and went back. That was the night Grandpa died."

"You needed a body guard. Animals *know* things, don't they?"

"Some seem to."

"Flash *knew* something."

"I didn't say you can't keep him. Think carefully and choose what's important: limiting social activity, and keep Flash, or, the youth club and weekday friend visits as well as weekends. If the latter, you can only hire and care for Flash at weekends – not daily."

I hung my head. "I don't know if Heather's mum will let me be a weekend rider; she could rent him to someone else," I muttered. "Besides, they like to get the horses ridden daily."

"Not all their horses get ridden daily, do they? I'll ring and ask what our options are."

Heather's mum would be cross. She was mean when she got mad. "Tell her he's a bit sick." A deep emptiness washed over me.

I banged my hand on the clock and squashed its clattering.

Five-thirty. I only knew that because when I reached for it I also put the lamp on. It was as black as coal outside. I could see my breath in the room like the steam from a saucepan.

The hand that reached beyond the bedclothes felt like an icicle. I grabbed my suspender belt, grey stockings and the rest of my underwear from the chair. I pulled my

79

bundle of clothes under the covers so I was cocooned against the icy tentacles of Yorkshire weather for operation dress.

First I took my Marks and Spencer's bra, which matched my suspender belt, then my liberty bodice, and started putting them on in bed. Next, my vest and suspender belt before I rolled on the school stockings. Finally, my new red bloomers. They were ever so mod. I had another pair in royal blue. They were almost knee length and the modern version of what my grandma and granny used to wear in their day – only theirs were white, and baggy.

Mum would have a fit if she knew I didn't have a strip-down wash first. I'd wash the bits that showed afterwards; I hated shivering in the bathroom. Some people who lived in the south of England, or who had more money and had that new central heating, wouldn't know the level of cold I was talking about. It's a sort of damp, biting, ancient empty Church cold.

Putting on all those layers was all so exhausting I nodded off again.

"Andrea!" Mum called up the stairs. "You'll be late for the stables."

I started coughing. "I'm tired."

"Thought you might be."

I flung myself out of bed, finished dressing at high speed, then ran into the bathroom and switched the heater on while I washed essential places, moving clothing where I had to.

"Is it raining?" I called down to Mum.

"Y-e-s."

She liked the sun too.

We'd ride wearing our wind-proof rain capes over our ordinary coats. I could already feel my wet gloves holding the reins. On the way home Heather's mum's car would smell damp and musty, like wet carpet.

I muffled myself up with my padded dressing gown over my clothes then went downstairs and coughed my way into the kitchen.

Mum raised an eyebrow. "That doesn't sound good. Hope it's not bronchitis again."

Radio Caroline's disc jockey said it was blowing a gale out there on the North Sea and snow was expected in the next few days. I sat down at the kitchen table. "I don't feel fab."

I had a bad feeling.

"I rang Heather's mum. She'll call the vet. I mentioned your homework was suffering. You could still rent and care for Flash just at the weekends unless they have visitors who ride – if that's what we decide to do. I need to let her know."

I could *never* stop seeing Flash.

The alternative wasn't great. I stirred my tea. Weekends would still be two full days out of seven. I scraped the spoon back the other way. What was I going to do? I'd miss him during the week. But I'd miss the *youth club* if I didn't go. *Everybody* went. "Don't make me choose," I whispered, coughing.

Five fifty. I should have been leaving for Heather's. I looked at the table. "It's hard to go *every* morning."

She held a spoon of red medicine towards me. "It's your decision," she said softly.

I sucked the bittersweet mixture. *Bloody hell.* How did *I* know what to do? I was so tired I couldn't think. I sighed. "Weekends then. Tell her I'll even go if it snows at the weekends." It was pretty in the country when it snowed. I rested my head in my hand.

Was I doing the right thing?

Condensation ran down the bus windowpane. I rubbed a little space in the dampness as we cornered Carrington Road. Although it was almost dark, I could see Brendan. My heart pounded. From the top of the double-decker I couldn't mistake the shape of his shoulders – and the Beatles cap, half way up the street. A big bag was slung over his shoulders; he had a paper round. I grabbed my school bag, hung onto the railings and hurried down the stairs to the bus platform. "Next stop, please."

I jumped down and rushed up the hill to catch up with him. The freezing air was like steam suspended in the darkening sky and the edges of the houses blended into the foggy background. On either side of me the street lamps made a ghostly orange glow. "Brendan! Hello!" I puffed.

He put his collar up and looked straight ahead. "Hello."

"How long have you had a paper round?"

"Just a couple of days. Look, I've got to keep moving. Besides, you don't want to get into trouble with your mother."

I had to run to keep beside him. "It's okay. I want to, you know…" It was on the tip of my tongue to say 'I want to be with you' and 'I like you' but he looked so angry.

"I've already been in trouble with your mother once – almost twice. I don't want to get you or me into trouble. You're too young, Andrea," he said, as if he were twenty.

"No, I'm not!" If I hadn't got a big duffle coat on I would have puffed out my 32A chest but he'd never see it under the layers of quilted lining. "I'll show you I'm not!"

"No, Andrea."

I was sliding down into that black hole again, like when I heard the news about my dad. How could he say no?

Thick, damp fog was closing in.

"I..." my voice cracked. If only he'd pull me inside his Beatles jacket and wrap his arms around me so I could breathe in that boy-soap aroma.

Brendan leaned into the wind and kept going.

"I'm dating Betty."

I couldn't speak. I bet the *Frizz's* mother didn't monitor *her* time or tell him off.

"Andrea, I don't dig you in that way now. Go home."

He didn't want me. Some invisible door slammed into my chest and stomach. I tried to breathe but my nose was blocked with icy fog. I opened my mouth. My breath came in and out in quick gasps as Brendan widened his stride. *Don't go*. Please don't go.

He never saw my eyes brimming because he didn't look back. Bitter damp air lashed my forehead and cheeks as his back disappeared into the fog. A sob rose inside me but the wind blew it back down my throat and the sound was muffled by nature's howl.

My head dropped lower into the neck of my navy blue duffle coat and I searched for a tissue in my coat pocket.

Something felt like pieces of cold mashed potato but they were used balls of Kleenex – not the sort I would have pulled out in front of Brendan. I wiped my eyes on the back of my gloved hand and my nose on one of the hard snot-knotted tissues. There was no one to see or hear me. I hugged my duffle coat close to stop the wind getting in then waded through the heavy fog. The eerie glow from the pallid orange lights made it like a very alien planet on *Doctor Who*.

Everything was so different – so – *wrong*.

CHAPTER EIGHT:

BREAKING SEAS

Sandra and I picked our small milk bottles out of the crates then walked across the playground and leaned against the railings.

I peeled off the silver top from my bottle. "He's going out with Beaming Betty the Frizz," I said.

She put her arm around me and squeezed me a bit. "I'm sorry."

"I couldn't bring myself to tell you the day after it happened but now I can get the words out without crying."

"He wouldn't even talk to you?"

I shook my head. "He had to deliver papers so he walked off. He said he didn't want to get him or me into trouble again. I bet *she's* having sex with him. He thinks I'm too young."

"Try and cheer up a bit. The bell will be going in a few minutes. Look, Heather's coming over. Do you want her to know?"

"No."

Heather bounded towards us. Sandra and I put on bright smiles as if nothing was wrong.

"Hello," we both said.

"Hiya. What are you up to?"

"Not much. How're the horses?"

"Mmm…" She fiddled with the buttons on her grey cardigan. "We washed the rugs this morning. Star ran away with Ellen again. She doesn't grip with her knees enough."

"I'm looking forward to seeing Flash next Saturday. It seems ages even though it's only been days."

Heather looked up, down and then to the side. When she looked at me again with her round, golden eyes her face was dead serious.

"I've got some bad news."

"What?"

"Flash had to be put down."

"Down?"

"To sleep."

"Not…?"

"'Fraid so."

"But it's only a few days since I was with him." We had our heads together. "He can't be *dead*. I was going to see him this weekend." His big, blue-brown eyes came to mind, and the tear that ran over the veins down the side of his tan face as he hung his head close to mine. He knew. *Flash*. I wanted to lie down. "When?"

"Yesterday morning."

I could have sworn everything in the playground slowed down, and the noise came and went.

Sandra grabbed my elbow. "You all right?"

I shook my head. Why didn't they let me know? Why didn't they ask if I wanted to be at the stable with him? "Why? I don't understand."

"He had a heart disease. Remember we had the vet once before when he seemed a bit unsteady?"

Did we? I gaped.

"And the condition of his fur…that was all something to do with it."

The real fog that covered me when I stood looking at Brendan's back was there again, but in my mind. "Who put him down? Who was there? When did you first know it was bad? Why didn't you tell me to come…to…say goodbye?" So I could talk softly and hug him in the last hour and minutes. I looked at my shoes.

"I was at school. I only knew Mum was getting the vet at ten. She was there. Vet said it was best; gave him an injection. Puts them to sleep quickly."

Shouting and laughter echoed through the playground. I looked up.

Heather shrugged. "It's what they do."

How could she be so matter-of-fact? *Flash.* My body was heavy. He was partly *my* horse and they should have told me. "I can't believe your mum *did* that. I mean, I've been renting him for six months." Her mum was being spiteful because we were only paying for weekends now. "Surely it would have been fair to let me say *goodbye*?" My eyes burned.

Heather looked away. "Wasn't my fault," she muttered. "That's the way the mop flops sometimes."

Sandra's arm went around my waist.

I was drowning again, gasping to keep my head up. It wasn't *fair*. The bell went and Heather ran off.

Sandra and I filed into assembly like grey soldiers on another grey day.

Sodding youth club and flaming Brendan.

I took my chin almost to my chest so that my long hair fell down either side of my nose and no one could see my eyes or my face as I stopped it from screwing up. I couldn't cry *now*. My tears would have to be like the sea at Skegness, somewhere there, but far from the shore.

My breath sounded like a sob as we started to sing a hymn. 'And did those feet, in ancient times, walk upon England's pastures green...' I trailed off.

Flash's feet walked on England's pastures green. I certainly couldn't think of who *they* were all singing about – Jesus. He'd taken Dad and Flash away forever, and Mandy and Brendan because they didn't want to be my close friends.

The assembly hall was on the ground floor but when I finally raised my eyes I could see the distant hills and the two industrial chimneys, which dominated the horizon. They rose out of the gloom, laced with charcoal smoke as it spumed out from the summits, plunged down, zigzagged between the light and dark columns and made smoke rings, which expanded to gulfs. Yeah.

There were faces in smoke and they were floating higher and further away. One was Dad with his pipe and his quiff; another was Mandy with a fringe and long hair. Brendan was there in the smoke, as well, with the Beatles cap and leather shoulders. In front of them was a horse's face. He became clearer as the smoke swirled. It was my Flash walking away. He had big eyes and big, fine muscles like before he was poorly. I imagined his soft chin over my shoulder and his face next to mine.

He walked proudly, his tail swishing but then the smoke started to float higher and further. He was going towards the smoke figure of Dad with his pipe. Going away. *Don't go.* Flash. I'm *so* sorry. I dropped my head.

Someone accidentally nudged into my arm near the shoulder. I pulled away without looking up then raised my hymn book in front of my face. Then a kind of coldness came over the hall and the sky went very white. It started to snow. I couldn't stand it.

I didn't want to be there.

Grandma went to meet Mum in the hall. "She didn't want a cup of tea and biscuits today. Not talking much," Grandma said about me. I knew she would so I was listening by the wall.

"Let me get my coat and boots off, Mother."

"Yes dear. It's hard for you, being back at work full-time. I've warmed your slippers. How do you want the potatoes?"

"I'll be in the kitchen in a minute, Mother. Let's have a cuppa together, shall we?" Mum said then she came into the lounge. "Hello, love. I've bought you a frame for your bedroom."

I glanced up from the homework I couldn't do. Mum was holding a small square photo frame. She wanted to put my dad in *there*? "It's not right!"

Mum widened her eyes. "What do you mean?"

I shoved my books aside. "I want it bigger."

"That's how most photograph frames for close up shots are. It's standard."

"I don't want it standard!" I screamed. "It's not right!"

I was getting hot and red like a tomato about to burst its skin. I wanted my dad and I wanted the photo big on the wall, not a three by three-inch square.

The demon inside started to rise, pushing against my skin. "*I want* it bigger, with more space around it." Billy the budgie stopped saying, "You're beautiful," and, "Do you want a cup of tea?" Instead, he put his yellow head on one side.

"I want it how I want it. Can you hear me? It's not *right*." I screamed a few times for the hell of it and started throwing the maroon scatter cushions in Mum's direction as if everything was all her fault. I couldn't see where they landed. My eyes were blurred.

"School is like prison. I hate it. Daddy's died, Mandy doesn't want to be my best friend, Brendan doesn't want me – he said so last week. And today I was told Flash … Flash …died. He *died*." I narrowed my eyes. "*You* made me choose 'no going out' or my pony. Some choice! It's *your* fault I never saw him." I squeezed out tears like breaking seas then looked around for what else I could throw again, bouncing, vibrating. "They put him *down*. Heather's spiteful mother never asked me to come to the stable when the vet was coming. Never told me. If you hadn't made me choose I'd have known to be there," I yelled. Then I screamed at the very top of my voice: "How *could* you? And the *bloody* photograph frame isn't right." I went behind the settee and gave it a huge push sending it right up on its front legs.

"Andrea, calm down."

"I *won't* calm down." The words pierced the room before I pushed again and the long brown settee tipped over.

90

Two strides towards me and she slapped me across the face then held on to my shoulders. I brought both my arms up, knocking her arms off me and slapped her hard across the face back. I narrowed my eyes and glared.

Mum stepped back. "Andrea!" There were tears in her eyes. "I'm so sorry about Flash. I didn't know, and I'm sorry you weren't able to say goodbye," she whispered, and then her tears broke slowly, gently, and flowed over her face. "I feel very sad about it."

"*Everything's* wrong."

"I miss Daddy too. It's very hard."

She turned away and walked into the hall. Where was she going? The front door opened and closed with a click. I hoped she wouldn't go away. I loved her really. I sat and hugged myself but after a while I got up and peeped between the heavy maroon velvet curtains.

She'd gone across the snowy road to Mrs South. The South's curtains were still open and I saw Mum sitting down in their front room. Mrs South was bending over her. I quickly closed my peephole.

Grandma came out of her bed-sitting room into the lounge. I'd forgotten about her. "Go away." I'd never spoken to Grandma like that before. Never.

She retreated, her slippers softly padding back to her room.

What was I? Sometimes I was from another planet.

There was a knock at the door. Bloomin' 'eck. I bet it was Mrs South. I opened the door. Worse. It was her daughter, Caroline. Not that I didn't like her. I did. She was a year older than me and really nice. We used to go to

Bible class coffee mornings together on a Sunday, but that was before Dad died.

Dad never wanted me to go to Bible class anyway. I only convinced him to say yes when I told him it was more about being grown up with two older friends and sitting on cushions sipping milky coffee and talking than having an interest in studying the Bible.

"Are you all right?" Caroline asked.

Of course I wasn't bloody all right. "So-so." I walked back into the hall and left the door open. She could come or go as she pleased.

She came in, closed the door and followed me into the hall. I sat down on the stairs and she sat on the seat by the telephone table.

"Your mum's worried about you."

I looked at the patterned wallpaper in our hall. I was worried about myself. And Mum. And Dad, and Flash.

"Maybe you were a bit unkind to her," Caroline said.

I stared ahead. "I didn't mean to be."

"Are you feeling sad about your dad?"

What a stupid blooming question. "Of course." I was burning from the chest to the eyes. I wasn't going to cry in front of *her*.

"We can talk about it if you like."

I hung my head and looked at my slippers. She was friends with Lynette next door to her and I was, too, out of school, but not in school. Lynette and I used to go riding together ages ago. She was good friends with the Frizz, alias Beaming Betty. I wasn't going to tell my most special thoughts and feelings about Dad and everything awful to Caroline – just in case. I looked down at the hall carpet, which Dad used to walk on when he came home from work, and flipping hell, a tear escaped. I quickly flicked it away. "I'll be okay."

How could she understand? Her life was okay. Her family was normal like four tidy pillars: a mum, dad, a brother and her.

"I'm really sorry to hear about your pony," she said softly.

Oh don't. I bit my lip and nodded.

"You've had a lot to put up with. Your mum knows that."

I let my hair hang forward and started to push the skin at my cuticles back with my thumbnails. Mum didn't tell *her* about Brendan and Mandy, did she? "What do you mean?"

She fiddled with the curly wire of the black telephone. "Well, your dad dying so suddenly and your pony getting put down while you were at school. All within six months. It wasn't your mum's fault, you know."

I looked away.

"Your mum says you're going to see Herman's Hermits soon. That's something to look forward to, isn't it?"

I nodded.

"We should all get together in the field at the end of the road and play cricket, like we used to," she said.

But everyone else could take their dads. I used to like the smell of the newly mown grass. Things were simple back then: ball games in the fields, tomboy climbs, playing on the new buildings. If I got stuck up the big tree in the field, who would climb up behind me to help me down now? It didn't matter anyway. I was far too old for trees and ball games. I shook my head. "I don't think so."

"Perhaps you could apologise to your mum. She's hurt."

"Might."

"She'll come back in a minute. If you want to talk to someone else about things, you could talk to my mum whenever you feel like it." She got up. "What about coming back to Bible class with me?"

I squinted.

Fat chance.

CHAPTER NINE:

SILHOUETTES

The lights came up and coloured the concert hall.

Sandra and I waited in our seats. The hall was warming now we'd listened to a few support groups. I took off my best blue coat with the mock fur collar and put it on the back of the seat.

Deep red curtains went all the way across the stage. "I bet they're behind there," I whispered to Sandra behind my hand. She had make-up on for the night, like me, and she looked so much like Twiggy. We both had our mod dresses on with our boots because more snow had settled today. I wiggled my toes to warm them up a bit more.

Seats of rich, burgundy velvet like our lounge curtains were arranged in rows like in the cinema.

"Look at those big doormen," Sandra said.

They were like boxers but in black suits. "I bet they're there to keep the girls off the stage. Will you try and go up?"

"Me? I don't think so. I like that girl's bouffant, don't you?"

She pointed to a girl a few rows in front. "She must have back-combed it for ages."

The lights went out except for a big round circle shining on the maroon curtain. The whispered 'hushes' were like the sound of the sea at Bridlington. We looked at each other then back to the round glow on the stage. It stayed there for several seconds, keeping us wondering, then a man in a dark suit and tie stepped out from between the curtains.

There was some music like a drum roll and then it stopped.

"Ladies and Gentlemen…"

Sandra and I looked at each other, hunched our shoulders up and sucked in our breath.

"Gerron wi' it," some boy shouted out.

"Without further ado, I'd like to present …Wayne Fontana and the Mindbenders!"

I held onto my hair and screamed. Wayne Fontana was *so* handsome. His fringe went over his eyes and he held his hands right around the microphone near his mouth and looked so – sexy, especially when he sang *The Game of Love.*

"I'm going to die," I sighed.

Sandra's mascara was running because she had screamed so hard that tears came. She mopped it with a tissue.

"Me too."

I screamed some more. The concert hall was like a playground with all our screams. It was hard to hear the songs sometimes but it didn't matter. Some girls were pulling their hair but Sandra's was short, so she couldn't. I got hold of my hair either side making bunches from the middle parting and pulled it with my scream when Wayne started to sing our other favourite, *Um Um Um Um Um Um.*

96

"Wayne! Wayne!" We shrieked.

When he took his bow, a couple of girls tried to clamber up on the stage. The bouncers made them get down again. "Look at that girl being carried out by one of the big doormen."

"She's fainted."

The whole show went far too quickly and then the curtain came across and that big round circle of light came back again. "Ladies and gents – Herman's Hermits."

I screamed.

"*Her*man!" Sandra shouted. "I love his baby face," she said to me but it was hard to hear her above the clapping.

He was so cute. He started singing, *I'm Into Something Good* and looked our way. I nudged Sandra, "Ahhhh!"

Nobody stopped us all screaming when we liked a special bit in the song. More girls tried to get on the stage and kiss the band members but the big men caught them before they had a chance. Then the music started for Herman's new song. We all knew what *that* was. The screaming rose to a pitch when he sang the words about taking a walk past a house.

"Sit down," the bouncers said when we stood up by our seats and screamed some more. Now *my* mascara started to run. "Herman!" I called, but so did everybody else.

"Weren't they fab?"

"Yeah. I could faint," Sandra said.

We filed out of Sheffield City Hall.

"Who did you scream most for, Wayne Fontana and the Mindbenders or Herman's Hermits?"

"Herman! When he sang, *I'm Into Something Good.* I screamed myself hoarse."

"Me too. I nearly pulled my hair out when he sang *Silhouettes,* and I loved Wayne Fontana and the Mindbenders earlier, especially when he made his voice low and sexy. We never bumped into Brendan. I think he's more of a Rolling Stones fan. Don't you?"

"Yeah."

A girl pushed passed us and knocked Sandra. "Sorry, love. Are you two going round 'back to get autographs? Most of 'em are going."

I nudged Sandra. "Let's stay and queue up for their autographs!"

"We can't. We've got to catch the 10.30 home."

"We can catch the next one." I nudged her again. "Go on."

"Our mums will worry."

"Oh, go on."

"N-o-o. I'm not staying."

"Well, I'm sorry, but *I* am. I'll catch a bus in half an hour."

Sandra gave me a dirty look. "I thought you were trying not to fall out with your mum again," she said.

She didn't disobey her parents like I did. I never used to. Well, not often. I bit my lip. "This is different, Sandra. They're *famous*! Tell your mum, if my mum rings, that I'll only be half an hour late."

She nodded with a sullen face. "See you tomorrow at the bus stop then."

I followed the other girls outside in the cold and around to the back-stage door. The courtyard was cobbled but you could only see the cobbles if you looked down because hundreds of girls' boots covered them. The queue was at least fifteen deep and many times as wide. I was near the back because I was younger and smaller and got shoved out of the way a bit. I hung onto my blue autograph book and waited for my turn to give it to the doorman to take inside and get signed.

It was boring just waiting and after a couple of minutes, for some reason – I don't know why, I turned around. Oh my God. I was going to faint.

It was Herman and his Hermits like a silhouette in the shade – but real. They'd been out to get some beers and Herman was carrying some brown bottles with dark green labels on them. They were sneaking back in like cat burglars.

Herman's twinkling eyes met mine and he brought his finger to his lips. "Shhh!" he went, *to me – Die!* Then he smiled and did it again because I was the only one who'd seen him so far. He didn't want me to tell the others.

I just looked, frozen with disbelief. *He is so lovely.* He kept his eyes on me and smiled, finger still to his lips as he crept by. I followed his sparkly fun eyes and was so shocked my mouth hung open. I couldn't even get my thoughts together to give him my autograph book or to hold his hand or kiss him – I was locked into those eyes. He was actually smiling at *me.*

They walked down the side of the crowd, Herman sharing his big secret with me all the way. A handful of people turned and saw them just as the back-stage door opened and a big arm hauled them inside. The doorman must've been watching for them through the peephole. The heavy wooden door closed and sealed them safely inside. Gone.

Everyone screamed. When I came out of my daze, I screamed too. *I loved him.* I still loved Brendan, but I loved Herman in a different way. "He looked at me and smiled and went, Shhh!" I said to the girl next to me.

"Why didn't you tell us?"

"I was too shocked. I just stared."

"You lucky devil. I wish he'd looked at me. I'd probably have been stunned too," she said.

I was special.

I gazed at the stage door. After a while it opened and the bouncer's be-suited arm stuck out for the umpteenth time.

"Next four autograph books. That's enough. Four at a time, I said."

I hugged my arms across my chest while we waited. The icy cold air didn't matter. I had Herman's smile to keep me warm.

The door opened again and the bouncer gave back four signed autograph books and took four more. I had to wait quite a bit longer until it was my turn to hand my book over.

Finally. My pale blue book was passed over the heads back to me with Wayne Fontana's and all the Mindbenders' autographs, and all of Herman's Hermits, scrawled on the blue book's pink and yellow pages. Now I could go home. What time was it? Buses were frequent from the city, so I crossed the road from City Hall and caught the 51. Herman filled my daydreams all the way back. I'd remember him for*ever* and ever.

My watch said it was a few minutes after midnight. I should have been home over an hour ago. I jumped down on the icy pavement. I bet we had colder weather than any other suburb because we were 700 feet above sea level. The two inches of snow had become partly frozen. It looked like iced sea waves. I walked as quickly as I could in my boots. I hadn't been out that late before and the street was quiet and deserted.

The only sounds were my breathing, when my warm breath puffed out into the atmosphere, and my feet as they made light crunches through the semi-frozen particles and into the softer snow. How late and dark it was – how still.

CHAPTER TEN:

STRANGER IN THE MIST

The icy stillness was like the end of the world, or a different world. A cloud-like mist made a blanket, which sat about head level. I suppose it was because we were so high above the city. I'd never seen it quite like this before. It was like walking in the sky, and it was very lonely.

I walked a little quicker.

I couldn't run because of the iced snow. Even though my boots gripped, I didn't want to fall.

Uh-oh.

I wasn't alone.

From somewhere behind me, out of nowhere, there were suddenly large striding footsteps. A man's. I walked faster, pulling my mock fur collar up to my neck. *Oh God.*

Where did those footsteps come from? They came nearer, almost right behind me, and a strange male voice said:

"You didn't know I was behind you, did you?"

"No." I kept walking.

"It's a bit late to be out all by yourself."

He strode up beside me and walked by my side. Something in my stomach galloped. I looked straight ahead and marched on like a soldier.

"I missed a bus. My mum's waiting for me." I didn't turn to look at him but out of the corner of my eye I could see he had on a gabardine and a trilby hat with a feather in it, like Dad's. I could see the feather blowing in the wind like a small silhouette of a leaf. I wasn't going to slow down to look at his face. I didn't want to see his face. I wanted my mum.

"Where do you live?"

I wasn't telling him the number. "Cliff Road."

"I live on Cliff Road, too. I have a daughter about your age. You'd be about twelve wouldn't you?"

"Nearly thirteen."

"Does your mum know you're out by yourself this late?"

I walked quicker despite the ice. "She'll be worried. I'm a bit later than I said I'd be."

"What number do you live at?"

He might come and murder us. "About half-way down on the right hand side from the top corner." The words came out between a wheeze and a pant.

"I live on the right hand side too, a few houses down from the end. Do you want me to walk to the house with you?"

I didn't want a stranger seeing my front door. I still didn't look at him properly because there was something eerie about him. "No, thanks."

We got to the corner of my road and both turned in.

"I'll just watch you from here then. Be careful in the snow. 'Night."

"Night," I whispered because I'd lost my voice. I heard two or three more footsteps and then the crunches stopped. Only when I reached the edge of our driveway did I look back. I wanted to see which driveway of the five houses before us he'd turned into, but I didn't see anyone.

He'd vanished.

I didn't know whether I was shaking from cold, fear, or something else. I started to put my key in the door but it flung open and Mum hugged me. She made a strange wail between a laugh and a cry.

"Where have you *been?*"

I hung my head now I realised what I'd done. "I stayed to get autographs." I was still shaking. "I'm sorry, Mum."

"I've had the police out looking for you."

"Why?"

"Sandra's mum rang and said you'd stayed to get autographs, so I gave it one bus – about twenty minutes, then I rang City Hall and they said everyone had left."

"We were outside the back stage door. It took nearly an hour to get autographs."

"You can't be out alone at this time of night. It's dangerous."

"I know." The cold, dry fear was still in my throat.

"Go by the fire in the lounge."

"Really sorry."

"You should have rung and asked."

"I will next time."

Mum picked up the black telephone in the hall as I went through to the fireside. I heard her ask for Sergeant somebody or other and explain that I was home and she was terribly sorry to have wasted his time. She replaced the telephone then Grandma's door opened.

"She's back, Mother," I heard Mum say.

"I knew God would look after her, darling."

She must've given Mum a hug because there were a few seconds silence, then Mum said she'd have to ring Sandra's mum to let her know I was home. While she did that, Grandma came into the lounge hugging her dressing gown around her. I gave her a big-eyed 'I didn't mean to' look. "Sorry for upsetting you both."

She bent to kiss me. "Praise the Lord! I can go to my bed in peace now."

Mum came and sat by the fire with me.

"You're as white as a sheet."

"A man walked behind me and scared me."

She sat forward. "What do you mean?"

I hugged my arms. "He was suddenly behind me on Lodge Road. He said it was late for me to be out and he had a daughter about my age. He said I must be twelve. He asked where I lived. I just said Cliff Road. He lives on Cliff Road too, in one of the first few houses on our side."

"There aren't any men who live in the first few houses on the right hand side before us. Did he say what number?"

I shook my head.

"There's Suzy and Mark next door, then a single lady called Jane, and in the last four houses they're all older widows. Tell me again what he said."

I was getting a funny feeling all over. "He only walked a little way on Cliff Road then said he'd watch me from there, and to be careful in the snow. When I got to our driveway I looked around. He'd just – disappeared."

She lit a cigarette and inhaled.

"No-one this side, and this end of the road, has any children your age. Did you see his face?"

Something like ice started to tickle the back of my neck. "No, I was too frightened to look. I saw the trilby hat with the feather and he had on a double-breasted gabardine with a belt…you know…"

As I turned from Mum back towards the fire my gaze passed the lamp on the top of the television and, beside it, Dad's photo.

Mum sank against the back of the settee and drew on her cigarette again. There was a chill in the room despite the fire. The clock struck one in the morning. An electric tingle rushed down my spine and back again, leaving a prickling coolness around my neck and throat.

Air blended with the fire and flames sparked and crackled. I jumped. My mouth opened and I turned to Mum.

Her head tipped to one side and she took my hand. "I don't know, darling."

We stared at each other and the clock went tick, tick and tick again. Apart from that sound, the silence buzzed.

"Don't stay out later than your allotted time again, and never, ever without phoning me. Okay?"

I couldn't get warm. I hugged myself and nodded.

The embers glowed and faded alternately and the light they gave came and went.

If who I saw was real but not real then perhaps there wasn't actually a heaven (or hell), and Earth wasn't that separate as in this side and that side. Was there a grey area in between what we could see and what we couldn't, where things overlapped?

Where they blended.

Radio Caroline was playing Bob Dylan's *The Times they are A-changing* on the wireless. Were they? It seemed that way.

I put my school bag down in the kitchen. "Guess what? Mr Fillmore wasn't there today. Mr West, the headmaster, came to see us in the afternoon. He said Mr Fillmore had had a boating accident over the weekend."

Mum looked at the teapot. "Go through. The new gas-fire's on."

I hung my coat up and went into the lounge. "And Mr West said we should all pray for him. It must be a bit serious."

Mum sat down with the tea tray and got her Park Drive tipped out. "It's worse than that. It was in the newspaper."

I got that awful dry throat. "What?"

"The boat was found without him in it. It was misty over the sea and he sailed off into the mist and was never seen again. I'm afraid that means he's lost at sea."

I gaped. *No.* "They'll look for him, won't they?"

"They have. I believe they're calling the search off in a day or so, if he's not found. I'm afraid that'll mean he's presumed dead, darling."

"Oh, not Mr *Fillmore*; I don't want him to die. He's my favourite teacher in the whole world. I can't believe it."

"There may still be hope. Fingers crossed, and perhaps we'd *better* say a little prayer for him tonight."

I stared out of the bay window. Radio Caroline played *I'll Never Find Another You,* softly from the transistor.

107

"And that's the Seekers on Caroline. Bright day out here on the waves as we come to the end of winter," Don Allen said. End of winter? It was still frosty.

It'd be *very* cold out at sea. Poor Mr Fillmore.

At least the snow had gone. The spring daffodils were trying to push through but the tulip bulbs were happy to stay in the soil a bit longer. I was like the daffodils: wanting to see spring but having a hard time pushing through. Every sad thing made it hard to push through. "School would be even more awful if Mr Fillmore wasn't there."

"You never know. The paper said it seemed strange. The sea wasn't *that* choppy."

We sipped our cups of tea as night started to fall and then there was a knock at the front door. "I'll go, Mum."

I tried not to groan. It was Christopher Howard, Mum's friend's son, with another boy. They were in Brendan's year. "Hi." Chris had pasty looking skin, but was good natured and always friendly. I supposed I'd better be polite. I did my best with a smile.

"Hi, Andrea. Do you know Michael? He lives at the back of you. Mike – Andrea, Andrea – Mike."

"Hi Michael." He had olive skin, dark hair, and was decidedly better looking than Christopher even if he had a squarish face. He wasn't as tall as Brendan but was stocky. I gave them both a 'Well?' sort of look.

"We wondered if you and your mate fancied coming to the pictures on Saturday afternoon?" Chris said.

"Don't know. I haven't been going out much, you know – hibernating." Everyone should hibernate in Yorkshire winters. Chris knew the story.

"Maybe we can change that. Come on, come with us. *The Party's Over* is on."

I hope this hadn't been suggested by our mums. "I'll think about it and let you know. I have to go. I haven't had dinner yet."

Michael started bobbing up and down in front of our bay window. "Yeah, I bet the old man's waiting for you behind the curtains. He'll be out here in a minute. Is he strict, your dad? Yeah, I bet he is. He'll be out here in a minute saying, 'What are you doing with these lads?'"

Chris nudged him in the back and rolled his eyes at me but Michael was on a roll. "Yeah, the old man'll be out here in a minute."

Chris jabbed him again.

"He'll be looking us up and down through the gap…"

He carried on with the theatrics pretending to peep through the tiny gap between the curtains then diving out of the way.

Finally, Chris thumped him in the back and led him away giving me an apologetic look over his shoulder.

I managed a smile, went back in and told Mum. "He carried on even when Chris had his fist in his back!"

"Oh no! You didn't want the teachers to tell the whole school so he wasn't to know. I think you made it harder for yourself."

I shrugged. "It couldn't be helped."

"*Chris* is a nice boy."

"M-u-u-m! Did you have something to do with them coming round out of the blue?"

"Mrs Howard mentioned Chris was at a loose end and perhaps it'd be nice for you and Sandra, and him and a friend, to go somewhere. I *had* to nod and agree. I know

109

they are not 'someone else', but there's no harm in being friends."

I rolled my eyes and made the Elvis Presley mouth.

Mum shook her head. Just as she was about to go to the kitchen there was a gentle tap at the door. We looked at each other and giggled a bit. I went and opened it.

This time Michael was upright and serious.

"I am *so* sorry. I feel terrible. I behaved like a jerk. I'm sorry, Andrea, and sorry about your dad. I didn't know."

"It's okay." I looked anywhere but at his face for a moment then folded my arms.

"I must make this up to you. *Please* let me take you to the flicks on Saturday. My treat." He frowned with a kind of passion, like an actor. "Please."

I had to smile. If I wasn't so nuts about Brendan James, I could like Michael. He probably was better looking – but, I was nuts about Brendan. "Okay, then."

Chris stepped forward.

"Can you bring your friend?"

"Mandy and I aren't *best friends* these days."

"The little one."

"There are two dainty ones."

"The one you catch the bus with."

"*Sandra*?"

"She's the one that looks like Twiggy?"

I nodded, ashamed of my gob-smacked mouth-drop. *I* thought Sandra was pretty, but like June, a bit underdeveloped for her age. June, however, knew how to flirt, courtesy of her big sister. "Great. I'll see her in the morning. Mind you, her mum doesn't let her go out much."

Chris pulled a silly face. "It's only a *matinee*."

"I'll let you know."

Michael stepped closer.

"I'll call for you after lunch on Saturday, whether she comes or not."

"I've got to go in for dinner." I smiled. "Thanks for coming back."

Michael put his hand on his heart but I didn't wait for more play-acting.

Sandra's eye make-up was just like Twiggy's. She had little lines like eyelashes drawn underneath her own lashes and white lipstick. Not that it was on now. She'd taken to the snogging business like a duck to water.

Michael's face came down on mine again and I leaned back against the velvety seat back. Over his solid neck and shoulder, I could see down the rest of the back row. All the other kids were at it. Some of them were girls or lads from our school and most of them were older. That was a friend of Lynette along there. Good. I hoped she saw me snogging with Michael. If she told Lynette it would get to the Frizz, and then Brendan.

Suzy Brown was further down the row with a lad. You could see she was in the family way now. I felt really grown up like her, especially with the older crew dotted around. It was like being part of the 'in-crowd'. I put a big effort into the next kiss. If being kissed by Brendan made me think of John Lennon, or looked like James Bond in *The Saint*, Michael was more of a cowboy-in-a hurry, or a pirate. Apart from that, my neck was killing me; Michael's hand kept clunking down on one or the other tit like a clamp: vuoom!

The lights began to brighten and there was a drum roll. Good. I nudged Michael. "National Anthem!" I disentangled myself and stood. Some grown-ups looked around at the back row because not all of them stood straight away. Sandra and I shared a secret smile through the words, 'God save our gracious Queen.'

"It's still early. Let's go back and have a walk on the Crags," Chris said as we came out onto the city street's tan pavers.

I looked at Sandra expecting her to make an excuse.

She nodded.

"Don't you have to be back for dinner?" I said.

"Not 'til about six."

I shrugged. "Okay." I didn't know if my chest was up to more grabbing.

Michael pulled me to him and whispered against my ear, "I want to kiss you – and more, in the long grass, away from the crowds."

My face heated. He was nice, in some ways. He took hold of my hand and swung it as we walked towards the bus stop.

Passing Strangers, an old record from the fifties, came on the radio as I walked in. Mum liked that. It reminded *me* of that man in the mist, and who it might have been. Perhaps it came on to let me know Dad would meet and take care of Flash. It also reminded me of Mr Fillmore. I hoped none of them became strangers in my mind. Michael on the other hand: he *was* probably going to be a passing stranger.

"How was the picture?" Mum said.

"The projector broke down twice." Not that any of us in the back were watching it.

"It happens. Did you go to the Wimpy Bar afterwards?"

Heat stung my cheeks. "Just for a bit of a walk." With an octopus.

"Did Sandra and Chris get along?"

"Like a house on fire." In more ways than one. "I think she was pleased to get asked out by a boy."

"What's Michael like?"

Strong, with a big chest and quick to undo things. "He's nice when he talks. He's more talkative than Brendan, but he's not Brendan. And that's who I like." I slouched through to the lounge. No, he just wasn't Brendan. Pity.

"Oh, darling!" she called after me in the 'don't be ridiculous' tone then followed me through. "At least I *know* Chris. I'm sure he and Michael were well behaved and trustworthy."

I looked at my slippers. "Mmm."

"Don't look so fed-up. Remember that night we talked about all the unhappy things after Flash…?"

I nodded then stared at the gas fire.

"You've toed the line as regards parties and so-on, and concentrated on school as best you could under the circumstances. I wanted to surprise you, but since Mr Fillmore has, well, gone missing…"

"They're collecting for a wreath next week."

She reached and held my hand across the settee. "I'd like to take you on holiday later in the year, okay?"

"Where?"

113

"I'm arranging for us to go to Hayling Island for part of the school holidays – it won't seem long once we start to plan it."

"Fab! Are we going to stay with Aunty Enid and Uncle Ron?"

"I thought you'd be pleased."

They weren't my real aunt and uncle but they were Mum and Dad's really good friends. Their daughter, Jocelyn and I used to play together and be special friends when I was really little but then Uncle Ron moved because of his job. Hayling Island was way down in the south of England, even south of London. We went down to visit them in Dad's car four years ago. "How will we get there?"

"On the coach."

It was warm and sunny there. There might be nice boys down south near Portsmouth. I might meet a handsome stranger on the shore. Things might be different when I come back too, mightn't they? The sea in the south might wash away the fog.

Or maybe I wouldn't come back.

CHAPTER ELEVEN:

TIME AND TIDE

I pressed my forehead against the windowpane as the coach pulled into Havant coach station. Jocelyn was waiting with her mum. I hadn't seen her since I was nine.

She still looked nine.

She had on a flared cotton dress, *ankle socks* and flat sandals like a little girl.

My chin sat back in my face.

Mum and I got up to take our hand luggage down from the racks. I smoothed down my mod Cilla Black dress and my lacy white stockings. I'd travelled in my high heel blue suede shoes – as high as I was allowed. The girls in my school would *never* wear ankle socks. Jocelyn was nearly thirteen; far too old for socks and flared cotton dresses. It wasn't even a *twist* dress with a drop waist, let alone a Cilla Black style. I bet she wasn't interested in boys.

I looked at her boring short hairstyle through the window as we walked down the aisle. Could I imagine her snogging with any of the lads at my school? Nah! Definitely not. She was brown though. I bet it was great living by the beach and sea.

"Jean!" Aunty Enid lunged at Mum and they hugged each other and both cried; long separated best friends.

Jocelyn eyed my clothes. "Hello. I *like* your Cilla Black dress and your suede and patent shoes."

What was she like now? "Thanks. Gosh, you're brown!"

She came and gave me a very quick peck on the cheek and I did the same then we both stepped back like it never happened. She went redder than me.

They had a car. It made me think of my dad's Ford Popular and our last holiday with them and all the days out in our car – the two families. Our car was brown inside and had a leather smell a bit like a saddle. Their car was a bit newer. I liked their car. Uncle Ron was waiting in it and we'd soon be crossing a bridge to Hayling Island. It was like going abroad.

Jocelyn and I squeezed in the back of the car next to my mum.

"Did you get my last letter? I posted it with Mum's to your mum," she said.

I nodded. "Thanks." I would never put *my* mail in with my mother's. "It sounds like we've got some good things planned."

"The beach is at the end of our road, and there's a fair at the Isle of Wight. We'll go there by ferry one day."

"Fab."

"I'm not thirteen yet. Lucky you, becoming a teenager back in spring. Does it feel different?"

I nodded. "Definitely. Some girls at school even get in the family way at thirteen."

She coloured and put her hand to her mouth with a gasp. "Not at my school. What did you do for your birthday?"

116

"Had my main friends Mandy, June and Sandra to tea. We played Beatles records. We all like one of them, so it's just perfect. *Mine* is John Lennon. Who's yours?"

"I don't have one really."

She didn't *have* one? I stared. What was the matter with her? "Oh." I turned to the window.

A few of the houses on the Esplanade had signs saying, Bed and Breakfast. On the other side was a row of deck chairs, then two railings, and beyond, the beach. It was made of round pebbles and they were beige, yellow and pinky-grey. "Look, Mum! The sea."

It was such a dark blue that it appeared to be more inky grey, probably because it was late in the day. The light of the afternoon sunshine sat on the waves so that there were shades of gold and grey. I didn't want to look at the grey parts. Instead I was drawn into the shimmering gold, the sun-kissed ripples of ebb and flow, gently rocking, light against dark. The beckoning gold shimmered like a moving pathway, always changing, shifting and merging.

You had to keep your eyes on the gold bits.

We turned the corner into their street. Their house was new and really modern. Ours was new too because we only bought it two years ago and we watched it being built. Theirs was bigger though. It had a really big garden.

"Take your things in there, love," Aunty Enid said. "You and Jocelyn have twin beds – no talking 'til all hours when you go to bed tonight." She winked. "Jocelyn'll show you the bathroom. I'll put the kettle on. Come and have a cuppa when you get unpacked."

117

I opened my suitcase. "My cousin bought me some tarot cards for my birthday. I've brought them with me. They tell your fortune."

Jocelyn bounced down on the divan.

"Fab."

She reached out across the space between the two beds. "Look, we can hold hands until we go to sleep, like we used to when we stayed over."

I smiled and had to squint to stop myself laughing. She was very sweet. I wished I had a sister. I shuffled the cards. "Cut here." She pulled the Page of Clubs. "You're going to meet a boy," I said.

"I don't go out with boys."

"Maybe that's about to change. The Page of Clubs is a trusted friend – of someone."

She coloured.

"It doesn't mean it's serious." Mandy, June or Sandra would have been pleased. "Just a meeting."

I spread mine and when I turned one of the centre cards up, it was the Cavalier of Swords. "I am too. Mine is brave and strong. Things are going to start happening."

I turned some others over. "Another one," I said. "The Cavalier of Clubs. But this one isn't directly relating to me. It's in a different set. I wonder if it's to do with Brendan."

"Is Brendan fair?"

"No, brown hair."

"This one's fair. He looks older."

"Yeah."

***

Jocelyn took hold of my hand. "We mustn't lose each other. This fair is huge."

Just because we'd held hands across the bedside cabinet at night while chatting, didn't mean I was going to do it in public. I kept her hand in mine for a few seconds as we walked through the entrance. "Look at *that*," I said and let go to point at the biggest candyfloss on a stick I had ever seen. I linked her arm through mine. "Hang onto my arm; that's safer." I didn't know if it was, but I wasn't going to hold hands with all those lads around.

I had my white hipster trousers on. Jocelyn was wearing shorts. We'd both painted our nails and had been allowed to wear eye-liner so I bet we looked older than we were – especially me.

It was fab walking through the entrance to the fair. You could smell the hot dogs and onions, sort of all mingled up with the smell of candyfloss. There was still the seaside smell of cockles and mussels, fish and chips and vinegar but the hot dogs and onions were the strongest. The boys selling hotdogs called: "Hotdogs, nice and hot, 'ere y'are lav." They had a different accent to how we spoke up north. Even Jocelyn had it now. A nice looking lad on the hot dog stand held up a sausage, laughed, and looked at us. "Want one, lav?"

"Not at the moment, thank you," I said. "We might come back later."

He gave me a funny smile and stuck his spotty chin out. The other one put his arm and fist up at an angle as if he was pulling a beer, but a bit lower. They were very funny. I think their eyes followed us.

I pulled Jocelyn closer. "We can go on the ghost train and the big wheel!" I had a few other ideas too. Lots of lads were passing us by and giving us the eye. Well, me, anyway.

"I'm glad our mums let us to go off on our own," she said.

"They wanted to talk while they had a chance. I loved the ferry ride over here."

We walked by the laughing clowns in glass cases and some stalls. Someone won two prizes; one was a big teddy bear. He gave it to his little girl.

There were dodgem cars bumping, ghost trains whining, carriages crashing back to the beginning again, lots and lots of jingles and juke boxes and music for the merry-go-rounds like the ones where the painted horses go up and down.

Jocelyn stopped and pointed to the carousel of horses. "Remember when we used to go on those? It was so exciting."

It was nice to have known someone a long time. Although Jocelyn wasn't far past the bucket and spade stage, it was like having a sister – a younger sister. "It was fun when we were five. I loved it." I looked away from the carousel in case she had ideas.

She put her arm around my waist and I put mine around hers as we walked along. "I do miss you," I said. "It was fun when we both lived in Roma Road."

"I wish we still lived near each other. It's great to lie in bed and talk about things when we're supposed to have the little lamp off. Maybe your mum will move down here now…"

"You never know. Which ride do you want to go on first?"

The bar came up and we got out of the swinging seat onto solid ground. "That was the most fab of all the rides." You could see for miles from the big wheel because we were stuck at the top while they did something to the mechanics.

"I'm glad we're on the ground. It was scary. Let's have a milkshake," Jocelyn said.

We walked over to the stall. Jocelyn chose a strawberry one and I had banana flavour; they were my favourite milkshakes in the whole world. We started sipping through our straws and walking around. There were a few nice lads at the fair and I noticed we kept seeing the same pair here and there.

We got to the bottom of our milkshakes and the straws made rude noises as we tried to get the bit up from the very bottom. Finally, we took the glasses back to the stall.

"We keep bumping into those two boys, don't we?" One looked about sixteen but the other more our age.

Jocelyn looked around. "I hadn't noticed."

She wouldn't. If they wanted to talk to us, why didn't they? We weren't far away. The crowds jostled us and we giggled about bumping into the people in front. Because I had hold of Jocelyn's arm it was easy for me to nudge her further and into the boys as they passed. She tried to resist but wobbled into them and turned to me with a mad look. The older one's eyes met mine. He smiled but he looked like he didn't do it often.

"Are you on holiday?" he asked.

He had lovely olive skin like an Italian or a gypsy. His dark hair was over the collar and he had big brown eyes, which made him look a bit sad but I supposed it was his natural expression. He was quite thin and had on tight blue jeans. The other one was similar but younger and had the same slightly scruffy look but not in a bad way. I couldn't imagine Mum would be impressed. "I'm from the Midlands and staying with my friend on Hayling Island; what about you?"

"I live here. Thought I didn't recognise you as local. So, it's just the two of you?"

"We're with our mums. We have to meet them at the bandstand soon," Jocelyn piped up. The younger one started chatting to her.

"What's your name?" the tall one asked me.

"Andrea. What about you?"

"Bisto. Want to come for a walk?"

"Bisto – like the gravy?"

"Yeah. My eyes. Like brown gravy."

His eyes bore into me and sparkled. "They're much nicer than gravy."

"Come on. Come for a walk."

When he smiled his teeth were white and nice. I'd got almost an hour before I had to meet my mum. "Um…"

"There are some sand dunes at the edge of the fairground where it joins the beach," he said, pointing.

He wanted to go there so he could kiss me and I wouldn't mind – it might help me forget Brendan for a while. I smiled. Should I? "Oh…"

"You can get some good photos of the sea and the fair with your brownie," he nodded down at my camera.

His brown eyes were really twinkling and lovely. I looked down. "Hmmm," I said, wanting to burst into giggles then I turned to Jocelyn. "Let's go for a walk with them Jocelyn, just for forty-five minutes; we can come back to the fair after lunch."

"We can't be late…"

She was such a good-goody. "We won't be. Come on." I put my arm around her. I was having such a great holiday: the sea, Jocelyn and Bisto. "This is my Cavalier from the cards," I whispered. "And you have your Page, the entrusted friend." I turned back to Bisto. "Just for a while…"

Bisto held my hand. *He held my hand. Die!* He was nice. Tall.

At the dunes Bisto pointed to the sea through the trees. "You could take a couple of photos from here," he said

I held my brownie up, looked through the lens and clicked the button. "Thanks. The sea's beautiful. You're lucky to live here." I turned the handle at the top to wind on the film. "Now the three of you with the sea in the background," I said. And I *had* to have one of me with him. I took the photo of them. "Jocelyn, could you take a couple?"

Bisto put his arm around me for the pictures and my stomach jumped. His arm was strong and brown like Michael's – but he was older, and much taller. Jocelyn handed back my brownie and I put it in its square camera case, then Bisto put his jacket down on the sand.

"It's a good spot here," he said.

I sat down and the other two sat a little way away. Jocelyn was trying to mouth something to me like, "Don't be long."

123

Bisto sat, put his arm back around me and turned his back on them. The sand was soft, warm and almost white there in the dunes. I could still glimpse the sea, enough to see that golden lace pattern of light, which danced on the surface of the waves.

He turned towards me and I got a funny feeling in my stomach. He was going to kiss me. His head bent and his lips met mine. At the same time, he eased me down and began lowering himself over me. I had to put my forearms and elbows in the sand at the sides of his jacket because he was almost on top of me.

His kiss was gentle at first, then stronger. I hoped I kissed back all right – him being older. At least I'd had a bit of practice with Brendan and Michael.

The cry of seagulls wafted over the tide as it roared out and swayed back again with a rolling shower of waves that broke against the shore. I imagined it taking away my sorrows just as the time away from home was doing. Yeah.

You could smell the sea too. It was salty, fresh and warm like Bisto's lips as they brushed mine again. The warm breeze carried that 'boy' type of smell of Bisto, the lad, not the gravy. He was squashing me down, my back moulded into the sand and he was breathing passionately.

I kissed like I had with Brendan yet tried to be like a film star from *The Saint*.

Bistos's kisses became harder like he was trying to eat my face and he was making it burn with his chin. I sank deeper into the sand as he pressed his bony hips into me. I didn't mind *this* kind of sinking.

We broke away and took a breath. I giggled a bit. I couldn't help it. He pushed a piece of hair from my face.

"So how long are you staying on the Isle of Wight?"

"We go back to Hayling Island tonight, and then I have to go back to Sheffield in two days." Time had passed quickly. I felt better than I had all year – since Dad died. I even had a suntan.

"Pity."

He kissed me again and this time his tongue went right in my mouth and I nearly bit if off because I wasn't expecting it.

He leaned up on one elbow. "How old are you, anyway?"

"Thir…Fifteen." I blushed as soon as I lied.

He went a bit quiet, eased his bony hips off me and kissed me a few times without his tongue swiping my tonsils. That was better. "What about you?"

Bisto sat up, closed his eyes and let his head drop back. He took a few deep breaths and breathed out through the mouth.

"Sixteen going on seventeen."

He took my hand and helped me sit up. "You're gorgeous. Better not be late for meeting your mum."

I looked at him for something – like – would I ever see him again, somewhere. He got out a biro and a piece of paper.

"Put your address down and I'll write to you. I do boxing. You never know, if I win a couple of tournaments I could be up your way."

"That'd be *so* fab." Imagine what Mandy, June and Sandra would think – and other girls at school when they knew. A boyfriend who was a *boxer*. He might be on television one day and we'd see him on the Saturday afternoon boxing that Dad used to watch. I wrote my address out for him. It might be a bit like him saying, 'If I win the pools' so I wouldn't count on it.

"This is my address," he said, "In case you come down again – next year." He rolled his bright brown eyes and smiled. "I have a flat. You could stay with me and get a season job."

I blushed. *Live in sin.* What would Grandma say? I wouldn't be sixteen next year like he thought. "I could…"

Our thighs brushed together as we stood. Maybe he could make me forget Brendan? I looked up into those dark eyes.

"I – don't want to *leave.*"

CHAPTER TWELVE:

NEVER GO HOME ANYMORE

Sandra and I nestled down into the deck chairs between the coalbunker and the smokeless-fuel bunker on my back patio. The transistor was between us on the little picnic-table.

"It's good to be protected from the wind. Not the same as the sea though."

"It'll help keep your tan. You'll be able to go back to school brown. It sounds like you had a fantastic holiday. Better than being stuck here."

The Shangri-Las' *Never Go Home Anymore* came on the radio. "This song makes me sad." I looked at the chrysanthemums and other flowers around the edge of our green lawn. "I nearly asked Bisto to let me stay there with him because I told him I was fifteen, but then I thought of this song. It reminded me of when Mum and I had a row about Brendan. I nearly ran away. I couldn't do it really. I wonder if Suzy Brown will ever go home again. She'll have left school this term, won't she?"

Sandra nodded and stared at the garden.

"Glad I'm not preggers. I won't 'do it' yet. This song makes *me* sad, too."

"You've never had a row with your mum over a boy."

Her big sigh made her chest rise up. "I saw Chris in the holidays. I'm still only allowed to see him once a fortnight."

"That's generous of your mum."

"We make up for lost time."

With no make-up on Sandra looked like a ten-year-old. I tried not to laugh. "Ooh, *Sandra,* really?"

Her face dropped and she put her sunglasses on.

"Something happened. I'm being sent away."

I sat up. *"What?"*

The Shangri-Las carried on singing the story of a girl who'd run away from home and thought of her mama tucking her up in bed.

"Mum and Dad went to a work birthday do last Friday, so I'd arranged with Chris to wait down the road for their car to go, so we could snog. He's a good snogger."

Not that she had any comparisons. "Great, you had an extra few hours then."

"Mum and Dad got half-way to town and she realised she'd forgotten the birthday present."

"Bloody 'ell."

"When she walked in he'd already tried, you know, and I'd said 'not yet', but he got me to …You know…"

"Actually…?

"We had the Stones on loud. By the time I realised that the noise outside was a key in the door, she'd opened the *lounge* door."

I snorted as I bit back a laugh.

"She marched in, switched the arm off the Stones' *Satisfaction* and said, 'Get off this settee now.' He was put off, you know, but was still…still…"

"No…he couldn't still be…?"

"No, but…out. Then he got his zipper stuck."

I bit my lip hard. Even Sandra laughed through tears.

"He took the bollocking as he tried to fasten up then escaped before she got my dad out of the car. Later that night Mum said they'd decided to send me to boarding school. I start next term so I won't be going back to Greenwood. It's religious; no hanky-panky there, she said. I'll learn to be more lady-like."

"Perhaps she means you should wear white gloves next time."

She giggled.

I reached over and hugged her. "I'm *so* sorry, Sandra. Seems daft to upset your school year. You're more clever than we three – *you're* in the *A stream.*"

She pouted. "And just when a boy has asked me out and I've been snogging like you three have. It's not *fair*. She's spoilt everything."

"Remember how my mum embarrassed me, having Brendan round for a bollocking?"

She removed her sunglasses and wiped a tear. "She didn't send you away."

"Might change their minds."

She shook her head. "Mum said I'll end up in St. Agatha's with Suzy Brown and bad lasses. My dad said, 'No she *won't*, if she gets herself in the family way there'll be a shotgun.'"

"Shotgun wedding?"

"So he reckoned they were doing the best thing to send me away. I'm scared."

"You stood by me after Dad …when Mandy didn't." I held her hand across the deckchairs. "Is it far, this school?"

"Couple of hours. Can we write?"

"Listen…" An echo of voices came from the driveway. "Do you want them to know?"

"Next week; when you three come to tea."

She had a more nonchalant, grown-up air about her. "At least that's still on!"

Mandy and June appeared in the back patio.

"Hi. How was your holiday?" Mandy said.

"Andrea's met a groovy boy," Sandra said.

June's eyes popped out of her head. "Andrea. *You* met a boy? Fab…"

"Have you heard the news?" Mandy said. "We brought a paper for your mum. Our teacher, Mr Fillmore is still *alive*; look."

I took the newspaper and Sandra peered over my shoulder.

The Telegraph and Star

Saturday August 21st 1965

Missing Teacher Fraud

Alan Fillmore, science teacher at Greenwood Secondary Modern School, presumed dead after his boat was found at Bridlington on Spring Bank Holiday weekend, has been found at London Heathrow airport. Mr Fillmore was about to board a BOAC flight. A search revealed that his wife, Lucy Jane Fillmore, had completed a claim form in preparation to claim on his Equitable Life

Policy, at some later stage. The policy was taken out two years ago. The pair had planned to meet in Bopal, India, en route to an unknown destination. Police and the insurers had been unconvinced....

"He's committed fraud. It wasn't an accident. He had a friend waiting somewhere nearby with another boat. It was all about him and his wife getting money out of an insurance policy," June said.

"Mr Fillmore? I wonder why? He's so good."

"And nice," Mandy said. "They were planning on starting a new life overseas with *thousands* of pounds. He'll go to prison. Probably his wife too."

"Prison. He can never go home anymore. How awful."

"He must have money problems," June said.

"Perhaps everyone's got some troubles," Sandra said, staring ahead.

I nodded. Sometimes people looked good and they had bad things going on. "He must have been thinking about how to pretend to be dead while he was teaching us science."

"Anyway, tell us about your holiday boyfriend," Mandy said.

"I knew he was coming. The tarot cards told me. I got the Cavalier of Swords. It can mean bravery. Bisto's brave. He's a professional boxer. He wanted me to stay with him in his flat." I lowered my voice. "He asked me to *live in sin*." I sighed. "I nearly didn't come back but I had to, really. I didn't want to hurt Mum."

"No, you couldn't do that to her. My sister lives with her boyfriend now, but she's seventeen. Have you got photos?" June asked.

"Sandra's seen them, here."

I passed the photos of Bisto to Mandy first. "Pass them on."

"Ooh, he looks nice," she said, passing each one to June. "Can you do the tarot cards for me to see if I'll meet someone?" Mandy asked.

"Okay. Maybe you're going to meet the fair man I saw in *my* cards. He wasn't connected with me so he might be coming for one of you. I'll do yours later anyway."

June's arm slipped through Mandy's while she was looking at the photos, meaning, Mandy was still *her* best friend not mine.

"You're really brown. Is it false?" she said.

"It's real. I got it sunbathing, except when I was with Bisto, of course. We had better things to do in the dunes." I flicked my hair back. "I got a letter from him this morning."

"Really?" Mandy said.

I yanked it out of the envelope. Never mind the spelling mistakes. "It was *fab* to hear from him." Even if he didn't say anything about coming up north to visit.

"I'll miss Jocelyn. She's really mature and goes to lots of night-clubs." I paused. "Still, it's nice to be exchanging letters and talking about the wild things we did."

"Hello," Mandy said.

It was Caroline South from across the road. "Hello."

"Andrea! How was your holiday?"

"Great, thanks."

"She met a boy," Mandy said.

Caroline looked between June and Mandy at the photos. "Let's see."

"And this is his letter." I held it up.

"Are you feeling a bit better – you know? It's almost a year isn't it?"

"Meeting Bisto helped." She would tell Lynette about him and Lynette would tell the Frizz and then Brendan would get to know. He might even be interested again if he thought I had a *sixteen*-year-old boy after me. Even though Brendan looked much older, he was only fourteen and a half, and at *school*, whereas Bisto worked. I lifted my chin. "He has his arm around me in this one."

"He looks nice. Lynette's got a boyfriend now. I still haven't. Mum won't let me, even though I'm older than all of you."

Caroline was nearly sixteen, but her mum was all churchy so she wasn't allowed to be with boys. "I wondered why Lynette wasn't wearing jodhpurs when I saw her. She had a *dress* on, and lipstick." That was so unusual for Lynette because she was horsey, like Heather.

"Her friend Betty packed Brendan James up because she heard he was going to pack her up," Caroline said.

My heart raced. I put some more Cool-tan on my arms and hoped Caroline didn't see the glances Mandy, Sandra, June and I exchanged. Then Mandy looked down so that her hair fell forward and hid her face, Sandra looked away and June stifled a giggle like me. "Oh." *Fancy that.* I rubbed the Cool-tan in and watched the white cream vanish into my arm. "Anybody want some suntan lotion?"

The sun was really shining today.

Yeah.

CHAPTER THIRTEEN:

WINDS OF CHANGE

Outside the classroom window, leaves were beginning to turn gold, titian and burnt orange. Some fell from the branches and floated down to the lawns where they formed little hearthrugs of smudgy shapes beneath the trees.

They'd turn chocolate and crisp on the ground. When it rained, which was often, they'd go into the earth and become soil and then new seeds would fall off and drop into the ground. Some might struggle against the air, gales and frost, and die. Others would grow stems anew, bud in spring and sway in the breeze, then bloom, lush and shady in summer. You could smell the green fields after the summer showers and everything was full and complete and pretty.

But it didn't stay that way.

Autumn came and even the healthy blossoms and leaves turned pale green, looked a bit battered and tired, then they went yellow, orange and shades of brown, and fell again.

Just like everything. Things in life were a bit like trees and nature because everything had died or floated away.

Yet the amber carpet outside glowed with a sort of warmth under the pale afternoon sun, as if to say, "Look how pretty we are; we're giving you this picture to make up for what has fallen away or died."

Dad used to paint pictures when he was young. The pictures were framed and hung on our walls. There were cottages with thatched roofs and gardens with lupins and red-hot pokers and trees, and then there were some with boats on the sea and rocks and things.

I had a feeling things were starting to grow again. Not that I could grow another dad, or replace Flash, but some things were taken away, and other things came.

The new didn't replace the old but they were different things and they made you feel a bit better than you had.

They were changes really, like the seasons.

Yeah. Changes.

Mum was back. I could see her through the kitchen window as I walked up the drive. She was smoking a cigarette. She opened the door and smiled as I swung my schoolbag onto the kitchen floor. "Did you have a nice time back down at Aunty Enid's?" On her own. Without me. I had to go to school because we were several weeks into the new term.

"I had a lovely time, thank you. What about you? Were you alright with Grandma?"

"Sandra came over on Saturday for half an hour and we talked." I wondered what Mum and Aunty Enid talked about. "She left for boarding school on Sunday."

Mum had a puff of her cigarette. "I'll check with her mum when it's alright to visit. She might be able to come home some weekends."

"Hope so. Suzy Brown is out of that home. She came to meet her friend Liz at the school gates. She looked distant, sad, quiet and old. They say she had her baby, but she won't come back to school 'til next year."

"Poor girl." She flicked her ash in the ashtray. "Jocelyn sends her love. I've just come out of Grandma's bed-sitting room. I had something to tell her. Now I want to talk to you."

"Is it about school?" I didn't get caught for daydreaming out of the window and looking at the leaves.

"No."

"What?"

"Let's sit on the settee in the lounge, shall we?"

I picked up Mum's Park Drive tipped and she took her glass ashtray through.

"Do you remember when I went out with those two men through the marriage bureau a few weeks ago?"

I giggled. She'd asked me first. "You said you were lonely and needed some adult company." One man was really short; the other had a heavy, hard-to-understand Yorkshire accent, and a loud voice. I mimicked him: "Does tha wont to go t' poob darn row-ad!" We'd laughed when she first told me and it was fun because, apart from our holiday, we hadn't laughed much all year. "That was so funny, Mum. You said you were going to stay in hibernation after that."

"I'd begun to think I'd stay on my own but Aunty Enid and Aunty Jenny don't think that's very healthy. The thing is, I'm not old, you know, even though you think I am. I loved Daddy very much but I might live for another forty years. It's a rather bleak thought. You'll probably leave home in a few years and I'll be all on my own."

I didn't want her to die or to stay sad forever. "Do you want to go back to that marriage bureau?"

She shook her head and pulled a face. "Remember when we stayed with Enid and Ron and we briefly met some friends of theirs called Bill and Mavis?"

"Yeah?"

"Well, I spent quite a bit of time with them again. We played records, the five of us, and danced, and Ron and Bill were very kind and both of them danced with me as well as with their wives. Now I'm telling you this woman to woman, because I feel you're grown up enough now, Andrea. I hope you won't be upset. It's a bit complicated."

"Yeah?"

"I liked Bill, but of course I didn't think anything of it, because he's married. The day I left I had a feeling he was going to turn up at the train station, although I had no reason to think that, so I purposely missed the first train."

I knew what she meant. We both had those feelings and then things happened, or someone said what we thought or dreamt about. I nodded. "Y-e-a-h?"

"I was right. He came rushing onto the platform. He wanted me to know he wants to spend some time with me and he's in the process of separating from his wife. Apparently they were just keeping up appearances in front of friends and neighbours until everything was settled. So, in a nutshell, he asked me out. He'd like to meet you. I wanted to ask you first, before I did anything. It has been a very lonely year and a bit. Would you mind if I went out with him?"

I knew that blank look came over my face while I thought. It was a very serious matter. "I don't know, Mum."

"If you don't want me to I don't think I will."

The last of autumn's crunchy leaves blew in the wind outside. I tried to imagine what life must be like for her now – especially with winter on the way again. "Well…I suppose so." I pulled my mouth to one side.

"I'm glad, darling. Thank you for being grown up and understanding."

I pulled my mouth to the side again. I was still thinking about that.

Mum hugged me to her and smiled at the face I pulled. "Bill works for a company that sends him all over the country."

"Is he rich?"

"He has a fairly good job. He's actually coming up here next week to train some staff and he'll be staying at a hotel in town. I thought perhaps I should invite him over to dinner. What do you think?"

"S'pose. What's he like?"

"Well, he's nowhere near as handsome as your daddy, but he's charming. He has fair hair, blue eyes and a Scottish accent – he's originally from Aberdeen."

"Och-aye," I said.

I was on my best behaviour for Mum. Under oath. No eye-rolling, mouth pulling or sighing by strict instruction. I'd got my grey hipster trousers on and my dark blue skinny rib jumper like I wore to the youth club. I bet Bill would think I was more grown up than Jocelyn.

Mum was all dolled up. She looked really nice when she was done up.

There was a soft rumble of tyres down the road. I followed Mum into the hall and hovered by the front door while she looked in the mirror and patted her hair.

A car pulled up and I peeped through the letterbox. It was a dark blue car. Mum said it was a Rover. I watched him close his posh car door. He was shorter than Dad; about Mum's height. "A bit short but not bad."

"Andrea! Quickly! Come away from the letterbox."

I was only looking. I let go of the letterbox. It tap-danced back into place as I jumped out of the way, just before the Scotsman walked into the drive.

Blooming heck. He gave her flowers. They were huge. I'd never seen flowers like that since the day of Dad's funeral when there were flowers all over our lounge and our dining room from family, friends, neighbours and other people. The Scotsman prized his twinkling blue eyes away from my mum.

"Hello, Andrea, I've heard what a gorgeous girl you are."

How did Scottish people make 'heard' sound like 'here'd' and gorgeous girl like 'godgus gearl'? And he'd have to be kidding. Mum probably told him I was a problem teen.

"I like your hipster trousers. Girls in London wear those. They're very fashionable."

He said it like 'fah-shon-ar-ble'. "Thank you."

"I hear you like the Beatles."

He sounded fairly mod. "I do. Especially John Lennon."

139

He laughed and the skin around his light blue eyes creased up. His eyes were really squinty and funny. He had sandy hair and a fresh face, which was sort of pinkish-white like porridge when you put jam in it.

"I was wondering if you'd like a record from the top ten when I come up next time?"

He was coming again? Well, he might as well bring a 'top *tern*' record, then. Maybe he was like nice porridge. I lowered my eyelashes.

"Thank you."

"Which one do you like?"

I thought for a minute. Porridge was quite fluid. "I like two, actually!" I giggled; so did he. He didn't mind.

"Andrea!"

"Well, I do, Mum! I like *Michelle* by the Beatles and *Groovy Kind of Love* by the Mindbenders. I can't make up my mind. Either would be nice." I smiled and showed him my dimple, thinking, 'Or both' then turned to go back upstairs, mess about in my room and leave them to it. Was he the fair man in the tarot cards? The Cavalier of Clubs said: a man in a hurry: change, alteration or a journey.

Perhaps he'd take us on holiday next year, if they were still courting.

Bill gazed at Mum across our best white tablecloth while he chewed chops, savouring each bite. I looked down at my Yorkshire pudding and vegetables, stifling a laugh. When he'd arrived he said, "May I freshen up, Jeanie?" But of course, he said it like, '*Frershern*'. So he washed up and stank out the bathroom. When I went in to wash my hands, it smelt of sweat in there. It was an animal-y pink and white very B.O. type of sweat smell. Not like Dad. He had a woodwork and honey and man-ness smell. Dad, like me, didn't eat meat, only a bit of chicken.

I bet all the pigs and cows and sheep oozed out of the little pores in Bill's skin when he got hot. He smelt a bit piggy. Yeah.

Bill said yes to more of everything from Mum's best serving dish then in between them talking about things to do with his work and the things on the news, he puckered up his lips and squinted.

"Ooooh Jeanie, thut was *wonderful*," he said, and blew kisses across the table to Mum. I was going to be sick, I was sure. He'd only had a chop and three peas. Och aye. I could feel my top lip wanting to go up like Elvis Presley. Although Mum had explained that even people *her* age did it when they had special feelings for each other, it was hard to imagine them – you know. I mean, she was nearly thirty-nine and he was *forty*. It didn't seem right. And worse, when I had told Sandra, Mandy and June about him recently, June threw back her head like a drama queen and said, "Oh! *I* could never love again."

Bill licked his lips and dabbed with a napkin. "You're a g-o-r-g-eous gal," he added, and his eyes shone like little marbles. She wasn't a gal. She was my mum. I wished he wouldn't drool in front of me. It wasn't as if he was my dad.

I cleared the table and took the things into the kitchen (being on my best behaviour) and when I came back into the lounge they were sitting on the settee holding hands. I rolled my eyes and he laughed. Mum gave me a warning

141

look about the eye-roll so I behaved while we sat and watched *Juke Box Jury* and *The Saint*, eating the Cadbury's chocolates he bought.

This time he was staying with us tonight and Sunday, not in a hotel like before. Did that mean they'd *do it* in *my* house? I wouldn't think so. It wouldn't be right. I certainly didn't want to think about piggy-pores doing it with my mum. Even worse, thinking of her *wanting* to, but she'd been down to stay in his new flat in London and he'd taken her to a posh hotel twice as well.

I knew what that meant.

They did it in London.

Mum looked over at me. "It's been a long day for Bill, driving up from London to Sheffield, and I'm quite tired too, so we'll have an early night. You can stay up 'til eleven thirty and watch television as it's the weekend."

Really? That was later than usual. I kissed her goodnight. "G'night, Bill," I said to him. I drew the maroon lounge curtains on the December sleet.

It was cosy in the lounge so I made myself comfortable, played the two records he'd bought me last time he visited, and danced the twist and the shake. A few dances wore me out, so I turned on the telly but there was nothing much on so I decided to wash some of the pots but not the pans. He called pots dishes where he came from but they weren't all dishes. How could you call cups dishes? They had strange sayings down south. I was putting away the 'dishes' but I didn't know where the dinner service went because we didn't use it much except at Christmas and things like that.

I padded upstairs in my slippers and turned the handle of Mum's door. "M-u-u-m. Where do I put…" The handle

142

didn't turn. The door was locked. How could it be locked? It was never locked. I always went in when I wanted to talk. Something rushed through my body and knotted in my stomach. I wanted to fight. My throat got dry and I banged on the door like a policeman.

"MUM!"

"Whatever it is, it can wait until tomorrow. We'll sort it out in the morning," she said behind the locked door.

No we wouldn't. We'd sort it out now. NOW.

How dared she lock me out? It was *my* house more than his. Why should he be more important than me? I grabbed onto the door handle with both hands and rattled it back and forth against the door frame. Surely, she wouldn't…? This was Dad's bedroom, after all.

She flung open the door.

"Andrea. Stop that this *minute*. This is despicable behaviour. I thought you were learning to be mature. Obviously I'm mistaken," she seethed.

The dragon in me, about to roar fire, evaporated into steam then became a water dragon. "I wanted to talk to you! How can I ask you something if you lock the door? It might have been really important," I cried. "It's *my* house."

"We've discussed this. You're behaving like a spoilt child. I understand how hard it is and I know you miss Dad but I'm not getting drawn into any dialogue now. Go downstairs and calm down."

"I expect you'll have *him* here for Christmas," I sobbed.

Mum opened her mouth and stared.

"Well, you ruined the last one."

I marched across the landing then clomped downstairs like an elephant, opened the lounge door and banged it shut. In between sobs, I shuffled, cut and spread the tarot cards. The first one I turned was La Maison de Dieu. I looked at the falling house and cried some more. Then I lifted the record player lid and put the Shangri-Las' *Never Go Home Anymore* on. It wasn't just Sandra and Mr Fillmore who couldn't go home. *This* wasn't like my home anymore.

Everything was changing. And I didn't like it.

CHAPTER FOURTEEN:

TIMES THEY ARE A-CHANGING

The candle flickered in the coral glass and ceramic container. Mum and I looked at the warm glow it made as we snuggled up on the settee.

"Did you know he was buying it for you?"

"No. It was all wrapped up. He gave it to me when I went down to London a few days before Christmas. He said not to open it until Christmas day with you."

"I'm glad we had Christmas to ourselves, just you, me, Grandma and Granny Hampton." I didn't mind her having New Year with Bill.

She hugged me to her. "I wanted it to be right *this* year – as much as it could be. It worked out okay; Bill was able to go up to Scotland and see his mum then come here for New Year on his way back to London."

I noticed a tear on her cheek. "Mum. Are you sad because he lives a long way away?"

She shook her head.

Her eyes were watery around the edges but she smiled.

"About Dad?"

"Partly. There's something else."

My heart jumped. "Who else has died?" Grandma was there so it had to be Granny Hampton or an aunty or uncle.

"No one."

I looked up at Billy's cage and my heart did another gallop. He'd just gone back in from a zoom around the lounge and had hung upside down on the mirror and talked to himself, so he was okay.

Mum took a Kleenex from the big box on the coffee table and wiped her tear away then reached for the red and white packet of Park Drive tipped. She changed her mind and took one of the new Benson and Hedges in a gold packet that Bill had bought for her. "I've just read a letter from Aunty Enid." She lit and inhaled. "I wrote after Christmas and explained about Bill and me. Bill's their friend; or was. Bill and Mavis had already decided to separate. As I told you, they were 'keeping up appearances' with their friends until it was sorted out, but once Mavis knew about me, she made it look like it happened because of our meeting – especially to Enid." She sighed.

"Uh-oh."

"She feels bad. It's difficult for Enid, caught in the middle; both Mavis and I are her friends. She said it'd be better if we didn't keep in touch. I don't blame her. She was very civil about it."

"What about Jocelyn and me?"

"She'd prefer to sever all contact – you girls as well."

The drizzle outside became more like rain and it blew and flattened against the windowpanes. Now I was losing another best friend. I'd known her since we were born. I thought we'd always be friends and be bridesmaids for each other one day – like when I married Brendan James.

I looked at my feet in my slippers and folded my arms. "I was looking forward to another holiday with Jocelyn." *And seeing Bisto.* After all, nothing had happened with Brendan since he broke up with the Frizz. Michael was friendly but not chasing me anymore. His love of football thrilled him more, and that was fine by me. "*I* haven't been since last summer. We planned to go this year."

People and animals just got taken away. And now little chance of seeing Bisto, bloody hell.

"I'm so sorry, Andrea," Mum said. "We've both had a big loss, and I know you've had other losses: friends and your pony, and separations. I feel those too. But Aunty Enid was my very best friend." She wiped a tear. "We'll have to make different plans this year."

Poor Mum, losing her *best* friend. I bet she felt like I did when Mandy dumped me. But Aunty Enid wouldn't even be just a regular friend with Mum. I gave her a hug and she managed a smile.

"Think of it this way – you did find Jocelyn immature and she's not really interested in the same things as you, is she?"

She definitely wouldn't shag.

I pulled my mouth to the side to stop myself laughing. "Not really. I never thought about grown-ups falling out."

"It happens sometimes."

I sat and talked to her so she didn't think about not having her special long-term friend anymore. It was still raining outside. That made it worse somehow when you

147

lost someone and it rained and rained. It was the greyness that really stamped home the loss.

Yeah, the grey.

"It's miserable outside. It's much milder down south," Mum said.

She should know; she'd been to London a few times now. People up where we lived didn't go to London often. It was like going to another country. "What's it like, apart from the weather?"

"Oh, there are lots of shows, theatres and large department stores. How would you feel about moving to London?"

"London?"

"Actually, a little village or town just outside London."

"I don't want to leave here."

"Why not?'

"My friends."

"You and Mandy aren't back as *best friends* are you? And Sandra has gone away."

"I said I'd visit Sandra."

"Bill comes up to Yorkshire to train people. We can come too, sometimes, and visit her on the way."

I shrugged. "Yeah, but, maybe – Brendan – one day."

She looked away and I couldn't see her face. When she looked back she had a little smile. "We could invite them down."

Could we? "Even Brendan?"

"With certain conditions."

That wasn't so bad then, but I still didn't think so. "No, I wouldn't want to move really. Why?"

The rain became finer and just trickled against the windowpanes and there was a damp earthy smell coming through the upper window where we let in fresh air when it was warm enough. The clock ticked like a heartbeat and it was nice and peaceful but I was still waiting for her to answer.

"Shall we have a cup of tea?" Mum asked.

I went and put the kettle on and the tea in the teapot as quickly as I could. "Kettle's on." I bounced down again.

Mum leaned into the settee back. "Well, Bill would like to have a family. He's always wanted a daughter and would like us all to live together and for he and I to get married when his divorce comes through."

Bloody 'ell. "Daughter!" She had to be kidding. I'd *never* be his daughter.

"He'll never replace Daddy, you know that, but I've grown to love him in a different way."

It was bad enough to smell his piggy smell in the bathroom, see him drooling at the dinner table and hear him calling my mum, 'Jeanie darrrling' on the odd weekend. But all the time? And Mum hated 'ies' on the ends of names. At least she used to.

I had my blank look in place, while I thought. "You mean we would have to sell our house?"

"Properties are more expensive down there so we'll both put in what we can."

I frowned and pinched my lips with my teeth. Sometimes bad people stole people's house money.

"Don't worry. It'll be in my name for the time being and he'll pay the mortgage we'll have to take."

"Hmm," I said. I couldn't imagine leaving certain people. "I don't really want to go." Yet something inside me was excited. What would London be like?

"It's only about one hour from the sea. Besides that, remember you saw a careers person about being a fashion designer? Well, there are lots of colleges for fashion in and near London and lots more job opportunities."

My mouth hung open. "When I told Granny Hampton I wanted to be a fashion designer she said, 'They dorn't mayke fashion designers 'ere, luv.'"

Get back in your box, girl.

They obviously made them in London.

"Typical of your granny," Mum said.

She and Dad's mum had never seen eye-to-eye, so visits had lessened since he died.

Mum drew the curtains and switched on the little lamp. A golden glow filled the corner of the room like instant sunshine through a tiny window.

"Of course, there are lots of night clubs and discothèques for older teenagers. Not that you're ready for that…"

"I'll be fourteen next birthday!"

So, the London area was warmer, and only an hour to the sea? Every January I thought, I'm going to live in Hawaii when I grow up. I didn't know where it was, but I'd seen it on television and it looked even better than Hayling Island. In the meantime, anywhere down south would do.

Hmm. And discothèques. I was thinking.

"I suppose by the time we moved you'd be fourteen, and there might be some discos suitable for young teens. Well, you have a think about it. I'll bring that cuppa through then I'm going to get dinner ready, okay?"

I nodded.

1966

I was still thinking about all that a few weeks later when Bill came for the weekend. After they did the kissy kissy thing in the hall Mum set the table and Bill opened some wine he'd brought. Mum never drank wine before. Bill sat down and smoothed Mum's best white serviette over his lap. We usually only had cloth serviettes for special occasions. "Can *I* have some wine, please?"

Bill's eyes twinkled when he looked at Mum.

"Italian youngsters have a dash of wine with soda water, Jeannie."

Mum had that half frown half smile again.

"A very dash."

I sipped my essence of wine while Mum served my dinner. "Sandra lightened her hair to blonde yesterday and June did hers dark auburn," I said in between forkfuls of food. "Another girl in my class is going golden. I want to dye mine." Brendan would really notice me then.

"Well, you can't. You know you're not allowed to have dyed hair at school; besides, you could ruin it," Mum said.

Bill sipped his wine. "If you don't mind me saying so, Jeanie, I think it would look wonderful on Andrea if it were done properly."

151

Scottish people don't say properly, they say, pro-perrly. Aye Bill. Mum's eyebrows lifted.

"Och. You're only a young lassie once. I'd be happy to pay for her to have it done at the hairdressers and to have the roots done every three weeks or so. It's nearly the end of term. We could get it done in the holidays. If they tell her off, we can get it dyed back again. She's nearly for'tin."

He winked at me and puckered up his lips to Mum. I held my breath. I bet she wanted to blow up and tell him to mind his own business, but not in front of me. Besides, if we were going to be family…

It was silent except for the delicate tinkle of cutlery on porcelain.

Dad would never have let me dye my hair. There would have been thunder under those dark bushy brows if I'd laboured the point and Dad's look alone was his word.

Bill wasn't a 'dad' type, but he was kind.

"Oh Mum! Say yes!" She'd bollock him later.

"Okay, Okay."

"Wow. Fab! Thanks, Bill – both of you."

Bill tapped the white tablecloth with his finger. He did that when he thought sometimes.

"I was thinking of taking you and your mum down to London next weekend – if you'd like to go that is…"

"London?"

"Yes, to Lorndon."

Mum cleared her throat. "We were thinking of looking for a house near London and we'd like your input."

"My *input*? You mean I have a choice about going or staying then, do I?" I slumped at the table and folded my arms.

"No, darling, you don't," Mum said. "You know I mean about the house."

The Cavalier of Clubs meant a man in a hurry and change. I got one of those little shivers that happen when something comes true like that.

Bill tapped on the table with his index finger again. Something important must be on the way. Maybe his finger softly brushing the tablecloth helped him pull his thoughts out. Here it came.

"I suggest we go down for your fourteenth birthday, take you down Carnaby Street to see the fashions and to a show at night. We'll stay for Easter, find a house, and then we'll get you into a good London hairdresser so you can go back to school professionally blonde after the break. What do you say?"

I wanted to say a swear word. "Wheeeee!"

Maybe London wouldn't be so bad. Wait 'til Brendan James saw my blonde hair. Wait 'til Mandy and June saw it. "We won't be moving straight away, will we?"

"It'll take about three months even if we find a house by Easter, which we intend to."

"Right," I said it with a sulk, but really I was beginning to like the idea.

CHAPTER FIFTEEN:

MY SECRET

"Bloody 'ell, 'Ampton's dyed her hair."

Brendan James' mouth stayed open as I swept through the school gates. It was the first time I'd seen him close up since I went blonde. He and his mob were leaning against the railings by the entrance. He didn't usually drop his 'h's' like some of the boys did, but he managed it today. At least he didn't drop all four.

"Hello..." It was a soft matter-of-fact 'hello' that trailed off into the wind behind me. I carried on walking. Mandy and June were waiting for me in the playground.

Brendan hadn't been saying hello since he told me he didn't care, and that he liked the Frizz. That seemed ages ago now.

He pulled himself away from the railings and walked beside me, adjusting his duffle bag onto his other shoulder.

"Very nice."

He was close to my arm. "Thanks."

"What's the occasion?"

"Oh, you know. A few things are happening all at once – moving to London in a few weeks and stuff like that..." I kept walking. We'd looked at seventeen houses at Easter and decided on the second one we saw. It was in a village half an hour from London.

Brendan marched to keep up with me and held onto my arm. "Hang on, hang on…"

Something jumped inside me like it did when he touched me.

"You're going away then?"

"Just before summer break." I was bursting out of the earth, dusting off the mud, being washed by rain and beginning to dry out in the sun. Yeah. I was getting more rays of sun, so to speak.

"How come?"

I didn't want to get into specifics that my mum was re-marrying because I hadn't told him my dad had died, had I? But even in a huge school like ours, he could have found out by now, I supposed. I swallowed my discomfort.

"Changes, you know…"

I could say, "My dad's job is taking him there," but that would be like saying Bill was my dad; I couldn't quite do *that*. I glanced at him and smiled. "London's more my style."

His dark blue eyes widened again and the creases appeared in his brow. His face was almost deadpan but the very corners of his mouth were turning up a little.

"I wouldn't mind coming down to London myself. I'm thinking of hitching down with Kev. We should keep in touch."

I wouldn't remind him that only fifteen months ago he told me to get lost and broke my wounded heart. "Good idea. I'll let you have my address before I go." I said it brightly as if I was just making a new friend and the past was forgotten.

He stopped me walking by holding onto my arm again and turned me round to face him.

Hold on heart. I shouldn't like him the way I did. I made my face look somewhere between friendly and blasé. Inside I wanted to b-u-r-s-t.

"Fancy coming to a big party in July? It's a mate of mine. His parents are going away for the weekend. He's not at school; he works. No-one from this school is going."

He tore a leaf out of an exercise book and wrote down the details. It was almost two months away, shortly before we moved house. I took the paper then looked up a bit as if I was thinking about it. My tongue was glued to my mouth and I'm sure he could hear my heart beat. *He* invited *me*. He liked me again, at least a bit. "Fab. Okay."

He gave me a really nice smile as if I was a girl he'd never seen before.

"My phone number is on the bottom in case you don't have it anymore."

I *did*. "Good." I'd wear my turquoise, flowered bell-bottom trousers and matching top. The colour looked fab on me.

He squeezed my hand so quickly I hardly knew it happened.

"I'll go early to help my mate; come as early as you like. I know it's weeks away, but I really want you to come, okay?"

I nodded. Would he change his mind before the event?

"Y' might like to come for a coffee down at Hills café on Friday nights before then? There's a new jukebox; plenty of Stones' music. Bring one of your mates, or your cousin."

Was this real? "Maybe in a couple of weeks."

"Come over to my house any time. My mum's there. You've got my number."

Really? "Okay." I watched the beginnings of his one-sided smile.

"Rather that, than me coming to yours!"

He pulled a scared face. His friends called something like, "Bren-dan, move your arse." He squeezed my hand again. Did he rub his fingers on my palm or did I imagine it?

"Okay? Don't forget."

I wanted to run and tell Mandy and June and phone Sandra and my cousin Jackie but I wouldn't tell *anyone* about THE night yet in case something went wrong. I had my plan for summer '66 now. I knew all along Brendan James would be the one. That was *my* secret.

Finally. I walked up the driveway to the house. How on earth did I get through the last few weeks? I'd thought about him every minute. Dark leafy foliage flanked the driveway either side of me. I was glad we'd already met at the café a few times. Not that we'd been alone; he always had mates with him, as I had.

I rang the doorbell and smoothed down my navy reefer jacket, which I wore over my bell-bottoms. My nails had new white nail varnish on with Mary Quant Op-art nail transfers in black and white. One half of the heart was black and one half was white with a black outline. That was because our hearts were half-black and half-white and sometimes we tipped more one way than the other.

I was going to be a bit black tonight.

I bet I wouldn't have been standing there with black eyeliner around my eyes and white nail varnish with transfers on if my dad were alive but then it was hard to say, because I was only twelve and a half when Dad died but I was fourteen now.

Brendan opened the door and took me by the hand. The hallway was crowded and noisy. The Kinks' *Tired of Waiting* blared out from the lounge. Squeezed in between people, we looked each other up and down with a smile. He had his bell-bottoms on too. His were maroon and he had a matching jumper on.

I could hardly believe it was me in the hall mirror. I looked *at least* sixteen, which seemed fitting, given what I was about to do.

Brendan led me through the crowded hall to the lounge. "This is Andrea," he said to some of his friends. They staggered about a bit. "They've had a few," Brendan said. He gave me a cheeky grin and added, "So have I."

I waved my hand in front of my face to get rid of the smoke.

"It's better in the kitchen. That's where the drink is. I'll get you one. Come on. It's packed in the lounge. Too small. You look fantastic."

I flicked my blonde hair back. It was almost waist-length now. The little bit of backcombing I'd done on top made me look older, I was sure. "Thanks." I'd used my big hair rollers to make it wave.

I clung to Brendan's hand as he steered me through the crowd and into the kitchen.

"Glad you were able to come."

"I said I was meeting my friends, which is sort of true!"

"What time do you have to be back?"

"The last bus. We looked it up. It's at 11.10."

"I'll make sure you're on it. What can I get you, shandy, cider, wine, or coke?"

"Shandy, please."

I sipped the drink and Brendan cracked the top off a beer.

"Tell me about where you're moving to."

He had one arm around me and he edged me against the kitchen wall. I could hardly think straight with him that close. "It's a country village close to London called Orpington. The Liberals won the other parties there so it's become well known – for a little place. Then in London there're lots of discos and fan clubs, and of course all the pop stars are down there."

He placed our drinks down on the kitchen table. Cold stone pressed into my back and I didn't mind one bit. Sandy Shaw's new record *Long Live Love* played in the other room. I blushed when his face came down to mine and we started snogging. I couldn't help it. He was very Neanderthal. I liked that.

My eyes were half open. People were coming and going to get another drink. I wished we were alone. Brendan came up for air. "I'm going to leave school in summer. I want some money. Most of my friends work," he said.

159

"You've definitely decided not to stay on and get O levels then?"

"Got the chance of work at one of the industrial furnaces. The work's a bit dirty but the pay's good. I'll save a bit then hitch down to London for a week, okay?"

It sounded good to me – the London part anyway. "Great. I'll be able to show you around." Fancy Brendan leaving school to work in one of those furnaces. "I always look at the furnaces out of the classroom window. Of the two huge ones, one's lighter and newer, the other older and blacker. They make me think about the opposites in things."

He looked a bit blank. "Yeah."

"Do you think you'll like working there?" I couldn't imagine he would. He was well spoken, had a nice house, his mum was lovely and I'd heard he was in the top few in his class so it seemed a bit daft to leave at fifteen.

"I don't know. I just want the money to buy clothes and a car and things." He pressed me further into the wall as his mouth came down on mine again until we ran out of breath. "It's the industrial age," he said, looking up. "Got to take it while you can. I'll need a break after the first few months though – in London." He winked.

I nodded. "Here, I've written down my address and telephone number in case we don't see each other much after tonight. I'm busy helping my mum pack up the house and visiting relatives these last few days."

He took out a wallet from his back pocket, folded my address, and put it inside. "Shame you're moving before the six week holidays …we could have done some things."

At last he was going to ask me out in the summer holidays. I swept my mascara'd lashes down. "That would've been nice." Bit late now. "At the end of the summer holidays I'm going away with my cousin Jackie and her mum and dad. Remember you came to her house with me ages ago for a small party?" I giggled.

His brows went up and wrinkled his forehead. "That was a *mini* party."

I hoped my soft laugh distracted him from my beetroot face.

"So are your cousin's family moving too?"

"No. I'll miss Jackie once we've moved to London." I'd miss him too. My eyes prickled.

"Come here…" he said, drawing me into his warmth.

After a lingering kiss he grabbed my hand.

"Follow me."

"Where?" I knew where.

"Here…"

"Where's here…?" I smiled.

He pulled me out of the kitchen and started to walk up the stairs. There were people sitting on some of the stairs, talking. Nobody took much notice of us. He opened a bedroom door and there were couples lying down all over the place, then another door – almost the same. The third door he tried opened into a room with just a couple on the bed and another on the floor at the side.

"Excuse me, all," he said with a little polite cough to the people lying down in the room. He said it like *Dixon of Dock Green* on television when he says, "'Evening, all," but Brendan didn't bend at the knees when he said it.

He led me by the hand through the darkness then turned and whispered, "This'll do."

It wasn't what I had in mind, but like he said, it would do. Time was too short to arrange much else, and we liked each other. I could say that was mutual now.

We groped our way in the dark around the foot of the bed where we discovered another couple on the floor. They were breathing heavily and writhing about. We stepped around them to the far side of the bed by the bay window. Ah. A space.

We settled down between the bed and the bay window.

Yeah.

CHAPTER SIXTEEN:

RITE OF PASSAGE

At least it was dark behind the heavy velvet curtains. You couldn't see anyone else at all; you just knew they were there because of the heavy breathing and occasional word or whisper.

No one was smoking or drinking in there, they were too busy. It was good to be away from the noisy crowds – to be with Brendan.

We lay facing each other and started kissing. Away from the smoky rooms I smelt the scent of soap, shampoo, wool and body and it was a good scent – the sort you wanted to hold on to. To blend with. Having his body on top was like being protected. I sighed because it'd been a long time since I'd pressed up this close to him. No wonder Mum had been lonely, not having anyone to cuddle for eighteen months 'til she met Bill.

"I want to make love to you," he whispered in between kisses. "Don't worry, I won't make you pregnant."

"Have you got…?" I didn't want the people on the bed to hear.

"Rubbers? I forgot. I'll be careful, I promise."

"Shhh! You will?"

"Of course. I know what to do – I'll pull out in time."

There was something magical about being touched and kissed by a person you really loved. It wouldn't be the same with any other boy. His lips sealed mine. Now I opened my mouth like him and kissed back moving my head this way and that. The more I kissed him and he kissed me the more I was aware of that man scent, the hardness of his body against the softness of mine, and I couldn't get enough. I knew he felt the same because he was holding me tight like he never wanted to let me go. His heart beat fast close to my chest and he breathed liked he'd started running.

At least our floor space didn't make squeaks like the mattress underneath the couple on the bed. It sounded like my granny's rocking chair.

Brendan's hands went under my blouse and passed over the lace in my Marks and Spencer's bra.

"I don't want you to take my clothes *right off* in case someone suddenly switches the light on," I whispered.

His smile hovered on my lips. "They're too busy."

I let him un-do the back. I knew he remembered about the cotton wool in the ends of my bra when he first grabbed me in the lane after school. I expanded my chest so that my bust – all mine, was full in his hand as he kissed me again. He held my head like they did in James Bond. His kisses were strong and warm.

I'd liked him since I was ten; he was one of the boys playing cricket in the field when I was there with my dad and other kids in my street. I'd probably marry him one day. Now I was with him again. He really was the only boy for me.

Both our trousers and underpants were off as far as we dared take them, after all, the party owner's parents could come home unexpectedly, you never knew.

My hands ran over his warm, lean body and he started to do it, just a little bit at first.

"Is it hurting?"

I wouldn't say if it were. "No." I'd been horse riding since I was ten, often bareback; I'd probably half lost my virginity.

"Just hold on tight, you'll be all right," he said, as if he were a riding instructor.

The writhing couple on the bed made the mattress go squeak, squeak, squeak like an old school trampoline.

Because I didn't want him to say things others might hear, I let him put his tongue in my mouth and I tested mine against his. He liked that. He stroked under my half-off bra then pushed a bit more and I wrapped my arms around him. He moved closer and deeper so that we were joined like the sky and the sea when you could hardly see the line between them – and I began to feel the waves. Brendan started to move quicker, which was kind of good.

He came up a bit more on his elbows. Now I was used to the dark I could see his face. He opened his mouth wide and the lines between his nose and mouth deepened. His eyes screwed shut and he frowned, curled back his lips in a strange way, and paused with his face like that, as if he was going to have a heart attack. Then he roared out his breath like a lion with a sore throat, pulled out, and fell onto me.

Oh. I was just beginning to enjoy it.

I cradled him in my arms. Did it always only last a few minutes?

"That was *great*," he whispered in my ear.

Was it? Well it was good, but I wouldn't have minded it being a bit longer – in time.

He kissed me on the lips again, rolled me towards him and fastened up my bra, then reached for his clothes. He pulled a neat square handkerchief from one of his pockets.

"It's clean."

He dabbed the stickiness on my stomach.

"Let's get back to the party. Come on," he said.

I'd rather have stayed. Couldn't he just lie there a while and talk in whispers and kiss? "Hang on." I pulled my clothes back into place and stood.

He squeezed my hand then led the way out, quietly stepping over bodies.

"Bathroom's there," he said. "I'll wait."

I closed the door behind me. Did I bleed? Only a spec. I quickly washed then tidied myself up and looked at my face in the bathroom mirror. I looked different, I was sure. Yeah, I looked different.

Brendan was waiting at the top of the stairs. He kissed me on the cheek.

"Let's go and listen to some Stones' music. Do you want another shandy?"

"No thanks. Just lemonade."

He grabbed a beer and lemonade from the kitchen then led me into the lounge. Everyone was dancing so we faced each other and moved with the music. The Stones' *The Last Time* hit home.

Brendan began to wobble and fall while dancing and we laughed.

"Sorry. I've drunk quite a bit."

It didn't matter because it was so crowded that people who were tipsy and toppling about just fell against each other. I didn't want to be with all these people anyway; only Brendan. I'd had enough dancing and besides, it was time for my last bus. "Are you going to walk me to the bus stop?"

He swayed on his feet. "I can't even stand up. I know I should walk you there. Sorry, I've overdone the drink. I'll crash on the floor here tonight."

His eyes half closed then opened again and he swayed some more. "But I am coming to London. Okay? *She's got a Ticket to Ride*," he sang, and then he pulled my hips to him, kissed me and flopped back against the wall.

Charming. I frowned looked at my watch. "Okay. Got to go." We had a small kiss and it was very beery. "Talk to you before I go away." I headed for the door.

The heavy maroon velvet curtains were drawn. I thought of the lacy net ones underneath and the warmth of our front room. I was glad to be home. Yet as soon as the door clicked behind me and I walked into the hall, a sense of guilt grabbed me. I wanted to sneak upstairs before anyone saw me. Mum and Bill were in the bedroom but the little lamp was on because a glow shone on the landing. Mum wouldn't be asleep. She'd be waiting for me. The bedroom door opened and she leant over the banisters.

"Hello. Did you have a nice time at the party?"

"It was great," I lied, calling from the hall. Well, it wasn't a great party, was it? I mean, I couldn't even say it was great sex – not that she asked me that.

"I danced heaps and I had one glass of shandy and then lemonade. I'm a bit exhausted though, so I think I'll go straight to bed." I looked up from the bottom stair, beamed a bright smile then clomped up the rest of the stairs looking down at my feet.

I reached the top and she came to give me a kiss goodnight.

"All right, darling. Don't forget to take your make-up off with cold cream."

I lowered my lashes so she couldn't see my eyes.

"Yeah!"

I was going to keep this black and white nail varnish forever. I had it on so thick that it would be easy to peel off whole. I sat on the edge of my bed and began to pick around the edge of each nail until I could lift the white nail polish and peel it off. They came off like little white plastic tablecloths with a black and white design on top. I carefully collected all ten nail shaped plastic-nylon transfers of black and white hearts on white, laid them on the bed and studied them.

Something to do with half a heart prickled the back of my mind. I still loved Brendan, but I knew he didn't love me as much. I was still cross that he hadn't walked me to the bus stop. He invited me so he should've stayed sober enough, especially as it wasn't a very good area there. If he hadn't been so drunk, he might have been able to do it for longer, you never knew. It should have made us closer and more like boy and girlfriend, or like family, but everything was still the same.

Perhaps love could be like the blackness of death and war as well as the whiteness of the good parts of life, and peace. I knew it was like a black death when he told me he didn't want me last winter, and like the brightest day when he asked me to the party this year. Yet even when you had the person you wanted, it looked like it could still be beautiful or ugly; incomplete – not right.

Sandra was really good and white, to me, but her parents thought she was bad. Mr Fillmore did a bad thing which gave him black edge, but he was such a good teacher. Sometimes it wasn't all one thing or the other. Maybe even a white heart could be tainted by a black edge, like the transfer outline of my Mary Quant heart.

I opened the lid of my shell jewellery box and placed the ten black and white heart nail remnants inside. Black, white, or somewhere in-between, I'd always be able to remember that these were the nails holding onto Brendan James' back, the night I first did it.

A black and white memento.

Granny Hampton moved over to the fireplace. It still had the old black warming oven at the side of it and sometimes she still used it to warm food. When my dad was little, it was their only oven. They even heated the iron in the fire, but irons weren't electric then. She stared into her small summer fire and stabbed the few toasted embers with the poker then looked up. Framed by her straight white hair, her prominent jaw was more set than ever.

"Is he alright, love?" she asked.

Granny couldn't be expected to love Bill, could she? Dad was her son. Even though Granny and Mum had never got along, Mum always encouraged me to visit, but it took two buses to get there and I knew I hadn't been as much as I should. "So-so, you know. He'll never be Dad, but he's nice to me and he's making Mum happy again."

Granny frowned and ran her hands up and down her checked apron. "I can't believe you've sold the house. What's t' new one like?"

"Similar, but older. It has a sunroom at the back and an attic like yours, a big garden and a double garage." I didn't tell her Bill had bought Mum a car. "It's on a long, winding country lane which goes up to an old village. There's a pub and a Church there. At the other end of our lane there's a slightly bigger village which is part of Orpington. It has a high street and a fish and chip shop. It's only half an hour on the train to London."

"You'll be a long way away, love. London's t'other end of the country."

Granny's broad Yorkshire accent was more noticeable after my few days away near London, where people said lav for love. Up our way a lav was short for lavatory, especially when they were up the garden path, like Granny's.

I gave her a hug. "I'll write and come and see you. Sandra's going to boarding school and Mum'll take me to visit her as well."

"Don't *you* be getting up to *nor* good in London."

I already had, without going to London. "'Course not. I'd like to leave a couple of special books up in your attic. Is that okay?"

"'Course y' can, love. I never go up there. Can't get up them there stairs with me rheumatism. It's bad enough wi' first lot just up to bedroom. You go up and have a

170

look round. See if there's anything you want. I'll make tea."

Her 'make' always sounded like 'mek'.

"Here's a duster. Y' might come across a couple of cobwebs, love."

I climbed the wooden stairs and waved the duster at the thin sinewy webs, which had formed on the top landing. The watered-down sunlight outside the attic skylight cast shades of light and shadow across the old trunks and chairs inside. I knelt on the hard, unpolished floorboards and gazed out of the skylight window at the rooftops and the soft, damp clouds beyond. Then, amidst cobwebs and silence, I scanned the room for an old tin of my dad's. I leant forward and pulled it towards me. The lid was stuck, but with a good yank it opened sending a tinny echo through the attic like a saucepan falling on a tiled floor.

Inside were the rest of Dad's tiny handmade horses and soldiers like I had in my special box: treasures of his childhood made in the 1930s. I'd be leaving all these little things that made me belong, leaving my roots.

I took the 1964 to early 1966 diary out of my shopping bag together with the sticky tape and scissors I'd brought. It wasn't just a day-to-day diary but more of a journal of important events and feelings. First I sealed it up then I removed the soldiers and horses from the tin, placed my diary inside and put the soldiers back on top to guard the fort. I shut the lid and sealed it with tape then I looked around for what else I could use for extra safety.

There was a hatbox in the corner. Granny would never use that. She didn't go away anymore. I gave it a quick dust then stuck the metal box inside and clicked the case shut. It could go under the old picture frames and mirrors that were stored in the corner.

I didn't want Mum to find my diary and read about what happened with Brendan, like before. I stuck a label on the outside of the hatbox: 'Boring Old Essay Study Notes.' That should deter anyone's interest. Just then a shaft of sunlight shone through the narrow attic window. It made a pyramid of light against the wall like a pathway, and you could see the little particles of dust dancing in the light. Then it faded.

"Yer'll get piles on that there cold wooden floor, love," Granny's voice echoed up two flights of threadbare stairs.

I took another look at the attic. This would be my last visit before we moved house and my life changed forever – again.

CHAPTER SEVENTEEN:

TWO BULGING CHIMNEYS

Interview with my new head teacher – yuk.

No one wanted to be 'the new girl'.

I looked out of my new bedroom window at the pretty garden. It was really long and had a wicker arch in the middle and flowers grew over it. I'd rather sit out there and sunbathe in a deck chair and listen to that song about wanting to go home. Let me go home, I want to go home, I sang as *Sloop John B* played on Radio Caroline. Thank goodness they still had Radio Caroline down near London; this pirate ship was Caroline South.

I admired myself in the mirror. Well? It was an interview at the school, not a school day, wasn't it? I stroked a bit more eyeliner on.

At least I didn't have to *start* until after the holidays.

Now I thought of school I really started to miss my friends and Brendan. He said he'd come to London at the end of the year or in spring next year; the latter was nearly nine months away. I could have a baby in that time.

I swallowed because my period was a bit late. I couldn't be. I mean, he didn't ejaculate inside – I know he didn't.

Not much anyway.

Since we'd moved house, it was on my mind all the time whether I was helping in the house or sitting in the garden pretending to read a book.

Mum called up the stairs. "Hurry up, Andrea, and turn that thing down." 'That thing' was my new, more streamlined, transistor radio. I got it for my fourteenth birthday earlier in the year. It was black with a silver grid. I turned the knob to 'off' because I was ready anyway.

I smiled at myself in the mirror. There was no time to spare for Mum to make me change now. We were just in time. I'd lingered there and planned it that way. I dabbed some powder on my nose and glided downstairs.

Mum was standing by the front door with her new car keys in her hand and her best silky looking daytime dress and jacket on. It was the one she wore when she went to my old school to complain about Miss Lane and the cane, and she wore it sometimes when she went to town with Bill. She had a very good figure really, I suppose.

"You look nice, Mum," I said to throw her off balance, but it was true, she did.

She clicked her tongue and her eyes went up to the ceiling.

"Oh God," she said, then looked at me again. "What do you think you've got on?"

I looked down at my crocheted holes and the bra beneath it then gave her a blank look. The brown crocheted jumper had big holes in it and you could see my lacy bra so I thought it was really sexy. I was wearing cream lacy stockings, my brown suede shoes and a beige mini skirt with thin brown lines on it. It had a big brown zip up the front and the zip had a huge gold ring at the top of it. If I were on another date with Brendan James I'd wear it so he could rip it off quickly. "I thought I'd wear my new top and the skirt I made. Do you think it's a little short, Mum?"

I knew it wasn't only the length. The zip looked like an open invitation for any boys that should pass by, quite apart from the top. I wanted to look fashionable in front of any girls I saw, didn't I?

Mum's lips were tight. I knew she was mad when they were tight. She looked at her watch then flung her hands and arms up like wings by her sides.

"Go and ch…"

She looked at her watch again.

"Oh for God's sake, get in the car. Get in!"

I lowered my head so my long hair hid my smile as I got into Mum's new pale green Triumph Herald.

"And take that smug look off your face. You know very well that isn't the way to dress for an appointment at your new school."

She pulled out of the driveway onto the country lane. "Now watch where we're going because you'll have to walk to school unless it rains. There aren't any buses but it's only a few minutes."

We drove up our lane. It was narrow and had grassy banks in front of everybody's garden instead of pavements. After a minute we turned across a new council estate.

"You'd better mind your Ps and Qs while you're at the school to make up for looking as common as muck."

They didn't say that down south. It was a northern saying, 'Common as muck'. "You sound like Granny Hampton when you say, 'as common as mook'. She has a little saying about make-up." I stuck my chin out. "It

175

goes…" I put on a Granny Hampton voice to make Mum laugh:

"'Little puffs o' powder,

Little dabs o' paint,

Makes a girl's complexion,

Look like what it ain't.'"

Mum's face relaxed.

"And your other Grandma said in her day they used to pinch their cheeks and their lips to make them ruby red, and wet their eyelashes with spit," she said.

"Uuurrrh! I prefer mascara. As for red lips, it's way out of fashion."

Mum parked the car and we walked up to the school. It was much smaller than my other school. "Yuk! It looks like a brick box with a few elongated garden-sheds around." I could see girls looking at me from the classroom windows of the box and that made me a bit nervous. I even felt a bit tarty, but not as common as muck. Some girls were still in the playground and running towards the doors. "You didn't *say* it was an all girls' school."

Mum clicked her tongue. "The boys' school is across the field."

The girls about my age had ankle socks on and no make-up. They looked like a lot of little Jocelyns. I turned my top lip up. "Ankle socks! I won't fit in here. They're just little kids!"

She shook her head.

Lingering about after everybody else and standing out like a couple of sore thumbs were two extremes, a blonde and a redhead. In contrast to the ankle sock brigade, these two looked like a couple of street workers.

I wouldn't fit in with them either – not even with what I was wearing today. They'd chew me up and spit me out. The blonde caught me looking and I quickly looked away.

The receptionist had dyed red hair and a nice smile. "I'll let the headmistress know you're here, Mrs Gordon." Mrs Gordon? The receptionist went through a door and came back again.

"You can come straight through now, Mrs Gordon."

It was funny hearing my mum being called Mrs Gordon when before teachers called her Mrs Hampton. I didn't know how she managed to look up. We'd both changed our name by statutory declaration so it wasn't confusing, her being one thing and me another. Soon, after Bill's divorce, she and Bill would be able to get married, but for now they were pretending so everything looked 'proper'.

I knew I'd always be a Hampton and my dad would always be my dad, but I didn't want every Tom, Dick and Harry knowing my business, did I? I could pretend Bill was my dad now so I didn't need to explain things to people. *I* hadn't used my new name yet though.

We followed the receptionist into the headmistress's office. I hoped the teachers were like her; friendly and smiling.

Bloody 'ell. It was a prize fighter.

"Miss Bolton-Fox," the receptionist nodded and then backed away.

Sandra thought she had problems.

I tried not to show surprise and I bet Mum was striving to do the same.

A huge, wide and round person rose behind the desk. Her hips were almost as wide as one of those chimney columns, honestly. Her chins were worthy of a tyre advert. She could have been a sumo wrestler.

She extended her fat arm and shook hands with Mum but didn't quite smile. "Please be seated," she said.

Be seated? Anyone would think we were in Church.

Each of her chins was the size of a baby's arm. Her bottom lip stuck out like those of some African tribes who wore a bone through their lower lip but there was no bone. Her greyish-mid-brown hair was parted on the side then scraped into hairgrips. Sprouting out from the clips were some tight curls like a 'Twink' perm. I'd seen a photo of my grandma like that in the 1920s when she was a young girl.

But Grandma was slim.

The dress on the hugeness was stretched tight. She was corseted in, I could tell. It was an old fashioned sort of corset that went above the waist. Mum had one of those when I was little, before panty girdles came in fashion. They were made in wishy-washy pink like the gas lamps on a foggy day. I bet if the headmistress didn't have corsets on she'd have soft fat rolling right over the desk when she sat down.

My mum was fairly curvy and had big hips but she would fit into this woman five times. I felt like a fly.

After we'd sat down the sumo looked down her nose and bottom lip at my clothes. "Hello, Andrea," she said in a horrible condescending way, as if I was a little tart.

Well, I wasn't.

My eyes rolled towards Mum. She knew I was glancing at her but she wasn't going to look.

I knew Mum would like to have reached inside her bag for her Park Drive tipped or the new Benson and Hedges she smoked sometimes these days, and she'd like to ask Miss Bolton-Fox for an ashtray. She always liked to have a cigarette when she first sat down, whether it was upstairs on the bus, in a café, on a park bench or in school. She wasn't game to ask yet.

I bet she wished she'd worn her dark blue and green tweed suit rather than the silky dress and jacket she had on.

Miss Bolton-Fox stuck her nose in the air. "I've received the paperwork from the Department of Education and your letter explaining Andrea's statutory declaration of her name change. I note you were *widowed*, and *re-married*."

Was there something wrong with that? 'Married' wasn't quite true yet, but near enough, and *she* didn't know. She looked down her nose and protruding bottom lip. "Y-e-r-s, I see." She folded some papers away.

"Good," Mum said with a taut smile.

I knew *I* had difficulty that Bill and my mum loved each other, but it was over a year and a half since my dad had died and I didn't think The Bulging Hugeness had any right to sneer at my mum.

She looked down her bottom lip at me now. "Although you've done your previous school's exam, Andrea, we'd like you to do ours, so we can decide into which stream you should go."

"I'm usually in the top few of the B, Miss."

"We'd still like you to do *our* exam." She turned to Mum. "Would one day this week before the school holidays be suitable, Mrs Gordon?

"Not a problem," Mum said and I nodded.

"Good." Hugeness looked me up and down. "And we do not wear lacy stockings to this school, Andrea," she said, and sort of bowed her head into her chins.

I gave her a candy smile. "Oh no, Miss. I just wore them today because I'm not *at* school."

She went on about school rules and that insolence was punishable by detention. What was new? Then she gave Mum a few pages of rules and stuff to read and sign.

"Certainly. May I have an ashtray?" Mum said.

The thud of a tennis ball went back and forth somewhere outside and Miss Bolton-Fox stared at my mum.

"Would you mind if I smoked?" Mum said.

"I would. There's no smoking in our offices."

"All right," Mum said, smile intact. She dropped her head and read her forms.

I knew what she was thinking. That it was very unusual to say no. Almost all adults smoked – and some teenagers. It was on the television, the advertising posters, film stars puffed their way across the television screens and you expected, if you smoked, that when you sat down somewhere for a few minutes, you could at least get your fags out and puff.

Naughty Mum. I pinched my lips to avoid bursting out laughing.

There was a glass window all around the office so Miss Bolton-Fox could see out even while she talked with Mum. The tough-looking blonde girl walked by and looked through the glass. She stuck her tongue out at me.

It was a bit childish but nevertheless I wanted to stick mine out back at her. I turned slightly side-ways. I couldn't risk it. I half pulled my mouth into a sort of a smile. Now Miss Bolton-Fox saw her pulling her tongue out at me, excused herself and walked behind us to the door, leaving very little room in the office. She opened the door.

"Have you nothing better to do, Sally Harper? I'll see you in my office after your next lesson," she said in that auditorium-loud voice like Miss Hubbard. The girl muttered something like, "You're all bleedin' wankers." I had to find out what that meant; it wasn't a northern saying.

"And detention tonight for your foul mouth. DO. YOU. UNDERSTAND?"

I wanted to put my hands over my ears. Now I sensed Mum's eyes roll towards me and I stifled a smile as we both sat awaiting Miss Bolton-Fox's return. Mum's look said, don't you dare laugh. Then I couldn't help it, it was just a nervous little giggle and shoulder shake but it was over before the sumo turned around and came back.

"I'd like you to meet my deputy," she said, and lifted the receiver of the black telephone and smiled into her chins. "Do you have a minute, Miss Roebuck?"

Roebuck was fat, too – but in a different way. Her face wasn't that bad except for an extra chin and she had mod glasses like my mum with wings on them. She had thin legs but a huge body in the middle which was sort of squarish fat and made her look as though she was a barrel on matchsticks. Because she had thin legs, she must have been thinner at one stage.

Miss Bolton-Fox was never thin.

Standing together they looked like giant salt and pepper shakers, or those two chimney columns, bulging, blocking your way and closing in on you. Similarly, one was a little brighter – a little nicer, than the other.

When everything was organised the two big ladies shook hands with my mum.

"Exam Thursday at nine-thirty, Andrea, then we'll see you next term for school," Miss Bolton-Fox said in an overly charming way, then she looked down her bottom lip at me and pulled her top chin into her other chins as if to say, "I know your type and I'll be watching you." The other one did it too but more subtly and not in such a mean way.

Mum and I walked out in silence looking straight ahead and not at each other until we were out of the building, then I raised my eyebrows and looked at her and she raised her one eyebrow like she often did. We laughed softly as we hurried to the car and it was really good because it was like being with a friend or an older sister and I knew we were feeling the same.

Mum went around and opened her car door and I got in my side. "You'd better watch yourself there. It doesn't look like she'll take any nonsense!"

"I must write and tell Sandra my school might be worse – even worse than prison for Mr Fillmore. She's awful!"

"She's not exactly personality plus," Mum agreed. We started to giggle as we drove home.

"I can't believe her size! I bet you're dying for a cigarette."

"You're not kidding."

Bill opened the door. "You two look happy. I'll put the kettle on."

"And Caroline!" He knew I meant Radio Caroline and he quite liked the songs. I got the teapot ready and Mum told him about Miss Bolton-Fox while she put the cups on the coffee table with her nice glass ashtray.

Bill's eyes creased up and his shoulders shook when he laughed, especially when I mimicked The Hugeness and her attitude. Billy the budgie chirped away in his new corner and said, "Do you want a cup of tea," and the Fortunes, *You've Got Your Troubles* played on radio Caroline South.

It was better with Mum's Bill there rather than just us three 'little women', me, Mum and Grandma. It was like having four walls instead of three and a gaping hole where the wind blew in. Yeah. Bill closed the gap.

It might not be the right colour wall, or the right strength. It might not resonate to the same tune as the other walls, but it closed the gap, sealed the boundary and made it whole, at least on the surface – on one level.

Bill tapped the coffee table. "I'll be going to Sheffield for two days in a couple of weeks. I have to train people for the northern region. You and your mum can come; you can see your friends. That'll make having to do an exam less painful. Afterwards, we'll get you a dress that's suitable for school next term, until we can get the proper uniform material bought," he said.

Bill really wasn't too bad. I'd better have a loose style, just in case. "How about a modern tent dress?" Wouldn't that be something to irritate the two bulging chimneys, a pregnant fourteen-year-old?

CHAPTER EIGHTEEN:

GRAMMAR, SOUNDS AND SAYINGS

I rolled my pen back and forth.

The entry foyer was light and airy, especially when my solitary desk was the only thing in it. Beyond the windows, lawn and car park was the nearby council estate and row after row of new houses. No hills and furnaces.

The nice secretary came over. "You have an English exam first, Andrea, followed by maths. This will help us assess which is the right class to place you in next term."

Show how clever I was – or not. "I love English, Miss."

"Good. You can turn the paper over and begin."

I wrote my name on the top.

Damn. I forgot who I was. I crossed out Hampton and put Gordon. I can't forget who I might be – a mother.

Still no period. Why was I worried? It was only a bit late.

Although I was looking through the exam paper, I couldn't help wondering if Brendan's baby should be called somebody James after Brendan, Hampton after my real name, or Gordon because that was my assumed name.

My chin rested on one hand as I circled the correct grammar with the other. That was easy. Mum always helped me with grammar and spelling. It was the next part I was worried about: comprehension. I slouched further over the paper and had to read it twice before I answered. Still, both that and literature were easier than at my last school. I bet I'd be top in English here rather than in the top few. My favourite was last, an essay. The composition had to have the words *Fall and Rise* in it. I could write about the rise and fall of my stomach. I started to draft it out on scrap paper.

English Essay: Summer 1966.

Rise and Fall of a Teenage Stomach

I watch it each week rise a little more, rounding and filling the flesh across the front of my body. I look down and slide my hands over it. It's like pictures of Da Vinci's angels in galleries or even 1911 Pears advertisements where all women had rounded stomachs.

He said I'd never fall. He'd be careful.

"Careful?" I said. "Okay."

And we fell to the floor and he rose against me. I longed for him, needed him and held him in my arms as our bodies rose and fell in tandem with our heartbeats.

And then he was gone.

Soon I'll rise no more, and the mound before me will fall away in two or three pushes like a balloon going down.

And a babe will be born.

Hmmm. If I submitted that they'd think I was a bit crude and I didn't want to be. Good job I did it on scrap paper.

The Secretary walked past and I slid my arm over it. After she'd gone I screwed it up.

English Essay: Summer 1966

THE RISE AND FALL OF SHEFFIELD CHIMNEYS

Look to the horizon and you'll see them. They loom up from the green hills behind the old stone city buildings, their towering strength dominating the skyline. Brick by brick the two chimney columns rise, majestic yet threatening, enclosing the city in the spiralling smoke they emit.

The outer edges curve from the top inwards, towards the centre, then curve out again towards the ground. One is a little blacker and older, with a line of thin angry red chimney columns behind it, the other, on the far side of the works, is newer, whiter and catches more sunlight. Its bricks beam brightly making it look like a white pillar next to the black one.

Angry fires burn to make tools in Blake's satanic mills and the brutal work crushes the souls of those who labour within. Smoke bellows out from the tops, into the distance, spitting out waste. Some pours down then circles between the main two columns forming a web of intricate corridors between the black and the white. My mind travels back and forth, buffeted from one to the other, caught in a pathway, knocked and jostled to the top and falling, a snake on a slippery slope, never missing the severe drop to a pulsing portal of choking ash.

It's too much. The pillars begin to shudder and shake then crack and break. Brick by brick they rumble and tumble down, stone and brick spewing out their frustration as they fling to the ground in a crumbling heap of rubble.

No more does its darkness rise on the hills, but is gone forever, battered into the ground and fallen – back to earth.

That was better. It was like my life: everything crumbling, tumbling and disappearing.

I still had time to spare so I set down my pen, folded my arms, sat back in my chair and made myself comfortable. The nice secretary came by.

"Have you finished your English, Andrea?"

"Yes, Miss."

"All right, here's the maths test."

When she handed me the paper I wrinkled up my nose. "Do I have to do the maths?"

"I'm afraid so."

She looked at her watch. "You can start – now."

She went away and I started reading; it looked really complicated. I hadn't paid attention in maths since I left private school at age eleven. I used to enjoy the lessons at The Oaks Collegiate even though they were hard, and teachers always helped you. Besides, Dad used to help me with maths. He could do algebra and logs and equations and fractions and problems and all those things. He helped me at secondary school too.

Mum was more of an English and history person, and the best speller in the whole world. I didn't think maths was Bill's thing because he spent a lot of money.

Well that was it. I'd read through the whole paper and I didn't know how to do any of it. The English was below the standard to which I was accustomed but I had to say the maths set by the London Board was harder.

I wasn't doing it. I wasn't. Why should I waste my blooming time? There was no point. I hadn't a *clue* what the paper was going on about and I doubted if it was anything I would ever use at the local shop, so bollocks to it. I put a line through each page. *Not interested*, I wrote.

I put down my pen and relaxed back in my seat again. That was that stress over with then. Now I could have a think about things – spend some time on myself.

A girl came past on her way to the headmistress's office. It was one of those two rough ones about my age. She was probably in trouble. She had bright orange hair like it'd been dipped in Heinz tomato soup and gone stiff. They couldn't be very strict about dying your hair at this school.

"What d'ya fink you're looking at?"

My stomach jumped. "Nothing; just looking around," I said it in a loud whisper, which was more than could be said for her.

She rolled some gum around in her mouth and walked over. "'Ere, aren't you s'posed to be doing an exam?"

"I've done English. I can't do the maths."

"Av dun Inglish. A carn't doo maths," she mimicked my Yorkshire accent. "You an' me bleedin' bowf mate."

I think she meant: me too.

"What's ya name?"

"Andrea."

"Where ya from?"

"Sheffield."

"I'm 'Azel. Do they all talk funny like you up there?"

"I don't talk funny, but yes, I suppose so."

"Ar dorn't talk funny. You say funny with a u like ugh."

"You say fanny and where I come from a fanny is something between your legs."

She cackled.

"When are ya starting class?"

"Not 'til after the summer holidays in September. I just came in for the exam."

"Bleedin' lucky bitch."

"Hazel Ford!"

I didn't see *her*. It was Miss Roebuck.

"What do you think you're doing? This girl is doing an exam."

"No she ain't Miss. She can't do it." She turned back to me. "You've all got bleedin' soot in ya throats, that's why ya can't speak proper. Know what I mean like? See ya."

"Come away this instant. My office. Now."

"Yes, Miss. I was already on my way – sent to you for somefink else I did."

It sounded stupid when she said 'somefink' with an f and a k.

In the playground that morning some girls said the word shag much more than 'do it', which sounded more grown up, but a bit bad because I couldn't say to Mum, "Do you like shagging Bill?" Whereas I could say, "Do you like doing it with Bill?" Not that I wanted to know. And Grandma would think a shag was a carpet.

Hazel came past again on her way back to the classroom. I widened my eyes to mean: don't talk to me; we'll get into trouble.

189

She walked past laughing to herself. "Facking bitch," she said nodding her head back to Miss Roebuck's office.

Fack didn't have the same punch as fook. I looked down at my blank exam paper and doodled. When you said fook off, up north, they knew you meant it. But fack would sound posh from some people – though not from Hazel. I bet her friend Sally sounded like a washerwoman saying it.

No punch.

When a lad in Sheffield said, "Do y' want to fook?" it sounded earthy and reminded me of the stone walled fields of Yorkshire and Derbyshire, the little blades of grass that poked out from the stones and stiles you climbed over, and the rich green moss like velvet patches. That was because out in the wild was a good place to 'fook' (not that I had – out there).

It reminded me of Dickon in *The Secret Garden*.

But if they were to say, "'Ere, ewe fency a fack? Know what I mean like?" I didn't think it would have the same punch for me because that would remind me of Colin in *The Secret Garden*, and he was a bit of a wimp. Then again, if the boy was from Yorkshire or London and he spoke really posh like Prince Charles and said, "I say Andrea, would you care to have a ...ehem... a fack?" I'd probably pee myself laughing.

I'd have to find someone who wasn't too rough, too Yorkshire, too London or too posh. Brendan would fit that category. He was well spoken but he could be a bit rough or basic on occasion, and that was okay.

Besides, I didn't think grown-up boys asked the question.

I supposed there were extreme sides to everything and then there was something in the middle. I stared out of the window. I missed seeing the two big furnaces across the green hills that I used to see from my other school, reminding me of the two sides of everything.

Like life and death.

The secretary came past. "Why aren't you writing, dear? You've only got twenty minutes left."

"I'm not doing my exam, Miss. Too hard."

"You won't get any marks if you don't."

I couldn't help laughing. "I won't if I *do* it!"

I smiled at a few teachers who walked past on their way to the staff room to pave the way for future classes next term and wondered how posh or how London they spoke. Then a girl with long blonde hair and a very short skirt walked past and waited outside the deputy's office. I figured she was in the year above me: Brendan's year.

The girl knocked on the door then looked across at me, pulled her mouth down in a mock intimidated expression and shrugged her shoulders. I smiled back then I saw Miss Roebuck come out and say something, looking her up and down. The girl rolled down the top of her skirt making it a bit longer.

As she passed me on her way back to class, she rolled her eyes, tutted about Miss Roebuck and smiled at me. Now there was someone I could be friends with.

I wondered what her name was.

CHAPTER NINETEEN:

BED BATH AND PRAYER

Guess where I was?

Standing at Brendan James' front door – a little detour after Mandy and June's houses.

I smoothed down my white dress then checked my hands before I rang the bell. There were no orange streaks giving away my *Tanfastic* false suntan, which had boosted my back garden glow. My heart beat madly.

Someone bounded down the stairs. Brendan opened the door and had a big smile on his face. That was good. I wonder if it'd stay there when I told him I might be six weeks pregnant.

"You look brown. Come in. I was surprised when I got your phone call."

I followed him down the hall. "My parents had to come up north for a couple of days. We visited Sandra's boarding school on the way. She's still got her boyfriend."

"Good for them. Where are you staying?"

"With my aunt and uncle last night and tonight – driving back to London tomorrow, but I have today. Glad you're here."

"I made sure I was. Coffee?"

"Thanks."

"It's just the two of us, my mum is at work."

I sat on a high stool while he made coffee and told me funny stories about where he worked.

"It's bloody hard work," he said.

I sipped my coffee. "You'll need that holiday then?"

"Not 'arf."

"They've still got Radio Caroline down south, thank goodness. It's a different ship."

He downed his coffee, stood and took my hand.

"Come upstairs. It's more relaxing."

I couldn't wait to be in his arms.

He led me up the stairs to the little bedroom at the front and we sat on the edge of the bed. Brendan ran his hands through my waist length hair. This was the perfect opportunity – the one I would have died for at the party when all those people were around. I'd still die for it; it was what I wanted. There was just one snag. I'd kind of made a promise to God – or whatever it was that made things go right or wrong. I said, and continued to say daily, "Let me not be pregnant and I promise I won't do it again until I'm sixteen, and then with protection." So I was in a bit of a bind really.

Brendan pulled back the covers and took his shirt off. His chest was lean and hard. I imagined him sandwiching me between him and the bed. Everything was the wrong way round. I mean, we (many of us, anyway) felt as randy as hell at fourteen, but we weren't grown up in other ways, we were told. We should've been allowed to marry and have babies and still go to school and have classes to learn how to be parents and do all sorts of other stuff that you had to do in the world like pay bills and look after

193

yourself rather than a lot of useless things that we did currently at school.

Brendan unzipped my dress and slipped it off my shoulders. I clung onto it as we lay down. "You're sure your mum won't come home yet?"

"Yeah."

"And your dad? I mean, he's not a shift worker or anything?"

"My dad's dead."

I sucked in my breath. "I'm sorry. I didn't know…" I watched the rise and fall of his chest.

"Few years ago," he shrugged.

Could I say it? Not *when* mine died, because he'd know I'd lied that he was alive when we first dated. I wouldn't have done that if I'd known he'd lost *his* dad. It would have been okay to say it. I took a deep breath. "Actually…" His alarm clock ticked. Then I had to finish it. "My dad – my real one, died too."

Brendan put his arm around me and I breathed in that maleness again.

"Life goes on," he said.

We stared at the ceiling.

"Come 'ere."

He rolled towards me and we started kissing then he peeled my dress down to my hips. My stomach jumped like always when my skin touched his. It was as if I'd never gone away, and this was the next day after the party. I wanted to stay there in his arms kissing and talking all day; it was perfect, but in the middle of a big snog he put his hand up the skirt end of my dress.

I pulled my legs away. "I daren't do it Brendan. I've missed a period and I'm worried I might be pregnant."

"No problem then, you can't get pregnant again."

"Very funny."

He held me close to his heartbeat.

"I'm fairly sure you won't be. I was careful. I've already made one mistake."

"Really?"

"There's a girl in Leeds I got pregnant. She's having the baby."

"Do you see her?"

"Nah. She's in some nursing home place in Allerton Park in Leeds. Says they're trying to make her sign stuff to adopt it."

"Are you going to see it?"

He shook his head. "I'm not that attached."

What? I knew he was sought after, but that was a *baby*. I rolled onto my back. "I see."

He propped himself up on one elbow.

"Don't let it get you down. This is the swinging sixties – we're here to have fun. It was a mistake. She's got a bloke now, anyway."

Before I moved house, and before I was blonde, I would have been intimated by all that. "You sound as if you don't care."

"I don't mean to but I was still at school when I found out, and even now I'm not on high wages – yet. We only had a one-night stand. Months later I found out."

What was I, a series of one-night stands and a long-term acquaintanceship?

I hugged my arms across my bare midriff. "Hmm."

"Andrea. If it really is the case, I won't run away, but I don't think you will be. I'm concerned, but not seriously worried yet. And if you were here, now, living here, maybe we could start again, but you're not. All I can say is that I'll come down to London for a few weeks and we'll see what happens. Hell, you're not even fifteen yet."

He said that as if he was twenty-six. He was only a year older than me, even if he did look nineteen. "I will be, if and when the baby's born. By the way, did Suzy Brown come back to school?"

"*That* baby's nothing to do with *me*. I heard her folks sent her to commercial college. They made her adopt the kid unless she wanted to be cut off. They're bloody rich."

They lived in a huge, old detached house with ivy growing all around the big front door. I nestled back down in the bed with him and we started snogging and touching again. Things got a bit heated and I broke away.

He stroked my hair. "You know I like you."

I smiled. "You won't mind waiting 'til London then, will you? It's not that I don't *want* to. If it's a false alarm, I don't want to tempt fate, you know, not yet. But when you come to London we could use protection." I wouldn't be sixteen when he came down, like I sometimes promised God, but fifteen was a bit nearer. I didn't think God would split hairs if I kept to the protection part of the bargain.

He pushed his face really close to mine, gave me a naughty smile and wrinkled up his nose quite a lot.

"Toss us off then!"

Us? How many were there in there? "*Bren*dan!"

The 'us' was so *Yorkshire.* Now that I'd been down south a few weeks it sounded strange but that's how some people said, 'me' in Yorkshire, like, give us that, instead of, give it to me. Toss off was also common north of the Thames. "Down south they say a different word: wank."

"Either or."

It really wasn't what I'd had in mind. I felt his hand move mine and hold it where he wanted it. I closed my eyes, turned my face into the pillow and thought of the word. Toss could mean lots of things and it didn't have to be rude like the 'w' word. You could toss a ball or a pancake. Some people didn't know what it meant in slang though. Grandma didn't bat an eyelid when she said my Grandpa used to toss all night.

We lay there holding and kissing until the day began to cool. Brendan yawned and stretched. "My mum'll be home soon," he said.

"I've got to go and do some visiting anyway."

I sat up on the bed and put my dress on. Brendan zipped it up then dressed himself.

"Who?"

"Other friends and my Gran."

"We'll keep in touch by phone. Good luck with the 'little problem'. I think you'll be okay. Let me know." He squeezed me to him and held me close.

I looked up and beamed a light, bright friendly smile to hide my dark spiralling fear and frustration – even at him.

The damp tan pavers spread before me as I jumped down from the bus. I got off at the stop before Granny

Hampton's because I wanted to walk past our old house, the one we used to live in when I was little, before we moved to the edge of the moors. It was my last chance for a while. We'd be driving back to Orpington tomorrow.

There was a special bridge near our first house that I liked to walk on. It wasn't really a bridge, but a stonewalled area, and beyond this wall, which made the road look like a bridge, you could see for miles over another area. Those two industrial furnaces were over there – the ones I used to see on the horizon from my school window.

It was like the end of one world and the start of another. When I was little, I used to wonder what was beyond the wall.

I looked at the two wide, inverted bracket shaped columns, the lighter and the darker. The dark, aged one was as black as ever. Behind it stood the tall, straight and narrow, angry red brick chimneys, also blackened by smoke, like a team of supporters for the dark side.

The furnaces didn't billow black smoke anymore because smokeless fuel had been phased in over the year. Even factories had to use it now, but you could see very pale grey heat waves coming up from the summits and it looked as sinister as ever as it wound around and down like a thin veil of strangling vapour.

I didn't know what I was going to do.

The almost invisible web-like grey circled and sealed the columns. That's how I felt. I was caught in a corridor between the pillars.

I kept my eyes on the towering furnaces as I began walking. From my last school, the lighter one was shinier because it was on the side that caught the sun. Yet from where I was standing just then, part of the lighter one was covered in shadow. That was a bit like my black and white nail transfers; like how the white heart had to have a black edge. And it was like how my date with Brendan now had a heavy cloud over it. From a few steps further on, there was a patch of pale sunlight on a small part of the dark one.

Some people said that from a certain angle, when the moon rose, it came up like a copper ball between the pillars. I'd never seen it.

I touched my stomach and walked ahead and a crow landed on the wall and went, "Harr – harr."

Bill pulled out the chair from the dinner table for Aunty Mary. "Come and sit in the lounge, Meree. Can I offer you a liqueur?"

Mum and Dad never drank liqueurs. Mum drank them now.

"No, I'll just help Jean with the pots then I think Lance will say we should start driving, Bill," Aunty Mary said.

I was looking forward to going on holiday with them and my cousin for the last week of the school holidays.

Grandma watched Bill flapping about like a head waiter. He was already tiddly on his wine. Sometimes Grandma said things without saying them.

"I'll do the pots Mary; you and Lance have a long drive." She carried some pots (or dishes to Bill) through to the kitchen with pinched lips as if to say, "We are not amused," like the Queen.

"We'll head off then. Should be in Great Yarmouth before dark. Lovely dinner, Jean. We'll pick Mother up on the way back," Uncle Lance said.

It was strange they'd be taking Grandma back with them for a couple of months. She'd lived with us for ages. Mum and Bill wanted some newly married couple time (even though they weren't, yet).

I handed my suitcase to Uncle Lance and turned to kiss Mum goodbye. I hadn't been away from her for a whole week before. There was a lump in my throat and my eyes felt hot. "Will you miss me?" She wanted to be with him. They'd be doing it a lot while I was gone.

She tipped her head on one side. "You know I will." She hugged me.

Yeah, she would really.

Jackie and I waved goodbye and settled down in the back of the car. Aunty Mary turned in the passenger seat.

"Come on girls, let's play 'I Spy'."

Jackie's top lip went up at one corner.

"I spy, with my little eye…" Uncle Lance said, looking at Jackie in his rear vision mirror. My uncle was about six foot four, had big glasses and used big words. His word wouldn't be something easy like T for tree or C for cloud. He'd make us think. All I could think about was how many weeks it had been since that night with Brendan, and, since my last period, but at the moment I was stuck with 'I Spy'.

"I don't know what you girls are doing sitting inside the caravan on a *lovely* day like today. Why don't you go and sit in the sand dunes?" Aunty Mary said on the first morning. *Because I want to sit here and tell Jackie I'm pregnant.* I smiled and looked at my knees.

"We don't want to," Jackie said.

Aunty Mary shook her head and she and Uncle Lance went off to the beach.

When the caravan door clicked behind her we watched out of the window until they were out of sight.

"I've got to tell you something."

"Thought so. To do with Brendan?"

"Think I'm pregnant."

She widened her eyes. "Are you late?"

"About eight weeks now."

"Really?" She pulled a scared face. "Oh *God.* Tell me."

So we sat up on the caravan sofa beds and I told her the story.

"Didn't he have a rubber Johnny?"

"He forgot. I know I should have waited…"

"Lots of people miss *a* period, but if it's two..."

"I get a sinking feeling when I think about it."

"Have you got your tarot cards?"

"I didn't bring them."

"I've got mine; hang on."

She reached in her bag, and pulled them out. "Shuffle well."

I cut and spread, but was afraid to turn them over. I had a bad feeling.

"Go on, turn."

I turned the first four and rolled my eyes. "Bloody swords…the ten, nine, eight, and three." I threw them down. I'm not doing any more."

Jackie put them away. "I've seen better. Come on, I'm nearly old enough to buy drink from the off-licence. Let's get made up so we look older. I'll buy you some miniature bottles of gin."

"What for?"

She went to the mirror and started putting eyeliner on. "I've heard if you sit in a really hot bath and drink some gin it helps to bring on your period."

"Oh." I joined her at the mirror, brushed my eyelashes with mascara and put some new off-white lipstick on.

"Take your sponge bag and towel in the beach bag. You can put the gins straight in there. When we get back, go straight to the bathroom building."

It was a drab, cold stone building in the middle of the caravan park.

"Grab a bath cubicle, not a shower," Jackie added.

"Okay. You can tell your mum I like a long soak before dinner."

The sea was swishing back and forth in the breeze. We were sheltered because of the dunes and the blue-green grass springing out of the sand. It was the warmest day we'd had so I was trying to get a tan.

I pulled off my beach towelling changing robe. "Hey, presto. Aren't these great to change in?" Aunty Mary made us both one. They were like sacks with a white cord around the neck but they were open at the bottom.

"Mmm. You could do all sorts in there, besides changing in and out of swimsuits. Mmmm, Paul …" Jackie said, soaking up the windy sun.

She meant Paul McCartney. I imagined being in the changing towel with Brendan but then a baby's piercing howl filled the breeze, drowning the cry of the seagulls. "I wonder what Brendan's baby will be like. I've bought a loose navy blue tent dress to wear to the new school. It has a white neck from the shoulders to just above the bust then the navy part starts at the bust. I should be able to hide my stomach under that for a few months."

"Probably. But what are you going to do once he or she is born?"

"The loft is boarded like a room except it hasn't got a window."

Her eyebrows lowered. "And?"

"Well…I thought I could keep her – I think it will be a girl, up *there,* and just pop home at lunch time and feed her. Mum will have a part time job from mid-morning 'til about four, so I could get in another feed before she comes home. The baby'd have to be quiet from then on though." I realised it was a stupid idea. Jackie looked at me like she wasn't quite hearing correctly.

"I *don't* know if that will work," she said. "She's going to cry. Babies start crying early in the morning – if not before. When our grandma is back at your house she'll think it's the neighbour's television and go and ask them to turn it down."

I giggled. "Or worse, she'll stand on the landing looking up at the loft hatch with an open mouth, think she's hearing things, and make a doctor's appointment."

"It'd be like hearing Colin wailing in *The Secret Garden* from behind a closed door," Jackie said, then her face looked more serious. "And your mum will know straight away."

"I suppose if the worst comes to the worst I'll just have to tell her."

"You probably will. Your mum would be much more understanding than mine."

"I don't know."

"She would."

"I wonder what she'd say."

"She wouldn't throw you out; you know that, don't you?"

The sun warmed my face. "She'll probably suggest I adopt him or her out."

"You're very young to look after it. Your mum's just got together with Bill; I don't think she'd be too fussed about having to look after your baby. She's done all that. It'd be sad to have to adopt Brendan's baby out though. What do you think?"

"I wouldn't want to."

"Don't listen to anyone who says to shove a knitting needle up, will you?"

I turned my head on my towel. "You're kidding?"

"Some people do it to abort the baby and it's dangerous. You could die."

I held my stomach and sat up. "I think I'm going to be sick."

"Forget I said it." She rubbed my back. "If the gin doesn't help, have the baby and things will sort themselves out. Your mum will think you've ruined your life that's all."

"It couldn't be much worse than it was – you know." No, it couldn't be worse. I lay down again and closed my eyes. But things were getting better now, and I was near London – the land of opportunity.

"You wouldn't be able to go to discos and parties and meet boys," Jackie said.

The Brendan thing wasn't the most sensible thing I'd ever done. I was beginning to get that heavy worried feeling like after Dad died but not as bad. But bad enough. "I don't want to wait 'til I'm *old* to go out to London clubs because I'm a mum. I want to go *now,* when I find a friend in Orpington. Preferably one who doesn't wear ankle socks."

Her shoulders shook when she laughed, like me. She rested her hand on my arm.

"You've had lots of baths and miniature gins this week, but you still have two or three to go. Don't give up." She started to get up. "Come on, it's time you got ready for the talent contest I entered you in. Let's grab our clean towels and sponge bags from the caravan and go to the bathrooms. Have you revised Twinkle's song, *Terry*?"

I sat up and put my Cool-tan in my beach bag. "Yep. *Ter-Ry,*" I sang the rest of the words then stood up. "I'll be able to support my baby if I win." I linked my arm through hers as we walked towards the caravan. "I'll practice some more in the bath before dinner."

"Don't forget the gin. My mum thinks you're such a good girl having a hot bath every night when you pad back to the caravan in your dressing gown all clean and red." She rolled her eyes, "Except for the time you take! But don't worry, she wouldn't have a clue."

"I like to lie there and think about the last two years when everything started to change." And kept changing. "Can I take your tarot cards in the bathroom?"

"Don't get them wet. I thought you were 'off' them?"

"I'll just work with picture cards – the major, what did you say?"

"Arcana. I'll be out of there before you. I'll come and check how you're going with the gins before I go back to the caravan." She lowered her voice as we passed some people. "If there's 'no sign' after tonight, you'll have to go to a doctor when you get back."

I gripped my stomach. "Yeah."

CHAPTER TWENTY:

GIN IN THE BATH

"*And*-r-e-a."

There was a frantic knock on the door bringing me back to reality. My stomach jumped so much the cool water moved and I began to shiver.

"Whatever are you doing in there?"

"Sorry, Aunty Mary. I was thinking."

"Good heavens, love! Whatever have you been thinking about for two hours?"

My life – at least, the last two years of it. "Just stuff."

"Jackie came back from her bath ages ago. I sent her back to ask you to hurry along. Didn't she tell you?"

She told me I'd only be twenty-nine when my kid was fourteen and we could go out on the town together. "Yeah, but I'm making myself beautiful for the talent contest, Aunty Mary."

"You do this every night. You can't monopolise the bathrooms like this. Other people want to use them. Dinner's ready. Get yourself dried and dressed and clean the bath quickly or you'll leave a grey rim after all that time. Hurry."

I sat upright in the cool water. It was only an hour and twenty minutes but I didn't say that. I stood up and put my sponge between my legs. Nothing. It was serious.

Mum would feel she'd failed Daddy. Granny Hampton would say it was all her fault. That wasn't fair. And what about Grandma? Was it a really big sin?

I turned the Hanged Man tarot over so he didn't look at me anymore then I let the water out. It went round and round in the plughole, but it wasn't grey. I imagined the water taking away all the things that weren't right, deep down into to the earth.

Seagulls soared overhead as we walked along the beach. "I'm going to miss them, the sea air and that seaweed sort of smell."

Jackie had a last look at the sea. "Last day. You were great last night."

"That's what Brendan said."

"Ha, ha. I meant in the singing contest."

"I didn't win." I linked my arm through hers. "I knew the words well but when someone handed me the microphone and you nodded to the pianist, I was nervous."

"It sounded good. Your voice croaked with emotion like you meant it."

"I thought of Brendan and when I'd see him again. Then because *Terry* is about a boy dying in a motorbike accident I thought of Dad dying in that street when a car ran over him."

"I still can't believe your dad's gone. He was such fun."

"I know. I don't think he'd be very pleased about the pregnancy, do you?"

She pulled a face like we were about to go on the ghost train. "No."

"It's funny how one sadness or worry pushes its way on top of another, like grief, and then even though you're still upset about both, the new one eats its way in a bit more." Yeah. Ate its way in. "And I imagined Brendan dying and me carrying his child, just to add to the drama."

"You got a big applause."

"God didn't answer my prayer, even though I wore my white trousers and whispered again, 'Please let me come on,' in my head. Mind you, I couldn't finish two *whole* miniatures of the remaining gins. Yuk." I stuck my tongue right out and pulled a face. "It never got any easier to drink."

"You've had about one a day. We tried. It's been great hiding in the dunes and talking. Come on. Let's freshen up in the bathrooms."

We headed for the stone building in the middle of the caravan park. The little empty gin bottles clanked when I tossed them in the waste bin. "So much for that." I went into the toilet cubicle, had a wee then stood up to flush; I looked in the pan. *My God.* "Jackie!"

"Uh?"

"Jackie, Jackie, quick!"

"What is it, have you come on?"

"No. L-o-o-k." My voice warbled. I let her in the cubicle then pointed into the toilet. My heart kind of beat and dropped and my stomach sank as if it had been kicked. I wanted to cry.

"What's *th-a-t*?" she said.

I was cold and wobbly. "I don't *know*, but it looks like a little half finger size baby, doesn't it?" My wailed whisper echoed through the brick cubicle. "Would a baby look like that at about eight weeks? A lump?"

"I don't know. I can't exactly ask my mum, can I? She'd want to know why."

We studied the thing in the toilet pan that was a mass of red and white, like a miniature thumb in a kidney bean shape, about the size of someone's little toe. It had red lines and tiny bulges on it that could have been the beginnings of veins and limbs, and then again it could have been nothing of the sort. Deep sadness welled inside me and my face started to crumple. "I don't know why I am upset," I sobbed. "I don't want to be pregnant. At least, I don't think so."

Jackie put her arm around me. "Oh. Brendan's baby. You'll have to get it out."

"It might not be. There's no blood coming."

"It looks like the beginning of something to me."

"I know."

"Get it."

"I'm not putting my hand down *there*." But I didn't want to lose it either.

"It's only wee."

I brushed a tear from my cheek. "You do it then."

"It's your wee."

"*I* can't put my hand in it. You. Go on! You're older than me." I nudged her. I knew she wouldn't.

"N-o-o. It's your wee – your baby."

I wrinkled my nose up. "Oh, I don't know…"

"It's Brendan's…"

"If it is what we think it is."

"I'd put my hand down and get it if it were my boyfriend's. And if it were my wee."

"What could I put it in to keep?"

"Get the gin bottle out of the bin."

"Do you think the opening is big enough?"

"Just about. It'll probably bend a bit…"

"*Bend* a bit? This could be Brendan's baby." I got the gin bottle and washed it.

"Take a deep breath." Jackie put her arm around me again then stood back. I used the lid of my soap box to try and catch the little lump of red and white but it slipped out of the top and further asunder. It went right underneath the porcelain and I couldn't go any further unless I stuck my whole hand in and half my arm.

I wasn't doing that. "I can't *get* it. It's *gone*," I shrieked.

"Oh, *no*," Jackie said, watching it disappear. "Bye-bye, baby Brendan."

The emptiness inside me was a bit like when you first heard someone had died. I stood and looked at the toilet bowl. "I *want* it."

"Come on. Don't look. There's nothing you can do now."

"I feel so…alone."

"You're not alone. You've got me."

"It's a different sort of alone…"

I was mesmerised by the tinted water in the pan. "Bye -bye baby, if that's what you are. God bless." A sob escaped like a huge hiccup. If there was a God.

I closed the toilet lid and came out of the cubicle then faced the whitewashed bricks behind the basins and washed my soapbox and hands with my head down. Soap bubbles popped and dispersed, becoming nothing. Jackie came and put her head close to mine as she put her arm around me.

"Don't cry. Maybe it's for the best and you'll come on soon, if it's what we think. I've never seen anything like it, so I think it was, you know."

I threw my soap in its box. "It's not *fair*. I don't *want* to come on now. I *want* Brendan's baby."

"You don't mean that. You're sad because it's part of you. Come on; wipe your face. You can't go back in a mess."

I splashed cold water on my face. "I wish we weren't going home just yet."

"Me too."

"There'll be no-one to talk to about all this soon. I'll be alone in the new school. On top of that I'll have to watch Mum and Bill being all lovey-dovey." I tossed things in my sponge bag.

Jackie hugged me. "We can talk on the phone and write."

We linked arms and headed back to the caravan then quickly brushed past her mum and dad to our section. I started to pack my small brown suitcase. The washed gin bottle was in my sponge bag to remind me of what I almost kept inside it, and as a memory of our holiday.

An empty bottle.

A souvenir.

CHAPTER TWENTY-ONE:

WISHING AND HOPING

Dear Jackie

No sign.

Everything is strange and new. Even Grandma is temporarily living with you instead of us.

I've just glided down to the sun lounge at the back of the house with a sulk on my face to let them know I hate it down here. My record player is out here so it's become like my special room. I've put on, *As Tears Go By*, by Marianne Faithful and the needle is dropping onto the record now.

It's perfect. I've got a bit longer to slouch around before dinner, so I'll play your favourite - Cliff Richard's *Constantly* afterwards. Like the song, I think about someone constantly. Not just Brendan but who is inside me. Perhaps it wasn't a miscarriage then? Still no blood. I was nine weeks late when we left Great Yarmouth; ten weeks now.

I pulled the card of the Moon yesterday and thought it meant the monthly, but then I read what it stands for – trickery, deceit and scandal. Scary.

I thought I'd made a friend called Lydia – one of the few in my class who doesn't wear ankle socks, but she's still just a child. Her parents won't let her out after seven. What good is that? She can't come on the train to London. And worse, when she met Bill, she said, 'Ere, you don't 'arf look loike your dad!' She didn't know he wasn't. I haven't told anyone.

You can imagine my look.

I sent Brendan a postcard saying 'no change' and he sent one back of the furnaces in Sheffield – in case I get homesick! He can't take holidays from his new job yet. Don't think he's enjoying it.

I've started typing classes at school and I'm fairly good because I can practice on Mum's Remington. The teacher might put me in for the Certificate of Secondary Education, in typing, early.

Are you still with Bob? You're lucky he lives near you.

I know you're thinking I should go to a doctor but I'd like someone to come with me. Wish you were here. Anyway, I've made a friend called Alexandria (no ankle socks), and we've been to each other's houses. She's not *that* mature, but she's really modern, bubbly and popular.

She likes boys too, although she's never had a boyfriend.

We're becoming good friends and I think I can trust her – so I told her my secret and asked her to come to the doctor's with me. I'll let you know. Now

I'm playing *Wishing and Hoping* by Dusty Springfield – how appropriate.

Lots of Love, Andrea

Maths class: time to draw and doodle under the desk.

Miss Lacy wouldn't even notice. She'd be too busy trying to control Hazel and Sally so we wouldn't get any maths done. I wouldn't anyway.

I knew it. As soon as Miss Lacy walked in, they started. It was because she was young. Sally scraped her desk so that it made a woody sound on the floor then she got up. She slouched down the aisle to where Hazel was sitting, pulled Hazel's red hair and started punching her.

"I'll fackin' do you 'Azel."

Where I came from, 'do you' meant something else. ''Azel' was no shy maiden. She was out of that seat in a flash, chest forward, fists up and nose flaring. Hazel's spiky backcombed orange hair was thin giving her an almost balding effect in between where the hair stuck up.

"'Ere, come on then Sally, put ya money where ya mouf is ya fackin' cow."

I rolled my eyes at Miss Lacy and settled down in my seat. She rolled her eyes back.

"Sit down Sally, sit down Hazel, now."

They didn't take a blind bit of notice. With their backcombed hair, they looked like a couple of spiky upside down toilet brushes jostling up and down the aisle. Everyone their side of the room leant away from the aisle and desks and chairs were scraping and moving. One girl who was really good at maths asked them to stop. Then I

215

chirped up. Blooming hell the words were out before I thought of the consequences.

"I don't know about you two, but I'm really hopeless at maths, so I need to listen even if I don't do too much! Could you do this later?" Then just to sound like them, I threw in the London, "Know what I mean, like?"

Sally's stiff white blonde hair was so backcombed it was like a glued nest. She must've been trying for the Dusty Springfield 'look alike' award (though failed) because she always wore really thick black eyeliner all around her eyes and white lipstick.

She opened her mouth and even across the classroom I could see brownish-charcoal edges to her teeth.

"You wanna fackin' fight?"

Uh-oh. I'm sure they both said it.

"I wouldn't lower myself," I yawned.

"Sit down Hazel. Sit down Sally," Miss Lacy said again. Hazel was slightly more gracious.

"Sorry, Miss – I got carried away. Me and Sally are mates really but she pisses me off, Miss," she said to the teacher then sat down.

Sally walked round to my side of the classroom. The ladders in her stockings appeared to be in the same place as yesterday.

Fook, I thought, and I meant fook, none of that fack business. She came really close to me and put her nicotine stained fingers on my desk, leant back and looked at me. She pulled her mouth like a real thug and then reached out and grabbed me by the shirt and tie like men did on the television.

The teacher strode down the aisle almost in tears. Miss Bolton-Fox would be down any minute because the noise and talking in the room sounded like a madhouse.

I looked Sally in the eyes, smiled in what I hoped looked like a friendly, confident way, grabbed hold of her arm, pulled her off my shirt and gave her a super quick Indian burn with both my hands around her wrist. Dad showed me how to do it. "Do me a favour," I said, throwing her wrist down but still smiling.

"F-a-rk. Ow'd ya bleedin' do that?"

"My secret. Maybe I'll show you at break time."

"Fackin' 'ell," she said on the way back to her desk. I think she laughed and said fackin' bitch and fackin' c as well and I hoped that meant she wasn't too mad. I didn't want her waiting around a corner for me after school.

It wasn't long before the bell went and we all stood up and got our schoolbags ready to go.

Alexandria looked across the classroom at me then giggled. A girl by her side nudged her then about six of them stared straight at me. One of them had stuffed a jumper up her skirt. I creased my eyebrows. What the hell were they doing?

Andre-a, Andre-a, remember the day
When y-ou and Brendan – had it away.

They sang to the tune of the Wayne Fontana's *Pamela, Pamela* then burst into fits of stupid sniggering. My heart beat fast and my throat got really dry. Betrayal. That was worse than someone just not being your friend. I narrowed my eyes at Alexandria. "You *little* cow." I walked towards her to give her a bit of a shove. Two giggling idiots stood in front of her and protected her.

217

Pathetic. I gave her one of those 'looking down the nose' jobs and tossed my hair back. "Ugh, Alexandria, you are *such* a child. Grow up."

It was bad enough when Mandy and I weren't best friends any more, but at least there were other people around and everything was familiar. I stomped down the corridor and out of the school gates. The card of the Moon warned me – dishonesty, craftiness, false pretence, slander and unknown enemies. So much for my so-called new friend. I started walking quickly. It was horrible not having any *special* friends that I could trust there in Orpington.

"'Ere, I want a word wiv you, Andrea," Hazel shouted after me.

Bloody hell. Sally wasn't far behind. Crickey. Two of them. I shouldn't have spoken up in maths. I stopped and scowled. "What do you want?" Hoped I look tough.

A few strides and they were beside me. Hazel walked round in front of me. My heart pounded. She looked me up and down and chewed her gum.

"There's this geezer wants to go out wiv you. Me an' Sal know him. He's seen you walking to school an' thinks you're a bit of all right, like."

I was stunned. I thought I was about to be fighting for my life. I lifted my chin. "What's he like?"

"His name's Con, short for Conrad and he's got big brown eyes, olive skin and long, dark hair over his collar."

"He looks a bit Gypsy like, don't 'e 'Aze?" Sally added.

"Yeah, he works at the fairground. He has an earring. What do you fink?" Hazel said.

I fink I daren't say no. Besides, I could have done with a friend. "Okay."

"Give us your number so 'e can ring you then. You wanna fag?"

I shook my head.

I stepped into the hall in the nick of time.

I couldn't help smiling as I thought of Con's face when I brought him to meet my parents earlier. He'd widened his eyes and turned the corners of his mouth down with a nod as he looked at our thick red carpet and the gold and white embossed wallpaper. I took him through to the lounge and said: "This is Con, Mum, Bill."

I started to go pink looking at Mum's face.

"Hello," she said and smiled like she would with any of my friends, but she had a beady-eyed look that went from me to Con's long hair and earring, and back to me. It meant, 'Good *heavens*, what on earth are you doing with *him*?'

He was on his best behaviour, but even Bill raised his eyebrows.

Mum looked at the large tattoo poking out of his shirtsleeve. "Why on earth do you want to go on the train to London if you're not going anywhere or doing anything when you get there?" she asked.

My face warmed. I didn't tell her about it the last few times we went. She might guess we went in the individual train carriages – and why. I was always elbowing him off.

Con shrugged. "Something to do."

219

Mum stifled an eye-roll then looked at me. "You're not to go on the train and I need you home at ten and no later." Well, I was. I shut the front door behind me.

Mum came into the hall as I was wiping Con's wide-mouthed sloppy kiss off my mouth. "On the dot," I said.

"Has he gone?"

"Yeah."

"He's *far* too old for you, Andrea. What is he, seventeen?"

"And a half."

"Grandma will be back from Uncle Lance's in a few weeks; she'd be horrified to see you with someone like that."

She would. *Never feed your pearls to swine.* "M-u-u-m!"

"What on earth do you see in him?"

"He's quite nice really. I like his earring."

"Don't be silly."

I wandered into the lounge where Bill was having a glass of his homemade wine and Mum followed me.

"I'd prefer you didn't see him any more. He's not appropriate for you."

She never even said that about Brendan. I wasn't madly attached to Con, but he was someone who wanted to be with me. I hadn't exactly scored the popularity prize at school with my Yorkshire accent, and going out with him made me acceptable by those hard to conquer toilet brush heads.

A muttered, "Fook off" slipped out of my mouth then I slouched out of the room.

I'd never heard Bill move so fast. He sprung out of his chair and was behind me in the hall then strode to catch up with me as I made it to the stairs.

"Don't you dare talk to your mother that way," which he said like: "Dunt you *dur* talk to your mother thut way."

"Oh go away."

"Go upstairs to your *rum*."

I already was, but he was at the foot of the stairs behind me and he grabbed me by the shoulder with one hand, and the other hand went on my bum but right in the middle almost between the legs and his push lifted me a few stairs up.

How *dared* he? I turned around from the middle of the stairs and kicked him in the stomach "You sleazy bastard. How *dare* you?"

He fell against the wall and the cupboard at the bottom of the stairs with a bit of a thud. It was only five or six steps and he was already on about the third. I continued up to the top.

"Och, Jeanie, Andrea's kicked me and I hurt my head," he called to Mum.

"Just a minute… Oh, darling, let me see. Where? Do you need a plaster?"

"No, but I'm winded. Perhaps something to settle my stomach…some hort meelk."

"Come in the kitchen and I'll make you some hot milk then."

I leant over the banister. "That's right Mum, make him some hort meelk; he's just about stuck his hand up my crotch and you want to make him milk and pamper him. Bloody great," I yelled. I nearly said, fooking great, but didn't want to get like the loo-brush heads and be saying it every other word.

Mum marched across the hall and closed the window.

"Calm down, Andrea."

I heard Bill huffing and puffing that he didn't think he did but if he did it was an accident and he didn't mean it.

Mum stomped upstairs. "You owe Bill an apology."

I folded my arms and sat up against the pillows on the bed. "No. He's the one who needs to apologise. I'll say I'm sorry to you for saying the 'f' word. I didn't mean it. I hate school, I miss my friends and Brendan not to mention – you know – things, and now you want to stop me dating a boy who likes me."

Mum sighed out her anger like a red balloon going down. She sat on the bed. "And do you really like *him*?"

I turned to the wall. Did I? I wasn't sure that I did really. "It's nice to have a boyfriend in the same area instead of two hundred miles away." I always *hated* it when Con tried to get his hand in my bra when we lay down inside the train carriages. I wouldn't have been elbowing *Brendan* away. *I should pack Con up.*

"Look, I know it's been a huge change for you on the one hand. But on the other, you're doing things that you wouldn't be doing if…under different circumstances."

She meant the singing lessons, the suede and leather coats and the grooming and modelling course I was about to attend at a model agency. We wouldn't have had the money or access to these things when my dad was alive. Not up north. *They dorn't mayke models and singers 'ere, luv,* as Granny Hampton would say.

And my dad would never have handled me like that. I turned back with a mad look.

"It was an accident, Andrea."

"How would you know? You weren't there."

"He was just protecting me."

"I was already half way up the stairs, Mum."

She sighed. "It was an accident. He was pushing you up the stairs and probably didn't think about what he was pushing."

Doesn't he know where a fanny is?

"He is trying so hard to make your life happy, Andrea."

Just then Bill tapped on the door.

"*What?*"

He poked his head around. "I'm very sorry, Andrea. I didn't realise I'd inadvertently mishandled you. I just grabbed and pushed because I was so mad when you were rude to your mother."

Mum nudged me.

I wasn't saying sorry for kicking him in the stomach. "Sorry you hurt your head," I half muttered, half snapped.

I got the better deal. It was quite a kick.

Brown made you feel down. The surgery walls were the colour of horse dung up to desk height, then a beige handbag shade on top of that. The chairs were brown pretend leather and the linoleum tan brown. No wonder I was getting that drab feeling.

"Linda Jones," the receptionist called, looking at me.

I dropped the magazine. It was me. I gave a false name when I made the appointment to come after school, instead of seeing Con. I felt relieved to have chucked *him*.

"The doctor will see you now."

I wondered if I'd feel relieved after seeing the doc? My hair was pinned up in a crocheted bonnet so no one would recognise me. It looked like I'd got short hair. On my face I put grey eye shadow just under the cheekbones because that's what I thought models in magazines did. It made my face look like I hadn't washed down the sides.

I walked into the surgery and in front of me was a big desk. The doctor sitting behind it had his head down and was writing. He was oldish. His brow furrowed and his eyelashes flickered as he sort of glanced up over gold-rimmed glasses.

"Take a seat," he said in a bored way and carried on writing.

I supposed if I were a grown-up he might have stopped what he was doing. I tried not to fidget but my fingers curled in my pockets.

Half looking up, he said, "What seems to be the problem?"

They all said that. It must be in the 'How to Talk to Patients' manual. He still had hold of his fountain pen and looked like he was about to carry on writing.

"I think I'm pregnant."

He put his pen down, took hold of his glasses and looked at me over the top of them. "I see."

Then he took them right off and gave them a rub with some material.

"Have you missed a period?"

224

He said it in that dear, dear, these things happen sometimes when you're young – until periods settle down, sort of way.

I managed not to roll my eyes. "I've missed four," I snapped and the words came out in my Yorkshire accent like, "Av missed *four*," and loud.

His chin retreated into his neck.

"Oh dear. Have you had intercourse?"

I stared. My camouflaging bonnet must've made me look so young and stupid that I'd believe I could get pregnant from a lad sticking his hand down my knickers. "Y-e-r-s," I said.

"When did you start your periods?"

"More than a year ago."

"Were they every month – before?"

"I think so."

Then he asked me some questions about my breasts. I'd never really thought about them as breasts. I mean we said bust, or at school, tits, but not breasts. It sounded womanly and motherly and I was getting butterflies in my stomach because I might be a mother soon and I'd have to go into special toilet rooms for *breast* feeding.

"They're bigger; so is my stomach."

"Any morning sickness?"

I shook my head.

He stood and partly opened a curtain.

"Hop on the couch and I'll examine you."

I lay with a sheet on top while he inserted a pencil-like rubber instrument a little way inside me.

"Hmmm. Hymen broken," he muttered to himself.

225

When that was over he felt my stomach and breasts. "Hmmm." He paused. "I don't see definite signs of pregnancy. Developing girls will have changes to their appearance, but a blood test will say one way or the other. We'd better be sure. I'll write a referral for the hospital."

He wrote on a form with his fountain pen.

"If there's no period in the next week, ring the hospital for a blood test appointment and take this paper along."

He handed it to me.

"Sometimes periods can be irregular. Then again... *if* it's positive, you'll have less than twenty weeks to go, in which case you'd better come back and see me – with your parents. There are queues of people waiting to adopt unwanted babies."

My throat went dry. The pregnancy wasn't wanted, but who said a baby would be *un*wanted?

Not me.

CHAPTER TWENTY-TWO:

RED MOON DRAMA

"Attention!"

Margaret's voice rose above the chaos. She was a nice prefect, not like some. "We're having this meeting in the domestic science lab as it's got more space. Mr Tomkins, your English teacher, asked me to select people for the school play. I have some experience in drama groups. *Quiet* please, Sally, I don't want you to miss anything."

Drama. That was exciting. There were a few people from our class and some from the year above me. The girl with long blonde hair and short skirt was there. Her name was Noreen. Eventually we all stopped talking.

"It looks like we have several interested girls from the fourth and fifth years. Good. I need people to audition for parts. Okay girls, sit in a semi-circle. Can those sitting on the laminated cabinets get a chair; there are more at the back. That's it."

Auditions. I used to be in drama groups when I was younger in Yorkshire, but not in school.

"'Ere, 'Sal, look who comes 'ere, Miss bleedin' prim and proper."

That was Hazel, spiky loo-brush head number one.

"Yeah. She'll be bleedin' useless at drama with 'er 'oop fackin' mill' accent, won't you? Ya frigid bitch."

Girls began to look at me. I scowled at her. "Who's frigid?"

"Con said you was, so there. He were going to finish wiv you anyway."

I'd like to have corrected her grammar. I folded my arms. "He's just peeved because I wouldn't give him a bit. *I* had a boyfriend before Con." I tossed my head in the air and looked away. I didn't usually speak like that. The words 'give him a bit' sounded really funny coming from me, but *they* said it a lot.

Sally opened her mouth and showed her chewing gum. "Y-e-a-h, the one that got you up the duff," she sneered loudly.

My face heated. Those who didn't know through big mouth Alexandria knew now. "Ha, ha," I said, quietly, as if it wasn't true.

"Sally, pipe down. We need to start reading lines. Start from the window side and take turns around the room. Okay?" Margaret said. She signalled to the first girl. "We're auditioning for Maria, the main part, first. Page two, halfway down. Start reading."

"Fine. Stop. Next."

Another girl read.

"Next…"

And another.

"Thank you. Next," Margaret said after a few lines.

That was me.

I was a bit dazed because I had a weird dream last night, after the doctors. It was so real, yet I couldn't remember it properly. It was something to do with those two big chimneys back in Yorkshire. I was on the bridge-

228

like road with my mum; there were stars, and Mum and I were looking at the moon but it was red. Because I paused to think, a couple of girls rolled their eyes.

"That's you Andrea. Continue reading the character Maria; the main part."

I'd think about it later. Suddenly I got flutters in my stomach and my face was burning. It was a mixture of stage fright and excitement. Margaret nodded at me.

Hazel looked across at me and went: "Wu wu wu wu wu wu," like a muttering sound as if I was going to be really pathetic.

"Oop fackin' mill," Sally muttered to Hazel behind her hand and laughed.

Well they were in for a shock.

I might have been a bit timid because I was from the wrong side of the Thames according to them and a few others, but as it happened, drama was my thing. Hadn't they noticed?

I pulled myself to my full height, which was taller than her and the other toilet brush, breathed into the whole of my lungs like I was about to sing an arpeggio in singing lessons, breathed out, then lifted my chin and paused a moment. They thought I was nervous. But actually, I'd get that part.

I cast my eyes slowly down and over the script then lifted my chin again. I pretended I had an audience of several hundred so my voice needed to be like Miss Hubbard's and Miss Lane's or like I was in one room talking to my mum who was in another room, like M-u-u-u-m, where's the –

No problem.

229

I began reading in my most posh theatre-loud clear voice that was neither Yorkshire nor London, but simply Queen's English, and I made regular eye contact with my audience.

Hazel and Sally carried on muttering and sniggering, but I swept them a look then ignored them and raised my voice and my chin.

"Shhh," people said to them.

The girl in the year above us with the long hair, Noreen, gave the loo brush heads a condescending look down her nose. "Shut up," she said, tutted, and then smiled at me. She flicked her hair back and looked at them again as if to say, "I'm older than you."

I continued to read. Voices lessened to hushed whispers then lapsed into stunned silence until you couldn't hear anything but the sound of my voice, steady, firm and clear with only the wind outside as a backdrop. I was Maria, a cripple in a wheelchair. At the end of the section I stopped.

"Read on Andrea, and when we come to Annie's part, can you read 'Annie', Noreen?"

Noreen's eyes were light blue and she had an intelligent air about her. I read the next paragraph, which was being spoken to Annie, so I looked at her a couple of times. She looked straight at me and only broke eye contact to glance at her lines then she lifted her chin like me and said the next part. Yeah, she was good. She read well. This made me put in even more effort. I *felt* like Maria the cripple. Annie was my carer. Noreen played up to me with the same level of emotion as if we really were two people in that situation, then she had to exit stage. I was alone with a monologue, reminiscing about when I could walk. I ended this by staring into space with my memory.

Everyone clapped, even *them.*

"Well done, Andrea. You have the main part, Maria, and Noreen – the supporting role of Annie. We've got a few weeks to rehearse. The play will be open to the public before Christmas break up. Let's take a two-minute break."

I knew I'd get it. "Up yours," I said to them under the rumble of clapping and congratulations.

Noreen came up to me. "Well done."

"Thanks. You did well too."

"Have you done drama before?"

"A bit. What about you?"

"Only at school last year. I like it. Here, since we've got the two main parts, would you like to come to my house after school, so we can practice?"

Somehow I didn't think she was going to be a false friend like Alexandria. She was more mature. "Thanks. Can I phone my mum when we get there to let her know?"

There was a bike outside the back door. "Is that yours?"

Noreen turned the doorknob. "My mum's. She cycles to the factory where she works. So does my dad."

"Same cycle?" I joked.

She pulled a face. "It wouldn't surprise me. Mum, this is Andrea, the new girl from Yorkshire."

Her mum turned around from the bench-top. "Have a pew. Cuppa?"

There was a blue and white smudgy-dot patterned Formica table in the middle of the kitchen. "Thank you."

"Andrea's got the main part in the school play and I've got the supporting role so we're going to practice."

She went up to her mum and said quietly: "Can she stay for dinner?"

"Yep. If it's okay with her mother."

She said it like, mavver.

Her mum put the knitted tea cosy on the teapot and Noreen got the cups out.

"My mum's a Cockney."

"What makes a person a Cockney?"

"It means you were born within the sound of Bow Bells in London. I'm from Bermondsey," her mum said. "Cockneys are very proud of their language." She poured our tea.

"Have you heard Cockney sayings?" Noreen asked.

"Only, up the apples and pears, for stairs."

"There's trouble and strife, which means wife, boat race for face and there are lots more. I'll teach you so you'll know when you hear them at school."

"You kids get on with your lines for half an hour. Dinner's in the oven. If you'd like to stay to eat you better ring your mum."

She pointed through the kitchen door to the black telephone on the hall table.

"And Noreen, set the table."

Noreen got tomato ketchup and HP Sauce out of the pantry and cutlery out of a drawer.

After I phoned my mum we read our parts, closed our books and tested each other.

"Do you like singing?" Noreen said.

"I can't make up my mind whether I want to be a singer, an actress or a model!"

She flicked some blonde hair behind her ear. "*Me* too!"

It was so nice to meet someone similar. "I've had singing lessons and started a modelling course. I go one night a week, in London. After Christmas I'm getting a photo portfolio done."

"Lucky devil. I've always wanted to do something like that. Can you show me how to do the catwalk walk?"

"Have you got a book handy?" I took her school dictionary and put it on my head then walked around the kitchen table doing my end of catwalk turns at each corner. "My mum got me to do typing and commerce at school 'just in case' I don't end up being a model or a singer. That is so Yorkshire." I rolled my eyes.

She put the dictionary on her head and had a go. "Poor you. That means you've got Mrs Benson and she is such a cow."

"She doesn't like me. There can be girls talking the other side of the room ten rows from me, but she'll say, 'Andr-e-a Gordon...'" I got up and mimicked Mrs Benson's walk. I nearly said Andrea Hampton because I still forgot sometimes. Noreen pulled a face.

"She and Bolton-Fox, the fat and the thin, are as thick as thieves, so watch it."

Something made me think of that huge, wide yet slightly shaped black furnace, and the row of tall, thin dirty red chimney columns behind it. "Mind you, I'm good at typing. Some of the really good typists are being put in for the CSE over a year early, before spring next year. I'm a reserve in case someone is sick."

"I'm doing English literature O level in January. If I fail, I'll get another chance in the summer!"

She stepped into the hall and came back with a guitar.

"Have you got a guitar?"

"Getting one for Christmas."

She sat on a kitchen stool opposite me and started strumming *Where Have All the Flowers Gone.* I joined in and sang the chorus with her and then we harmonised through the whole song. Noreen's fingers moved deftly over the strings then she did a few fancy chords at the end. I recognised the beginning of *Blowing in the Wind* and we started together. That was so *fab.*

She tapped the wood of the guitar. "What else can we sing?"

"What about Barry McGuire's *Eve of Destruction,* about war?" I loved that.

She strummed a few keys and we both frowned with passion, being the actresses we were. She knew the words as well as I did.

After the final verse she put the guitar against the wall. "That was great. It's damn true as well. Old enough for war and not for voting. All those poor boys sent to Vietnam."

"I've heard that there are *Ban the Bomb* marches in London. I'd love to go on one. We shouldn't still be having wars in the sixties anywhere."

"I'll find out when the next one is and we'll go if you like."

She was *so* groovy. "Fab."

Noreen picked up her guitar again. "Do you know Marianne Faithful's *As Tears Go By*?"

"Do I know it? It's one of my absolute favourites in the whole world."

"We both look a bit Marianne Faithful-ish with our hair," she rolled a shoulder. "Let's practice singing in front on the mirror in the hall. Here, use this pen as a mike."

We looked good in the mirror, singing together. I could just imagine us on *Top of the Pops* on the telly.

"Brilliant," Noreen said. "When you get a guitar we can go and sing in the park and on buses – we might get some donations!"

"I'd love to. It's great to sing."

"What about writing songs; can you?"

"I'm good with words and usually top in English, but hopeless with music – you know, 'Andrea tries hard.'"

"Trade you! Bye the way that Sally has got a mouth like a trap door and she's mean, as well as being *absolutely* common." She lowered her voice. "You don't have to tell me if you don't want to, but if you really think you're pregnant and you want some support, I'm not a blabbermouth."

"Thanks." I wanted to get to know her a bit better first.

"News is on in five minutes," Noreen's mum called.

"Let's watch the news before dinner. Did you see *Cathy Come Home* on TV last week?"

235

"Oh my God! Wasn't it *good*?" It made me think of how I might end up with my baby.

"It'll change things in Britain. The Government should help homeless people more."

I didn't know much about it. "I felt so sorry for Cathy when she lost her children."

We went through to the TV. Noreen nudged me.

"Mum fancies Harold Wilson. Harold's her man. My dad too, but I don't think he fancies him!"

"Hope not!" *My* mum and dad were always Conservative, and Bill was a business-man so he too preferred the Conservatives. "My mum and Bi...and dad are more into Ted Heath except they don't like the fact that Ted's always going off on his boat."

"What's your dad do?"

"National Sales Manager." It didn't sound right. I used to say, my dad, the real one, worked in an office. "He's not my real dad," I blurted out. That felt strange. I hadn't said it before. "My real dad died nearly two years ago." That felt worse, yet having the 'nearly two years ago' after it, made it less real. Why couldn't I have said that easily to Brendan and other people who didn't know during the last two years?

Noreen's eyes clouded over like Mandy's, June's and Sandra's had. "Oh that's *terrible*. I can't imagine losing my dad. I'm *so* sorry. What happened?"

Perhaps everybody would have been sympathetic like Noreen. Maybe I wasn't odd not having a dad, after all. It was still strange to talk about it away from the home. It was like putting your toe in a swimming pool and not knowing whether you'd fall in and drown. I took a deep breath. "He was run over by a car. He died almost instantly." I wasn't going to drown, but the water was cold, uncomfortable, lonely and sad. It was like walking into our old front room the day I found out. I looked down a bit.

"Oh no. How awful for your mum and you."

I nodded.

Noreen held onto my arm. "Here, tell you what," she whispered. "The *Ban the Bomb* march will probably be on a weekday. How'd you feel about wagging a day off school? Nothing much happens at *this* school during the last month of term. We could go to the Small Faces Fanclub and the *Tiles* as well. It has lunch time pop groups."

I'd heard of that. "Wag school? You're on!"

CHAPTER TWENTY-THREE:

RED MOON AND THEM

Mum put the tablecloth on the dining room table. "It'll be lovely to have Noreen to Sunday dinner. She's quite a bright spark isn't she?"

That meant interesting and funny. "We've been having fun these last few weeks." I got the cutlery out. "She's clever. She was top in her year for history and she's doing O level literature early next year. We're going to be fantastic in the school play at Christmas. We already know most of the lines by heart." I looked in the mirror above the mantelpiece as I put the napkins down. "Perhaps we'll be actresses – if I'm not a model first. By the way, can I go to *The Iron Curtain* in the afternoon and evening down at the bottom village – it's a sort of disco?"

"Back at ten."

"There's a pop group on called *Them*."

The phone rang and mum went to answer it. "Ph-o-ne, Sheffield!"

I bounded through to the hall. It was always great to hear from Sandra, Jackie, and occasionally Mandy and June. I looked at Mum. "W-h-a-t?" Then I took the phone. "Hello?"

It was a deep voice. "Andrea. How's it going?"

My hand curled around the black receiver. "*Brendan*. Great, I mean, well, you know, some things are the same…"

"Shit."

Mum went through to the kitchen.

"Quite. But apart from that, Carnaby Street and the fashions are fab! How are things for you? And how's the job, really?"

He sighed. "It's dirty work. Hard to get the grease out of my fingernails. It's really black. The blokes are good honest people though."

I thought about where his fingers had been and how I'd feel about being with him now – with dirty black fingernails. He should have stayed on at school then he would have been able to have more choice in jobs. Lee Dorsey's *Working in a Coal Mine* sang through my mind. "That's good, about the blokes, I mean." Not the fingernails. "Will you stay?"

"For now. It'll pay for a bit of travel like London and so-on."

I imagined his Beatles cap and that wool and soap scent when he held me. "When?"

"Can't say for sure; next year. What else have you been doing?"

Why wouldn't he say? I didn't know if I missed him because I was carrying his baby or because I really loved him despite the things he says or doesn't say. At least I could talk to him in my own language and accent, and we both knew what a tosser was.

"I had singing lessons with the instructor who trained Shirley Bassey and other stars. He's organised for me to make a demo tape. Sometimes I go up to Oxford Street and Bond Street with a friend." Slight exaggeration. Bill's secretary always met me at Charing Cross Station and saw me safely on the tube to singing class or modelling school. "On the underground it's like being a sardine in a can. Sometimes they're so full you have to hang by straps wedged in between people. Have you been out much?" I held my breath. He had money now. He could have been dating someone else.

"Here and there. Still go to the *Esquire* Club. Good to have a bit of cash. Had a few hangovers. Blokes where I work can put it away. Once or twice to their level was enough for me. What about down your way?"

"There's a club called the *Iron Curtain*. It's open on Tuesday and Friday nights, and Sunday afternoons. My friend Noreen is taking me today and we'll go in the Christmas holidays as well. They play ska, Tamla Motown and so on. Hold on a minute…" I closed the door to the kitchen. "I've been to the docs. He says I'll have to have a blood test. I've made an appointment at the hospital," I whispered.

He let out a breath that was almost a whistle. "Let me know. Phone me if you need to, otherwise I'll ring next year when I get holiday dates. Got to go; I'm on shift work. Hey, happy Christmas in case I can't ring you nearer the day."

I put the receiver down and stared at the black telephone. Why couldn't he have rung me *at* Christmas? He never *said* much whether we'd been on a date or talked on the phone, yet his raspy John Lennon voice still made my stomach jump. I didn't think love had to do with having everything in common or even with how 'nice' someone was. There was just a thread of something underlying the things you could see, feel and hear and it pulled you to someone like a magnet as if you were a puppet and someone was pulling the strings.

I wondered if that was how people lived and died, too, because someone or something was pulling the strings.

"THIS IS RADIO CAROLINE," Simon Dee said out of the transistor as we ate breakfast.

Bill sipped his coffee. "How was your night?"

He said it like, 'neet'. I looked up from my cereal. "It was wild! The walls and ceiling were black like a cellar. The whole place vibrated with ska and blue-beat music."

Mum pulled a face. "Lovely! What were the group like?"

"Great. In the break one of them talked to me and took my phone number."

"He probably takes lots of girls' phone numbers."

"That's what I said, but he said, 'It's not as glamorous as it sounds, you know, living out of a suitcase, never having time to have a proper girlfriend.' He said he'd prefer to have someone to come back to. He walked me home but he had to be quick because the rest of the group were loading the van and he was supposed to be there too." I ate a few mouthfuls of cereal. "There were lots of mods with green parkas on, and rockers, and lots of black people. The mods had scooters parked outside and they had bits of fur trim on their aerials. The rockers are called greasers now."

They still had the black leather gear, slick hair and walked like they'd got motorbikes between their legs, but I kept that bit to myself.

"Glad you had a good time," Bill chuckled.

"The black lads are really good dancers. I learnt to dance with a boy, partner to partner like you would in a waltz." But boy – that was no waltz. I blushed into my cornflakes. The first handsome black boy moved to the rhythm and moved me with him until I fell into step. Some of them pushed their hips against me and I ended up trying to push my bum away from them so they weren't constantly pushing their parts into me.

Then there was Warren. Mum would have liked him. "A nice boy who helps out at the *Iron Curtain* came and chatted to us. He's half Italian and has a really short mod cut." I could still whiff his Old Spice aftershave; it made me want to kiss him, but I didn't. "I'd like to get a mod boyfriend with a scooter." *Black, white, or in between.* "He asked when I was going down there again and if I'd like to go to the pictures. I said I'd let him know and he's going to ring. So I met two nice boys, one famous." Now I was thinking like this I almost forgot other issues.

"As long as we meet whomever, *before* you go out next time. Why so serious all of a sudden?" Mum asked.

I needed to have the blood test. "I was thinking I'd go for a hair trim down the high street after school."

I'd get the doctor's referral from my hiding place and slip it in my reefer jacket pocket.

"Okay. Is Noreen going?"

She'd be giving me a hair trim in the park on the way back from the hospital. "Think so. Oh! It's *THEM!*"

They both looked. "Who?"

"On the radio. Quick, turn it up. Turn it up." I turned it up myself. "It's the *group THEM* who we saw last night. And the boy who wanted to take me *out…*" Although he didn't know I was still at school.

Here Comes the Night played and Bill turned it up more for me.

"Good sound," he said, tapping his foot. "You be careful with these boys. They're probably after one thing."

"It's catchy," Mum said. "She wouldn't be silly, would you? Come on. Don't be late for school."

Sod the school. "*Here Comes the Ni-Ight* der-der-der-der–da," I sang, and I felt my eyes welling up because the lovely boy in the band had walked me home and kissed me on our doorstep, only last night.

"Yeah. School. I'm going." I rushed upstairs to clean my teeth. "Better not be late for meeting Noreen," I called from the landing. My skirt felt great. It was as short as Noreen's – she got me to roll it up a bit; being hipster it hid my slightly rounded stomach. I figured I might as well make the most of it before I got *too* fat. If the blood test was positive, I'd have to tell my mum. I'd be over half way there. I closed the bathroom door and quickly used the toilet.

What's this?

Blood.

My heart thudded. I looked again, put a tissue there then decided to stick a finger inside to make sure it was coming from *there*. Definitely. I could hardly believe it. I looked at the red blood for what seemed a long time.

Red. Now I remembered a bit more of that strange dream I had the night before the drama audition because I'd had it *again* last night. There was a red moon in it again – really red, like a sun. I was watching it and it seemed I was actually there – somewhere beautiful.

If I didn't have to rush, perhaps I'd remember.

I washed my hands, put on a sanitary belt and hooked up a pad by the loop then washed again and clean my teeth. I ran down and give Mum and Bill a quick peck.

"Bye…" I almost jumped for joy across our thick, red hall carpet towards the front door. Red was good.

Should I cancel the appointment for the blood test? I wondered. Sometimes pregnant people bled and yet they were still pregnant – but not often, were they?

CHAPTER TWENTY-FOUR:

BLACK IS BLACK

1967

I slid my right elbow on the desk.

Commerce was a lot more interesting than typing that year; pity it was the same teacher. Who cared? My main worry was over. I smiled to myself and looked out of the window. *Thank you God, for letting me have my periods again.* Perhaps there was something out there, after all. Things were *so* good. I liked London.

"Andrea Gordon. No doubt you're *still* day-dreaming about your *acting* career following excellent reviews in the Gazette since the school play," Mrs Benson said.

Heat rushed to my face and I looked to the front. *Actually no.* I was wondering why Brendan hadn't phoned through the winter. Didn't he want to know the outcome? As far as he knew, I could be *very* pregnant by now.

"However, it's more likely you'll be in an office, like everyone, so pay attention."

I folded my arms. Benson was peeved with me earlier. I couldn't help mulling over it. I'd stood by her desk when summoned and she'd carried on writing as if I wasn't there.

"Andrea Gordon, I've called you into this room so you can take a place in the exam," she said without looking up. She had that dry scrape to her voice.

"Liz Goodfellow is sick," Mrs Benson added, looking at some papers on her desk. When she paused for a moment her mouth went into a tight line.

"As you know, Andrea, really talented students are allowed to sit the CSE typing early. Liz was scheduled for today's exam, along with a couple of others, as she's exceptional. You're reasonably good, and would only be given this opportunity a year earlier in summer. So given that you're not the best, you're very fortunate to be a reserve for the *spring* exam."

Grinning goody-goody ankle socked Liz couldn't suck up enough. "We have a typewriter at home and I use it. I'm sure I can do it well, Mrs Benson." I didn't wait for an answer. I sat down at the allocated typewriter desk, lifted the lid and slid out the black typewriter. When I took the cover off I checked the ribbon, put the paper and carbon paper in and typed my name on the top then waited for the nod to start. All the typing and setting went well. No mistakes. I didn't think I'd ever done so well in typing so I was feeling really pleased with myself that afternoon.

Mrs Benson handed back my commerce project. "Excellent work," she said without looking at me. "Today we are going to talk more about Roneo machines, telex messages, and POP which means 'Post Office Preferred' size envelopes."

There was a knock on the door and it swung open. Miss Bolton-Fox filled the doorway.

"Excuse me, Mrs Benson. Might I have a word?" Her chins rested on her sternum as she sort of smiled.

Mrs Benson stopped her demonstration about envelopes. "*Certainly*, Miss Bolton-Fox."

She turned back to us. "Read page nine, and quietly," she said, and the word 'quietly' was really loud like a controlled shout, then she pranced out like she was going to a tea party.

She and Bolton-Fox talked in hushed tones outside the classroom for a couple of minutes and then the door opened again. Mrs Benson beckoned me out. Me? I stared. Mrs Benson nodded.

What the blooming hell had I done now? Another detention I expected. The last one was for wearing my lilac suede shoes. Cassie Felton had the same lilac suede shoes on the same day so we both stood in detention and laughed, looking at our fantastic shoes. Well? They were comfortable and I had a long walk to school.

I left my desk and walked out into the corridor. Mrs Benson closed the door behind us and she and Miss Bolton-Fox edged closer together, facing me, like a wall.

Miss Bolton-Fox looked down her lip at me and she even smiled into her chins. "Andrea, as you know you were a reserve for the typing exam this morning."

She said it as nicely as I've ever heard her speak to me, yet it sounded smarmy.

"Yes, Miss. I think I've done really well."

"Ah, but now Liz Goodfellow has turned up and her father would like her to do the exam."

"Well, it's too late Miss, isn't it? I mean, the exam is over."

"Well Andrea, it's not that simple. Liz's father is on the school board and puts a *lot* of money into the school, and he insists that we allow her to do the exam. So, we're going to rip your exam paper up and you can enter next time."

"But you can't do that, Miss. The exam is closed. She wasn't here," I squeaked.

Mrs Benson piped up. "Now, now Andrea, don't start any nonsense. You were only a reserve. Liz is *much* better at typing than you, but you'll get another chance."

They loomed over me like two chimney columns, blocking my path, Bolton-Fox the big coal stained furnace, and Benson the thin angry red one behind it, also blackened by coal.

The deputy head was like the big, lighter cleaner furnace. She wasn't bad like them; she wasn't there.

"We don't want any repercussions Andrea," Miss Bolton-Fox said. "There's no need to go worrying your mother and no need for her to be telephoning the Department of Education *now is there*?"

They inched further together, blocking my view of the isolated corridor beyond. "No Miss, well, I don't know."

"There's *no* need, Andrea. You'll get another chance," Mrs Benson said in her slightly brisker dry scrape tone and then she opened the classroom door. "Off you go now. You'll take the exam again in a few months."

I hovered and opened my mouth. Wasn't it illegal to rip up an exam paper after the exam was completed?

"You'll get another chance," they chimed in unison, nodding their heads.

I raised my voice. "But, Miss…" It was wrong.

248

"No answering back, Andrea. You don't want another detention." Benson held the door open. "Back to class."

I slid down in my chair and looked out of the window. Mum had said I could do modelling as long as I had typing to fall back on. If I qualified early, I could even leave school, if I wished.

I imagined those industrial furnaces and the thinner chimney columns behind them spewing out smoke from the top and it zigzagging between the pillars of light and dark like snakes and ladders. Noreen said those two were as thick and thieves. Yeah, pillars of support for each other – on the dark side.

"They did *what*?" Mum raised an eyebrow and went red in the face. "How dare they? They're supposed to uphold ethical behaviour and standards. Turn that down."

I always liked Radio Caroline on when I came home from school. Los Bravos were singing, *Black is Black*. Apart from Brendan's fingernails, it fitted the deed of the teachers. "It's a good song for Miss Bolton-Fox and Mrs Benson, as in black and evil." I turned it down and put the amber glass ashtray on the coffee table for Mum. "Imagine if it had been the other way around and goody-goody-two-shoes ankle socked flaming Lizzie Goodfellow was the reserve and I the actual entrant. And *I* came back ready to roll in the afternoon after missing the exam time."

She took a cigarette out. "Quite."

"Noreen couldn't believe it either. We named them the crook and the crim on the walk home. Noreen said she would have walked out of school and gone straight home

249

and told her dad. He would have gone up the school for something like that."

"Why didn't you say something?"

"I didn't know what to do. You're always telling me not to answer them back. Besides, it's Friday. I didn't want to be in detention."

Mum lit her cigarette. "Bill's working on his sales reports at the dining room table." She raised her voice. "Did you hear that, darling?"

Bill came through. "I most *cert*ainly did. We can't have that, Jeannie. What they've done is illegal." He pursed his lips, sat in the easy chair then tapped a finger on the chair's arm.

Mum flicked her ash. "Your exam paper belongs to the examining board. We'll have to do something on Monday. What do you think, Bill?"

I didn't have a dad but this is where Bill could come in handy. He could march up to the school and give them a bollocking. I looked at him while he did the finger tap thinking. I looked back at Mum. On second thoughts, she was much scarier.

"We should ring the Department of Education and I'll talk to my solicitor," Bill said.

He had his good points. I *suppose* I was quite fond of him, really, apart from the bum poking episode.

"Depending on his advice, we might contact the *Gazette* for some press coverage."

Help! I could end up in the paper and on television.

Mum widened her eyes. "I don't know about that. She's still got over a year to go. It could make things worse for her…"

"I'll think about it during the evening if that's okay," I said.

Then the phone rang. "I'll get it." I was hoping it would be Brendan and his black fingernails. I dashed through to the hall. "Hel-lo?" I put my head back round the door into the lounge. "It's Mandy in Sheffield." I closed the door. "Mandy. Good to hear from you. How are things back in Sheff?"

"So-so. We haven't chatted since Christmas. Seems funny you not being here. What about you? How's life?"

Mandy was fed up, I could tell. "Great. I made a demo disc one night last week, singing the Seekers *Morningtown Ride,* and I'm on the second part of my modelling course. I'm going to get photos done! A few weeks ago," I lowered my voice, "I wagged school with my friend for the second time and we went to Carnaby Street in London."

"Wish I were there. I went out with Alan Barnes a few times but it's finished now." She sighed. "June is going on holiday with another girl after the school exams."

"Oh."

"We're supposed to be best friends, and she's going on holiday with someone *else* and her family. I can't believe it. She didn't even *tell* me 'til after it was booked. She just dumped me," Mandy said.

Interesting.

Had Mandy got a short memory? I looked at the gold and white embossed stripes of the hall wallpaper. Did anything prickle her conscience? "That's not very kind for a best friend. She's old enough to know better," I said, letting her off the hook. I supposed I'd forgiven Mandy even though I didn't like what she did. She *was* only twelve and a half when she dumped me because I wasn't 'fun' in my grief. I sensed her silent penny dropping.

"Yeah," she said quietly.

"You've still got other friends, including me, Mandy."

"Yeah."

"I met a nice girl, Noreen. She's in the year above me. That's the girl I wagged school with. I met a boy too." I giggled. "I've met several at the *Iron Curtain*. The singer of *Them* walked me home while his band started to load the van."

"Really?"

"He's gorgeous, but he's gone on tour. He phoned before he went, just like he said he would. Pop star aside, I like one other boy."

"What's his name?"

"Warren. He's half Italian."

"Lucky thing. What about Brendan?"

I never told her about missing my periods. "He phoned a few times last year. Might come down. He's not in regular contact, really. Hey, would *you* like to come down for a few days in the summer holidays?"

"I'd love that, thanks."

It'd be great to have Mandy down and show her around without June hanging onto her.

Grandma came downstairs for dinner as I replaced the receiver. She nodded at the phone.

"Is that a friend in Sheffield?"

"My former best friend."

We went into the lounge together. "You'll never guess what, Mum. Remember Mandy dumped me after Dad died? Well now June's dumped her!"

"Don't gloat."

Grandma looked over the top of her brown-framed glasses. "You reap as you sow."

Now that had happened to Mandy, I thought of Bolton-Fox and Benson. Would they reap as they sowed? Mr Fillmore had; he was paying for his mistake.

Mum relayed the story about the teachers to Grandma. Her blue eyes bulged and her chin drew back into her neck. "*Goodness*, gracious me," she said.

"You think my teachers will reap as they sowed for tearing up my exam, Grandma?"

"The universe has a way of evening things out, even though we can't always see the reason behind it. Mark my words."

I thought the crim and the crook would get their due. It'd been ages since I played with my tarot cards so I got them out while they all watched *What's My Line*.

Grandma sucked in her breath, looked at the window then back to me. "Don't let the vicar see those."

"We don't have a vicar come here."

She stared into space. "*No*."

"Oh Mother, they're just a bit of fun," Mum said.

"They're more than that, dear," Grandma said in her more superior, former history teacher voice. She had a little smile like Mona Lisa. I spread my cards on the modern fitted carpet. All swords. The miserable ten of swords was in the distant past position, the upside down four was now, that was reasonable, and the seven was for

253

my immediate future. "That's a nice card." It was about new places, hope, confidence and wishes coming true. "But, what about the teachers?"

Grandma took her eyes off *What's My Line*. "Ask the God within," she said.

Well, I supposed if you looked at it like *that*, I *could*. I stared at the trees outside the window and concentrated then pulled a card.

It was the scales – Justice. Good. I collected them up and put them in the packet.

The adverts came on the telly and Mum turned it down.

"I can send you to commercial college where you can do English O level as well, if you'd prefer to leave," she said.

That might be good – if I wasn't a famous model. Noreen would leave school later in the year because she was older. "I don't want to waste my energy on this *petty* little school. I think the bad deed will come back to the teachers. Don't worry about doing anything. What goes around comes around."

"If you're sure…" Mum said.

"You're going to be a model anyway," Bill said.

It sounded like 'mawdel'. I probably was. A model and an actress. I had choices.

But I'd still like to see Brendan James.

CHAPTER TWENTY-FIVE:

RED MOON RISING

Mr Anton, the photographer and owner of the modelling school, came towards me in the studio. "Ah, An-d-ray-a," he said.

He was even older than Bill, portly, had yellowy-olive skin, slick black hair, bushy eyebrows and a huge black moustache like a cat's tail.

His eyes squinted a bit like they would if he were smiling but he wasn't actually smiling – he was just looking. Then his big black moustache with the curl on each end went up one side towards his cheek.

"Darling," he said, rolling the 'r'. "Do you have the four outfits?"

I wanted to giggle because the moustache looked like it was stuck on.

"Yes, Mr Anton. I've been practising my model walk on the way to school with my friend just like you showed me on the course."

"Ve-ry good. You look beautiful and very 'appee."

"I am."

I was like a feather, light and free. And, I was going to be a model.

I was.

Mr Anton tweaked his moustache. "Start with the day dress. We'll take about twenty shots with that then you can change into the evening dress followed by the culottes and the nightie."

He stroked his chin on the word 'nightie'.

"Where shall I change?"

He pointed to a screened off area in the corner of the studio.

There? "In the corner?" Really? I went behind it and changed quickly, looking over my shoulder all the time in case he was peeping. Finally, I stepped out in my short red day dress.

Mr Anton arranged the paper backdrops for me to stand on and the big, hot lights on tall stands around and in front of me.

"You know how to pose in front of the camera, Andrea; we've covered that on the course." He pointed to the centre of the huge paper backdrop. "Stand on this chalked cross."

I did as he said. He came up to me and fondled my hairdresser perfect ringlets and moved them here and there. I was glad I'd had it tinted back to my own colour; I didn't need to be blonde anymore. The gold showed through a bit, looked like a shine and was just a shade darker than Noreen's natural dark blonde.

"Your eyelashes look ve-ry good," he said.

They weren't mine. I stuck them on that morning and they looked like spider's legs. "Thank you."

Mr Anton walked backwards to his camera stand, looking at me all the time then started taking lots of shots.

"Smile – good; with the teeth; mouth closed; side-ways; chin up; head on one side; good, good. Now the culottes."

I darted behind the screen and changed. When I returned Mr Anton arranged my curls again.

"Let's take this just a leet-le lower," he said, adjusting the zip down the front of my all-in-one, turquoise culottes. "Beautiful." He went back to the camera.

It was warm and bright under the lights.

"Think something sexy; puff your lips out; put the left hand over the edge of your hip; Ve-ry, ver-ry good."

He walked away from the camera and came and stood right in front of me. He was a bit close. He tweaked his moustache to one side. At the same time, he looked at me with a really creepy glow in his eyes and then his left eye twitched. So did his face.

"Andr-ay-a." He stroked his moustache. "Some girls your age can make a *lot* of money in this business," he said in his lyrical accent.

It sounded like, '…a lort orf marney in thees bizziness...' He reached out and touched my curls and twitched again.

"Would you like to make a lot of money?"

Dirty bastard. I widened my eyes like I was stupid and looked straight ahead – at the door. My eyelashes were sticking to the space below my eyebrows.

"'App-in-ess is something you should always 'av, And-ray-a."

The way he said happiness, it sounded like, *A*-penis. He knew how old I was, and that I was still at school. Filthy git. He'd even met my parents. I bet he thought I

257

was a *virgin*. "I know Mummy and Daddy have paid a *lot* of money for the course so I expect to get some work from this agency," I batted my spiders' legs, "And make money from those jobs you send me to." My voice was squeaky with nerves and I bet I sounded about ten.

Noreen would probably have said something like, 'Just take the photos' and given him a snooty look. Apart from his position as owner of this school and my age, his wife, who ran the agency side of the business, was seven months pregnant. He did the rest of the photos in relative silence in the way that an artist might have been absorbed in painting a picture.

Colleen Brown, Mr Anton's pregnant wife, had straight chestnut hair in a bun and red lips and nails but no eye make-up or false eyelashes like all the models whose photos were on the walls. She was talking on a modern cream telephone that wasn't quite as big as our black one. I sat and waited, but not to tell her about *him*. She wanted to send me for a couple of interviews. Finally, she finished talking.

"Now Dahr-ling, if you get offered work, they'll want you to show their spring collection, so the start date will be soon – just after Easter. You'll be on school holidays. They think you're leaving at Easter if you get a job. Don't tell them you'll be going back to school. Take the job and get some experience."

If I went back, I still hadn't decided. I nodded.

She wrote out an introduction card. "We'll think of an excuse when you have to go back."

I picked up my big black model bag containing changes of shoes, bags and outfits, and carted it down the

258

busy London street to the first fashion house just off Bond Street.

When I walked inside the showroom another very dark non-English-looking man met me. He had those heavy lines either side of his face between the nose and the mouth, skin like a well-worn tan-brown saddle and a big hooked nose.

He took the introduction form from the model agency, "Ah, sweetie," he said. "You are very pretty but not quite tall and skinny enough for our range. Our girls are *very* skinny, like Twiggy."

He reached out and ran his hand over the top of my tummy. "You need to lose just a few pounds from here first then we might not worry about the height so much. Do you exercise?"

I was in shock. "Well, a bit, once a week." At school, I thought. "And I walk." To and from school.

"Ah. The agency tells me you're still at school, but leaving soon, no?"

My face prickled with heat. "Yes."

He nodded and smiled. "Ve-ry good. I will show you the exercise you must do, then come back and see me in a couple of months, okay?"

"Okay."

Well, I didn't know. Were all modelling job interviews like that? I looked down at my stomach. I wasn't bloated. It had gone down a bit since having monthlies again and looked reasonably flat to me. My hips measured 35" and my waist 25" or 26".

"Good. Slip off your dress."

Well, this was a bit odd.

"Slip off your dress so you don't crease it while you exercise."

I stood there looking a bit blank.

"Sweetie, you don't want to crease your dress. I assume you have another interview after this, no?"

"Yes."

He held out his arm for the dress with a bored expression on his face and big droopy eyelids. I supposed his models must hand him dresses all the time then.

I slipped it off and handed it to him. He placed it carefully over a dress rack.

"Okay, lie down on your back just there on the floor then I'll show you what to do with your legs."

I lay on the floor on my back like he said.

"Okay, now take both legs over your head then bring the legs down slowly, holding your tummy muscles."

I did it a couple of times.

"Widen the legs more. Wider. That's it. And keep your legs straight. Now pause."

I had my feet behind my head, my white lacy bum in the air and I looked at him from under my legs because he'd stopped shouting instructions and the showroom was quiet.

His left eye was twitching like Mr Anton's. In fact, his whole face was twitching in the muscles in his leathery cheeks above those deep-set lines as he stared at my bum and my pantyhose.

Silly, stupid me. I swung my legs down, went for my dress and put it on in seconds.

"I'm going," I snapped and it came out in my Sheffield accent, like, *am* going.

He gave me a horrible smile that made my skin crawl. Another dirty bastard. London must have been full of them. I marched out and back up the road to the agency.

Miss Brown frowned, her head rolled back and her red nails rose to her temples.

"O-o-h, Andrea, *darhling*!" she gasped through contorted red lips.

She picked up their cream phone, dialled, and tapped her angry talons on the desk. "I'll never send you any girls again."

She went on about me being not even quite fifteen and still at school. What did he think he was playing at? How dare he do that and give her agency a bad name?

I heard his cackle in the background. I imagined him leaning back in his office chair and eating something with an open mouth and food stuff falling out.

Miss Brown hung up. "Andrea, *never* ever do that at an interview again."

"I won't."

"On a brighter note, don't worry about today's second interview; you have a job offer. Remember the lady who came in to give a talk during the course?"

She was really nice. "She and a man interviewed me and four others after their talk on the rag trade and seasons for clothes. She has a fashion house down the road."

Miss Brown sipped from a coffee mug with red lip marks on it.

"She rang twenty minutes ago. She wants to offer you a job as showroom junior to start as soon as possible.

You're the look they want. You'll be doing some modelling and looking after clothes and so on. A letter is on the way to you."

I wanted to jump up and down. "Fabulous."

"It's ten pounds a week, which is quite good for your first job – even if it's for a short time."

"*Ten* pounds!" I'd be able to buy that new bloomer dress outfit that Noreen and I saw in Carnaby Street and a maroon leather coat. "I'm so excited. Thank you."

"I know you have a train to catch, so don't be late. You'll be able to tell your parents the *good* news," Miss Brown said with a nod and a smile.

I carted my black model bag to Bond Street tube station. Never mind about the weight. *I'm going to be a model.* Whee!

London seemed good but some of these fashion people – the men – were pretty bad. Brendan said the factory people where he worked, even though rough, were good, honest, and helped you out. Sometimes you assumed people in certain jobs would be good but they turned out to be bad, like the teacher and headmistress at my school, and yet other people might seem bad, or rough, like Brendan's factory people, or Hazel and Sally, but they weren't really bad people, mostly.

I supposed it was like black and white. But sometimes it wasn't all one thing or the other, but a melding of grey like the smoke that travelled between the chimney columns; like Mr Fillmore because he couldn't be all bad.

I remembered my encounter in the mist, some weeks after Dad died, with the 'man' who maybe wasn't a real man. Even though death was still death and life was still life, it wasn't as black and white as that.

I stepped onto the plush red carpet in our hall and flung my heavy model bag down. "I'm b-a-ck. Is Noreen here yet?"

Mum came into the hall. "She's been here about fifteen minutes. We've been chatting. Did you see the note?"

I turned to the telephone table. Mum's handwriting on the small pad said the time of the call and, *Brendan James says he's coming down next week.*

Fancy that; at last. I hadn't thought about him quite so much this last few days. "Really? What else did he say?"

"Not much."

"Mum!"

"He's hitchhiking to London. He'll call later tonight from another phone box with the details. How were your interviews?"

I couldn't wait to tell her and Bill about the day. "It's a long story." I rolled my eyes. "I'll tell you all together."

She followed me into the lounge. Noreen was arguing politely with Bill about Ted Health and Harold Wilson. She knew a lot about politics. They liked that she held proper conversations with them, unlike a couple of earlier school friends in Orpington. Noreen was more like me, a bit of a rebel without being totally over the top like the toilet brush heads.

"Have you got a modelling job?" Bill asked.

I jumped up and down. "I've *got* one."

"Well done," Noreen said.

Mum gave me a big hug. "That's wonderful!"

Bill got some glasses out of the china cabinet. "If you like the job you don't have to go back to school; it's up to you. Now, this calls for champagne to toast your modelling career."

He went to the kitchen and returned with a bottle then uncorked it.

"Get your mum in for a glass, Jeannie."

He started pouring.

"M-o-ther, glass of champagne before dinner to toast Andrea's modelling job," Mum called.

Grandma came through and accepted a glass. "For such a special occasion," she said.

We all clinked and Billy the budgie said, "Billy's a good boy. Do you want a cup of tea? You're beautiful."

I felt like the bubbles – sparkling and rising upwards. It was a double celebration for me.

Noreen clinked her glass to mine, "Congratulations," she half turned away from Mum and Bill and almost closed her mouth. "And to *the other* fairly recent success."

I almost closed mine. "I know."

Mum tapped me on the shoulder. "Hey you two, it's rude to whisper in public."

"Sorry. Noreen said it's nice that Brendan is coming." After they'd all toasted me for getting the modelling job I took a few sips. "Let me tell you about a day in the life of a model. I went to an interview and this bloke said I needed to lose a few pounds…" I acted out the 'exercise saga' as if I was on stage but made it a bit less sleazy, especially with Grandma being there. The adults were

264

gasping. Noreen was laughing so much she was doubled over and crying.

Finally, there was a gap in between the, "Oh you didn't," and, "Oh no," chants.

"Oh God, I don't know about this rag trade," Mum said.

"Unfortunately, Jeannie, Andrea's going to come across that sort of thing in the fashion world." Bill turned to me. "Sometimes, you need to stand up for yourself even though the people interviewing you or your bosses are older. You need to let these chaps know when something is not acceptable," he said, but it came out like 'accerpterble' in Scottish.

That was the first bit of fatherly advice Bill had given me. I took a slurp of champagne. "I will next time."

"You're quite capable of standing up for yourself."

Our eyes met. He knew.

"I can't believe you did that exercise." Noreen closed her eyes and bit her lip before spluttering into more laughter.

"Nor can I; I'll know next time."

Bill tapped the white tablecloth. "I hear your friend Brendan from Sheffield will be in London next week. Don't go rushing to see him. Make him wait a couple of days."

He winked at me.

"I will."

CHAPTER TWENTY-SIX:

MOON BETWEEN THE PILLARS

Trafalgar Square was teaming with people and pigeons. There was traffic noise all around from the red buses and cars, and then there were the mingled sounds of many different languages with all the foreign people who came there. On a bright and sunny day, Trafalgar Square had a holiday feel.

"Be careful you don't get dive-bombed. You don't want bird poop on your lilac suede coat, for meeting Brendan," Noreen said.

She and I looked good together, a bit like Mandy and I used to look, but more mature. "No, I don't. Mind you, it's supposed to be good luck."

"For you or the bird? Are you excited about being with him?"

"I'm not sure. I still love him a bit, but I like Warren and his brown eyes. He's so mod. It was great to see him again last Sunday. And I really like the guy in *Them*, especially since he phoned me like he said he would."

"He's gone abroad on tour. That's worse than having a boyfriend in Sheffield."

"Yeah. He'll be too busy to go steady."

"If Brendan's better than them, no pun intended, he must be quite a stud."

I nudged Noreen. *He's here.* "There he is, sitting on the wall by the fountain."

"Oh."

It sounded like, E-o-w. That was probably because he looked a bit scruffy in denims. We headed towards Brendan through people and pigeon dirt. My heart jumped a bit – but not a lot. Not like before. Pigeons flew and swooped between Brendan and us. I saw him duck and laugh then he looked up and saw me.

"Hello," I said.

He got off the wall and smiled. "Hi, Andrea. You know Kev."

"Kev, this is Noreen. Noreen – Brendan, Kev."

"How was your trip down?" she said.

I knew that snooty look she had. She wasn't impressed but she was acting friendly, for my sake.

Brendan looked skinnier in those denim jeans and a matching jacket. He was skinnier. He was holding a big winter jacket over his shoulder. Somehow he looked a bit unkempt compared to the boys I'd met at the *Iron Curtain,* especially Warren. He was nowhere near as trendy as the lads with scooters around our way.

And he didn't look like John Lennon anymore.

Still, John Lennon had changed. He didn't wear a Beatles cap anymore and he had longer hair and was skinny too. Even the Beatles music was different these days.

"Took eleven hours. We hitched. Had a few gaps in between lifts."

I couldn't help thinking, I'm not surprised. "Noreen and I hitched to Margate for the day not long ago.

267

Secretly of course. We wagged the day off school today as well; we hitched along the A23. It's more fun than catching the bus."

Conversation was very basic while we tried to find some common ground. I didn't think they were even trying that hard.

"Have you been to St. James's Park yet?" Noreen asked.

"No. Any sights you can show us would be good. Suit you Kev?" Brendan said.

He shrugged. "Nice day. Might as well."

"Lead on!" I said to Noreen.

She strode out in front of them and gave me a quick glance. Her lips went up slightly making a wrinkle between her nose and mouth. I thought so. She didn't like Kev. She'd had better offers.

I glanced up at Brendan. Actually, I'd had better offers, come to think of it. Warren's sparkling brown eyes flashed through my mind and I blinked. I'd waited ages to see Brendan. Was I saying I loved him out of habit?

I strode up beside Noreen leaving Brendan and Kev to lag behind. I gave her a questioning look.

She turned her head slightly. "Make the most of it. I won't be making up a foursome with *him* again," she mumbled with almost closed lips.

"Right," I said in the same manner then lagged back to be with Brendan and try and make conversation. Noreen and Kev walked ahead down the tree lined central pathway. Kev never was much of a talker. She'd be doing all the work 'til she got bored and gave up.

The pale sun was still shining and a newly mown grass smell blew through the park.

Brendan looked around, then at the middle of my mauve suede coat. It was a mini, but very loose and straight-up-and-down. Was he wondering if I had an eight month bulge hidden underneath? He should have phoned more then he'd have known he didn't need to look worried, wouldn't he?

"So, how's life near London?"

He frowned as if that wasn't really what he wanted to ask.

"I like it now. It was hard at first. I hated school. Our school was much better."

Brendan stared ahead at nothing in particular. "Easier than working in the furnaces."

There was mingled talking of walkers and bystanders and branches swayed as the breeze picked up. We passed a man strumming *Blowing in the Wind* on his guitar. Perhaps Brendan never said much about anything important. He was a bit moody. "Are you fed up with the job, then?"

"It's pretty dirty."

"Anything else?"

"Money's reasonable." He sighed. "Should have stayed on."

"I've been offered a modelling job to start on Monday. I was thinking of not going back for O levels."

"I should've stuck it out."

"You're earning money though."

He sighed. "I'm thinking of leaving the furnaces and training to be a shoe shop manager."

269

I nearly spat with laughter. It didn't fit with his image. Or the image I had. "Oh."

"Stay on. More choice."

"I don't know. Perhaps I will then."

He took my hand in his; there was still *something* but it was different. We carried on walking down the avenue, looking at trees and people on both sides of the park. Radio Caroline was on at one of the ice-cream stands and Chris Montez's *The More I See You* played. Once, that would have been perfect. I glanced at him. I wished he'd be more – I don't know.

He looked at my coat again. Time to relay the good news. It was like trying to tell a stranger. I took a deep breath. "The most recent news is: I *came on* a few weeks before Christmas, soon after you called that last time. I'm definitely not pregnant."

The corners of his straight mouth turned up and his face relaxed. "I said you'd be okay. You were just late. Very bloody late! You could have rung me!"

Then I might *never* have seen him again. "You said *you'd* phone *me*. You didn't – until last week."

Was I just late? I stared at the grass in front of us and remembered the blue-green blades in the dunes at Great Yarmouth – when I was only seven or eight weeks overdue. Maybe what happened there was what Jackie and I had thought: the mass of what would have been a baby. But perhaps it was merely congealed blood and tissue from me. It wasn't as if I could ask anyone what they thought. I looked at Brendan but didn't say anything.

He squeezed my hand and swung it as we walked along between the trees. "Phew! Bet you were pleased. I might have a few beers at the hostel myself tonight. Do you want to sit down for a while?"

"Okay."

We sat on a park bench and watched people go by. I looked at him out of the corner of my eye. I *was* glad I wasn't pregnant. "It wouldn't have gone down too well at home."

He wrinkled up his forehead. "I know. Same here. I should've had a packet of rubbers on me."

The Bachelors' *Sound of Silence* echoed through the park over Radio Caroline.

"Yeah. It probably wasn't the best time and place…"

"Still, turned out okay in the end," he said.

"It was quite a scare. I'd make sure I got…" I couldn't quite say, "Got *you* to wear a condom next time," because it didn't feel right. It might not be him. "Got…my boyfriend…to wear…" I muttered the words and blushed. I didn't want it to sound like I had a boyfriend either.

He squinted and stared ahead as if he felt more uncomfortable than I did.

The *Sound of Silence* uttered the final lines through the loud speakers. I wanted to get to re-know him again but it wasn't happening – not unless I wanted to sound like an interviewer. It was like trying to unpeel an orange then finding there was thick white pith underneath that you couldn't get off, and even if you could, you had a feeling that the orange might not be very juicy – not worth the trouble. He used to appear so fabulous and grown up. Things could change, like the leaves and the seasons. I'd changed.

To think I was so crazy about him I was too embarrassed to tell him the truth about my dad. He probably knew later and thought I was an idiot. The pale sun warmed my face. "Do you remember before I even started at our school, when I was about ten, and we used to play cricket in the field at the end of the road with Caroline across the road and her friends?"

"Vaguely. I chased you with a mud ball and Lynette said, 'You'd better not, you don't know her mother!' I certainly got my telling off a few years later!"

A good laugh always eased things. "I've always liked you."

He squinted again and looked ahead like he used to when Mandy, June and Sandra used to push me into him. He looked kind of angry and he was very slightly red.

Noreen looked across and smiled and even though she had no idea what I was talking about, that helped me go on.

"I did a silly thing. I don't know why."

He frowned even harder. "What?"

"Remember at the beginning of last summer holiday when you told me that your dad had died, and I told you mine had too, over a year ago?"

"Yeah."

He was leaning forward and looking around the park. He really wanted to get up. The expression on his face looked like it might have if he were about to do serious business on the toilet. "On that first date at the end of '64 when we went to my cousin's small party, you asked about my dad, and I told you where he worked."

"So?"

272

There was a long pause and I didn't know why I had to make it all 'right'. I screwed up my nose. "I lied. He had already died just a few weeks earlier, but I couldn't say, somehow. Silly, wasn't it?"

"Suppose it was easier. Doesn't matter." He gave me a quick smile. "Do you want an ice cream?"

I stared at him but couldn't help frowning. *Ice cream*? "Sure. Thanks."

"Hey Kev, I'm going to get ice cream," Brendan called.

Kev said something to Noreen and she nodded, then he joined Brendan and they headed towards the stand.

Noreen strolled back to me. Her sweeping fair eyelashes lowered in a haughty look. "Do you *really* want an ice-cream?"

"What do you mean?"

"Well, frankly Andrea, that Kevin can't string two decent words together. And your Brendan isn't quite the stud I thought he'd be. Can you imagine taking *him* to the *Iron Curtain* or one of the parties we've been invited to by the boys we've met?"

I looked around. Did Brendan sparkle? Was he interesting? I stared at Brendan's back at the ice-cream stand. He and Kev looked lanky, bored and scruffy.

Sparse branches swayed in the breeze. The Mamas and Papas, *California Dreaming* played from the stand and although the leaves were brown in the song, it had a happy sound. I let out a big sigh. "I see what you mean. He wouldn't fit in, would he?"

Noreen lifted her head back and looked down her eyelashes and her nose. "Not really."

He was my yesterday man, as Chris Andrews sang. "Brendan's not the good conversationalist he was – or I thought he was."

"I don't think *Kevin* ever was."

"If Brendan really liked me he'd have made more effort." I had to admit what I'd always known deep down. "I know he likes me, but not madly. Not as much as I have liked him." I'd thought he was 'the one'. "It's a bit sad but I don't care much anymore. For the new me to like him, he would need to do some work."

"You don't owe him anything. From what you've told me, he hasn't treated you well. Besides, *you've* been asked out by one of *the* mods of Orpington, Warren Peters, and by a pop star!"

The boys were still in the queue at the ice-cream stand. "It's awkward to say anything, to get out of it, isn't it?"

She wrinkled up her nose. "I don't think they'll be that bothered if we leave."

She was so cool. To think if I hadn't moved down south, I'd never have met her. It was strange how life took special people away and gave back others. But it could never take away the memories. "I get that feeling too. I suppose I don't need that ice cream. I'm going to tell him."

"I'd just go."

"No. I'll tell him."

I walked up and pulled on Brendan's sleeve. "Can I have a quick word with Brendan, Kev?" We left Kev in the queue and I steered Brendan aside.

"I'm going." I took a deep breath. "I'll always remember you." I had my black and white nails as a memory of him, but I didn't say that. "It's not the same anymore. I'm still friends with you, but not in *that* way. Someone else has asked me out."

His eyebrows went up and made a couple of lines in his forehead. That had given him something to think about. One day, he might want to win me back. Maybe I'd be interested and maybe not. But not now. Not as he was.

I rushed away from the awkward moment looking at branches ready to bud. The afternoon sky turned crimson. It'd be another sunny spring day tomorrow.

"Come on. Let's go." I put my arm through Noreen's and we walked down the avenue beneath the overhanging trees. "Thanks for coming."

"I hope you aren't too disappointed."

"I feel free."

The way a red cloud sat in the sky between the two rows of trees reminded me of something. I wanted to jump into the sky and touch it; it was so beautiful.

Noreen looked up. "What's so fascinating up there?"

My heart skipped. The *dream* about the red moon. "When you looked up, it made me remember my dream."

"What about?"

"I dreamt it twice before, and again this morning. It was one of those where you feel you're really there. I was standing on a bridge-like road near our first old house with my mum. We were looking at two industrial chimneys and in line with them, and about five shooting stars went up into the air and down again. We thought about my dad and his soul, and Flash, my pony, and other people who had died but then my mum said in the dream it was to do with me and my future.

"The stars showered brightly and beautifully from the sky down in front of me then a red moon came up between the two chimney columns. It rose *exactly* in the middle, balanced, and became a rosy, coppery red."

"Really?"

"And between the red of the moon and silver of the stars there was a shimmering pathway between the pillars – a bit like this pathway between these two rows of trees, in perspective, tapering off in the distance. I was able to start walking through."

"Great. Look, if we run, we can catch the express from Charing Cross then we can plan our social life in comfort!"

And who knew what was along my path? I ran down the sunlit avenue – towards my future.

About the Author...

Pamela Mariko grew up near UK's bleak moors, where *Red Moon: Secrets of a sixties schoolgirl,* (formerly *Red Moon Rising),* is set.

She's a 2011 semi-finalist in Amazon's Breakthrough Novel Award and gained five star reviews from Amazon panel editors and Publishers Weekly.

In 2010 she won the Olvar Woods Fellowship Award, and in 2008 the Varuna Longlines.

Besides this book, Pam also writes women's fiction. A former freelance travel and property writer, she is now driven to follow her heart and concentrate on novels. Pam lives on Australia's Sunshine Coast and enjoys spending time with her partner, family visitors, good friends and her cat.